*Was the ste*

As if sensing my weakening, Jim put his arms around me. Ashamedly, I did the same. I gazed up into his eyes.

*Could we work this out?*

Leaning down for a kiss, he murmured, "You're too darn nice for me to ever let you go again."

*Nice?*

I pushed away.

It was being "nice" that got me in trouble in the first place. What was I thinking? This guy was nothing but trouble. How could I even consider taking him back? *Had I lost my mind?*

I looked around and spotted a glass of wine on a nearby table.

"Excuse me," I muttered, and much to the astonishment of the woman obviously enjoying a bottle of wine with a date, I picked it up and threw it in Jim's face.

"Get lost, jerk. Instead of trying to get me back, you should fear a lawsuit."

I could feel my lips turning up into a grin as he stood there, dripping red wine, a stunned expression in his eyes. I knew at that moment it was completely over. Through. Done. I'd never get that money back anyway. Jim had now been relegated to a past mistake. It was onward and upward from here on in.

"So here's where you've gotten to, sweetie." An arm wrapped around me and a kiss landed on my head. "I've been looking all over for you."

Shocked, I looked up to see Red, sporting the most dazzling smile I'd ever seen. He leaned in for another kiss. This time, right on my mouth. My heart raced so fast, I wondered if there was a defibrillator around, just in case I went into cardiac arrest.

"Just play along," he whispered, as he raised his head.

*What They Are Saying About*

## *Nice Girls Can Win*

This is a sweet story of love and forgiveness, of redemption, and of making lemonade out of the lemons that life tosses in your path. It has triumphs in unexpected places and a fairy tale ending wrapped up in shining paper at the end.

A striking feature of ***Nice Girls Can Win*** is Hurley's heroine, Jessie, whose voice is authentic in every way. The reader can believe she is a real person, whose world and friends and struggles are as familiar as her own, allowing the reader to care deeply about her.

This book is charming, humorous, uplifting, and, at times, heartbreaking. Just like life. *Nice Girls* ***Can*** *Win* takes a well-deserved place alongside the author's previous best selling *Shades of Envy.* Don't miss this one.

**Dorothy Bodoin**

**www.dorothybodoin.**com

**Nice Girls Can Win** is a delightful, feel-good novel that celebrates female friendships, love, and the power of forgiveness. You'll enjoy it from beginning to end!

**Marilyn Levinson**

**www.marilynlevinson.com**

***Suzanne M. Hurley*** steps aside from her usual *Samantha Barclay* M*ystery Series,* to produce this poignant dysfunctional family saga. Jessie White struggles with tough-reality when her insufferable boss fires her from her lawyer's position; her conniving boyfriend dumps her; and to top it all off, she is evicted from her cozy apartment…all on the same day. You can't help but root for Jessie as she struggles to get back on track. I found this a touching read as Jessie works at finding herself and mending her broken relationships.

**JoEllen Conger**
**www.congerbooks.com**

*Other Works From The Pen Of*

## *Suzane M. Hurley*

**Changeable Facades** – September 2007 – A murder has been committed! No one believes it but a young boy and his high school counselor. Will they catch the killers before he or she strikes again?

**Delusions** – October, 2008 – Narcotics are sweeping Milton High! A student is dead! Lies and Deceit take over, as high school counselor Samantha Barclay is immersed in yet another deadly drama.

**Chances** – August 2009 – FBI Agent Ryan Leam's son is missing. Psychologist Samantha Barclay risks her life to go undercover at Sacred Heart Academy, seeking truth. The results are shocking and unbelievable.

**Shades of Envy** – November, 2010 – Dead bodies are stacking up! Teenagers want to be vampires! The sheriff is acting secretively! Psychologist Samantha Barclay sets out on a wild ride to uncover the truth. Her discoveries lead to confrontations of the deadly kind. Will she survive with her life, as well as her heart intact?

*Wings*

# Nice Girls Can Win

by

Suzanne M. Hurley

A Wings ePress, Inc.

Women's Fiction

**Wings ePress, Inc.**

Edited by: Cheri Jetton
Copy Edited by: Jane Merrill
Senior Editor: Anita York
Executive Editor: Marilyn Kapp
Cover Artist: Trisha FitzGerald





Wings ePress Books
http://www.wings-press.com





ISBN 978-1-61309-943-8

Published In the United States Of America

April 2012

Wings ePress Inc.
403 Wallace Court
Richmond, KY 40475

## *Dedication*

To Mike and Rico who bring great joy and love into my life.

To my family for their never-ending support - my sister Maureen who promotes my books relentlessly, my brother Brian and Charlotte who provide numerous story ideas with their B&B and Bakery, and author brother Peter, who provides valuable insight into my writing.

To Lynda Simmons – an outstanding author, friend and mentor. Her enthusiasm and wisdom expand my view of the world.

To Mary Lou who helps me dig deep, as I explore the various relationships in my writing.

To Sheila Mazza who spurs me onward with her humor, wit and knowledge.

To Dorothy Bodoin who is a steady, calming influence during the writing of my books.

To Teresa Thompson who is a fun, kind and enthusiastic support.

All of you have aided me in the creation of imaginary worlds that end up in my manuscripts. Thank you.

# *One*

"Get rid of these cases," barked James Kite, top criminal lawyer at *Kite, Packer and Sims*. He tossed a handful of folders across his desk.

"Why, sir?" I asked, puzzled by a request seemingly out of nowhere.

"They're all pro bono, Miss White. A waste of our time." He picked up the folder closest to him and flipped it open. "A teenager caught stealing." He opened another. "A woman beat up by her husband." He rolled his eyes. "Who needs this? All they do is suck up your time." He banged his fist down hard on the desk.

I stared in his eyes, twin pinpricks of disapproval, not believing what I was hearing. I knew disagreeing was not a good thing when still in the midst of probation, especially with a boss who had a reputation of being a hard ass. He was tough, with little tolerance for us new lawyers who'd just joined his firm. Oh, at first he came across as Mr. Wonderful but we'd all soon seen his dark side.

*But how in hell could I just drop these cases?*

The brown paneled walls, oak bookcase and massive desk made his spacious office seem small and suffocating. I felt closed in, bordering on claustrophobic. Trying to remain calm, I drew in a deep breath and almost gagged. The air reeked of expensive cigars, despite the firm's health and safety rules.

"Did you hear what I just said?"

"Sorry, sir. Yes, I did." How could I forget rule number one when securing a job—*pay attention to what your boss says.* "But you also agreed I could do pro bono cases when you hired me. That was part of the deal." I tried to keep my voice calm and steady. Surely, reminding him of his original offer would create an understanding of what I was doing. Maybe he'd forgotten our negotiations.

A disquieting smirk eased across his face. I'd seen that look before. Something was up. It was the expression he wore just before pouncing on someone or something.

"The operative word is 'some.' I recall saying you could do *some* of them. Like one or two a year, if that. Not three or four a week," he clipped out. "Why you feel the need to represent every person with a 'poor me' story, I'll never know." He wrinkled his nose in disgust. "Quite frankly, I'm tired of your riff raff hanging around, dropping their cigarette butts and coffee cups at the front door. Have they never heard of cleaning up the environment?"

*He should talk.* Opening my mouth for a rebuttal, I shut it quickly when I noticed his lips start to move. I'd let him finish his tirade first.

"This is a respectable law firm, and I'll have you know, I won't put up with weakness."

"Weak?" Insulted, I sat straight up. "You must be kidding. You know how hard I work."

"You never learned to say no. That spells out weakness to

me. You screwed up. You need to take care of the paying customers first. Get rid of these." He tossed a file on the floor, then stood up and stepped on it for emphasis, leaving his shoe imprint. Did he purposely step in dirt on the way in, planning this demonstration, so as to drive home his point? Drama was his forte. I'd seen that in court.

"*Now,*" he added, sitting down. "I want these cases terminated today.

He looked away, eyed his box of cigars hungrily, lifted up the lid, picked one up and smelled it. His eyes closed in ecstasy, then popped open just as quickly. His eyebrows rose as if he were surprised to see I was still in the room, not jumping up to do his bidding. I just sat there, stunned, not knowing what to say or do.

"Call these people and tell them to go somewhere else," he said, even louder and more insistent, brooking no argument. "Legal Aid, perhaps. Anywhere. I don't care. Then get working on bringing in paying customers."

He clicked on his intercom. "Mrs. Whitmore, would you please come in? I have a letter to dictate."

With those words, I was dismissed. It was obvious he was not even going to take the time to discuss this. But really, why should he? He was the boss. He'd made a decision and that was it. Finito. My pro bono cases were gone.

*What a crock!*

The door opened in approximately two seconds flat and his stone-faced secretary walked in, dressed ultra conservative in her usual attire of beige suit, white blouse, gray hair tied back in a tight bun. She looked at me, mirroring the same smug smile Kite wore. She'd probably been listening at the door. Everyone knew she was his spy and this was probably all her doing. Always nosing around and reporting back to Kite. He never lowered himself to visit my office, and never entered through the front door, so how would he even know how I operated? Couldn't just mind her own business. She had to know everything going on.

Aunt T's face shot through my mind, as it often did whenever I was discouraged. She was the reason I'd gotten into law in the first place. I wanted to defend people who needed help but didn't have the money for pricey lawyers. No way would I let my clients down. They depended on me.

"Can't do it, sir."

I stood up, also trying to incorporate a little drama.

Whitmore gasped in shock, just as Kite rose as well. Hands on his hips, at least a foot taller, he faced me down, his eyes glaring.

"I beg your pardon," he said slowly, emphasizing every word. "Can't do what?"

"I can't terminate my representation. You know how long they'll have to wait if they go elsewhere. They need me. They have no one else."

"I think you've misunderstood me. I'm not giving you a choice. This is an order."

He watched, fully expecting me to bow down to him. *But the haunted eyes of my clients floated in front of me. I couldn't give them up.*

"Sorry. It's one I can't morally obey."

They might be just a pile of brown folders to him but to me they represented the very people I wanted to help. What would Christine do? She'd stolen to get back at her father and it had taken ages for me to win her trust. What about Sylvia who had finally come forward to testify against a husband who beat her up on a regular basis? Too much was at stake for them. Kite applauded my passion to help others when he hired me. Surely, when he saw I didn't intend to give up these cases, he'd understand. Surely he'd relent.

He sat back down and I expected to see a grudging smile on his face, even pride and an "Okay, keep them." Instead, he clicked on his computer, brought something up on the screen, opened his drawer and pulled out what looked like a small leather folder. He flipped the cover up, looked at the screen again as if verifying something, and started writing. Then he ripped the paper free from the rest and placed it on the desk in front of me.

"You're fired. There's your last check." He nodded towards the paper. "I want you gone today." Glancing at his watch, he added, "I'll give you one hour or I'm calling in security to remove you. I won't put up with insubordination."

What? Was this a joke? I looked around the room. Were there hidden cameras? Was I being punked? Surely, he didn't mean it. For sure we'd be doing some more negotiating. My boss wouldn't let me go, just like that.

I kept staring at him, hoping he'd back down. Nope. He looked dead serious.

*Think, Jessie. You're a lawyer. Plead your case.*

"Just last week, you told all of us to stick up for what we believe in, sir. That's precisely what I'm doing."

"I'm also the boss and I expect obedience. Go on. Get out of here." He pointed toward the door.

I finally got it. He meant it.

*The arrogant SOB actually fired me.*

Astonished, I wanted to storm out of his office with a 'who needs you' attitude, head held high, ripping up his check and telling him to shove it where the sun don't shine. But I was now unemployed and would need money badly. Instead, I grabbed the paper, shoved it in my pocket and walked out, slamming the door. Childish, yes, but did it feel good? *Yes.*

Furious and not wanting to waste time waiting for the elevator, I pushed open the exit door leading to the staircase and sat down on the first step. My legs were shaking so badly that it was either sit or tumble down the stairs. Tears threatened and a headache pounded away as I rested my face in my hands and attempted to fathom what just happened. The word 'fired' rang in my head.

*What in hell was that all about? One minute I had a job, the next I didn't?*

Surely, this was some kind of dream? Hallucination? Nightmare?

I reached across and pinched my arm. Nope, I was awake. *Dammit!*

So what do I do now? What do you do when your dream collapses?

*Law school doesn't prepare you for this, especially being fired for trying to help those less fortunate. People in great need.*

"Is she gone?"

Oh, no! I could hear Kite's voice outside the door.

"Yes," said Mrs. Whitmore. Her voice sounded excited. Guess he'd sent her out to check whether I'd left the area.

Damn her. That woman never liked me from the beginning. I tried hard to get along with her but we never clicked on anything, butting heads on every single office rule, particularly the one about how to treat a client. She never offered them a cup of coffee, for fear they'd hang around, and resented the fact that I had beverages—hot and cold—plus cookies available for everyone. She'd be glad to see me go and be replaced by some poor sap she could control.

Glancing at my watch, I realized I now had fifty-five minutes to get out of there. Being escorted by security guards didn't appeal to me and I was sure he'd stick to his guns and call them.

Not wanting to hear anything more, especially any kind of trash talk about my work, I stood up; willing my legs to get their act together I quickly ran down the stairs, all the way to the bottom. I needed to get far away from them. Wiping away a stray tear, planting a smile on my face, I pushed open the door.

The basement was the domain of the legal assistants. It was where they all worked, in a series of rows. Cubicles were marked off with partitions and what looked like hundreds of tiny workstations stretched out, up and down the floor, like a giant maze. I quickly headed to the last desk in the last row by the far wall, where my favorite, John Layton, worked. As usual, he was nose deep in a law book for I could see his spiky blond hair standing up over the pages. Scouting out information was my guess as I drew nearer and took in his intense look, pen in hand, pad of paper at his fingertips. He glanced up as I approached and a smile spread across his face as he pushed his glasses up on top of his head.

“Howdy, Jessie. Tried to call you earlier. Wanted to thank you for that gift certificate to Sobeys. Sure came in handy on grocery night.”

“No problem. I imagine trying to feed five children can be tough.”

“Sure is. Can’t believe you won it in a twenty-five cent raffle. Mighty kind of you, giving it to me.” He reached out his hand to shake mine. It was bony and lean like the rest of him.

John was a sweet guy, a hard worker, assistant by day, law student by night. I was sure he never had a moment’s rest with a demanding household to oversee, as well. Who even had that many kids these days?

“Ahem,” John said, clearing his throat loudly.

“Hey, you’re the kind one here,” I gushed, realizing he was sitting there, waiting for me to say something. “Just wanted to pay you back for all your help. I never shop there and it would just sit on my kitchen table until it made its way to the garbage can.”

Watching his smiling face, it hit me like a hard slap that we’d never work together again. Not a great or welcomed thought. He’d been a wealth of knowledge when I first arrived and saved my butt on many the occasion with his attention to detail. That was why I tried to help him. As a payback. I never really won the certificate in a raffle but purchased it for him, knowing he had a hard time making do every month. I figured he wouldn’t take it, if he knew. A white lie, but at least a forgivable one.

“Well, it’s been my pleasure working with you.” He beamed. “Now what can I do you for? I’m sure you didn’t find your way to the ugly bowels of this building for recreation." He pushed his glasses back on his nose, his eyes gleamed with excitement. "Got a big case pending? Research for me to do? Something shady and mysterious? L.A. Lawish?"

"Ahhh... no. Just wondering if you have any boxes you don't need. You always seem to have some hanging around." John was a packrat and had a deal with the caretaker to give him empty containers where he filed every scrap of research he uncovered. Figured I'd need a few for my belongings.

"Certainly I do." He looked surprised and disappointed at no impending work. "Two or three?"

"Two, please."

He leaned over and picked up a couple of medium sized ones stored behind his desk. "These do?"

"Just what I need."

"You bringing stuff up from your car? Need me to help you carry something?"

"I'm okay for now."

"Well let me know if I can do anything else for you."

"Good to know."

Within two seconds, he was lost in his book again and I didn't have the heart to tell him I was gone, history, canned, let go, and all those other horrible termination words. I was barely holding it together so decided I'd give him a call later and explain. Yeah, I was chicken.

I picked up the boxes and took the elevator to my office. Luck was with me. I got there without running into anyone. Tears openly ran down my face and I didn't want to have to explain. Just wanted to get out of there, away from my scene of failure. I had some heavy duty thinking to do.

On impulse, I pulled out my cell phone and called Jim, hoping he was free to meet for a drink. It was only ten in the morning, but he'd know of a bar open this early. Surely, there was one somewhere, available just for emergencies. And wasn't that what boyfriends were for? To comfort you? To be as Dr. Phil says, "your soft place to fall?" Jim would make things all right and alcohol would sure come in handy at the moment; so would a listening ear, but nope, he didn't answer. Too bad. I could do with his way of making light of everything. He'd find the humor somewhere in all of this. I considered calling his office but he'd told me not to. Said he was always in meetings and it would only be a distraction, so his cell phone was the best avenue.

Disappointed, I wiped away my tears and went back to my desk, pulled out my drawers and dumped the mismatch of things I'd collected over the past couple of months, into the containers. My silver pen set, a graduation gift from my mother, a special notepad that I'd purchased with my name on it, buttons, small sewing kit, pair of unopened nylons, and loose change. Not much at all.

"Oh, no!"

I looked up to find Emma Blake standing there, hand to her mouth in shock.

A reluctant smile forced its way out of my traumatized state as I took in her lime green sequined top, yellow tights and knee high black boots. Her outfit clashed with her dark hair streaked with orange highlights, but somehow she made it all work. Having a gorgeous figure helped. A lot. Her bright, gaudy getups always managed to startle me and I often felt I needed sunglasses when in her general vicinity, for the glare disturbed my eyes. But she really was a dear. Outlandish, but the most efficient secretary in the world, who had also become a good friend. Her advice ranged from torts to contracts to dating and I valued every word.

Luckily, she'd been away from her desk when I'd arrived back, so didn't see me at my worst. Unfortunately, she still beat me to it before I'd come up with a viable story. I dreaded telling her the news and was trying to figure out how, just before I made my escape.

"Jessie! Say it isn't so?" She leaned her arm against the doorframe and looked like she was about to collapse. She was in the wrong profession. A soap opera filled with drama and angst was more her style.

"You heard already?"

I should have known, since Emma always had her finger on the pulse of the law firm. She had one of those sweet, non-threatening faces and a way of focusing, as if you were the only one in the room, so much so, that folks ended up telling her more than they intended. Every little nuance of color went her way. Next to Google, she was the second avenue I used to get information, as she was a font of wisdom and knew all the gossip. I'd spent many the night, over drinks and nachos, being filled in on what went on at the firm and who went out with whom.

"A few rumors flew my way. So it's true?" she finally gasped out. "You got fired?"

"Yes."

"Damn." She stamped her booted foot hard. "Why?"

"Too much pro bono work."

"Since when is being kind a bad thing?"

"I wasn't bringing in enough revenue." I broke free with my Mr. Kite impression, which I'd perfected over the past few months.

At least that coaxed a smile out of her.

"But what about the clients you did bring in?"

"Not enough, I guess." I knew I sounded curt and Emma didn't deserve that, but I could barely even think about it without my stomach doing flip-flops. And I didn't want to have a repeat crying jag. We could gab about it another time.

"Aren't you out of here yet?"

We both turned to see Mr. Kite standing outside the door, arms folded at his waist, his eyes emitting sparks of rage. Probably still pissed that I'd disobeyed him, as well as slammed the door in Mrs. Whitmore's face. I wondered if he'd heard my imitation, but then decided I really didn't care. He had no hold over me now.

"Do I have to call security?" he added.

*Yeah, like I was really a threat.*

"I'm going, I'm going."

I threw my purse in one of the boxes, piled them on top of each other, picked them up and marched past him, once again holding my head up high. But my hands trembled, my legs shook and my heart thudded.

Going down on the elevator, I had only one thought.

What in hell should I do now?

Hadn't a clue and little did I know... *the worst was yet to come.*

## *Two*

Was that my landlord?

I tiptoed a few steps closer. It was!

The tiny baseball capped man, dressed in a blue shirt and overalls, construction boots on his feet, tool belt wrapped around his waist looked stressed as he stood in front of my apartment knocking loudly, sighing repeatedly. I could hear Sadie, my pet Havanese, barking up a storm at the commotion outside her home, probably indignant, thinking, "how dare someone interrupt my naptime?"

What was he doing here? He knew I worked during the day.

I had half a mind just to turn around and take off, making a run for the stairs. He was an okay guy but I just couldn't deal with anyone right now. All I wanted was to be alone and figure out my next step.

It looked as if he hadn't heard the creaking of the elevator doors opening, but as they whirred shut, I realized it was too late. He looked around, saw me and stormed down the hall, waving an official looking document. I hadn't made my escape fast enough.

"I need to have a word with you, White. Saw you pull in so figured I'd get here before you took off again."

What did he do? Watch the parking lot all day?

"Sure, Mr. Parletta." I smiled warmly, hoping to disarm him. Something really had him in a tizzy, especially since he was addressing me by my last name, which he'd never done before.

"Can you just let me put these boxes inside? They're kinda heavy."

"Yes, yes. Do that," he muttered.

Putting my load down on the floor, I took my time as I slowly opened the door, struggling to get myself under control by staving off tears, as well as blocking Sadie's attack. She'd be on red alert protecting me, especially after hearing my voice. I reached down to pet her, saying soothingly, "It's okay, Sadie," but she ducked around my hand and growled at Parletta, standing up on her back legs like a tiny black bear cub protecting her turf.

"Real scary, Sadie. Now back off," I said firmly, as I swooped all thirteen pounds of her up into my arms and held tight, kicking the boxes in with my foot.

Was someone suing him? Did he need my help? If so, why did he sound and act annoyed with me?

Stalling long enough, I turned to face him. Sure hoped it wasn't another problem.

Having my full attention, he stamped his foot and said, "You need to cough up rent money today. If not, you're outta here. Pronto." He shoved the paper in my hand. "In case you've lost the previous notice, the deadline was yesterday. You're late. Again."

"What notice? I've paid my rent."

"Not for ninety days. A few weeks ago I gave that boyfriend of yours this same sheet of paper to give to you but you never responded. What are you trying to do? Duck out on your rent? Hoping I wouldn't notice?"

"What are you talking about?" Was he crazy? Early onset Alzheimer's? I always paid on time. Cash, even. And Jim would have told me if he talked to the landlord.

He pointed his finger. "You know what I'm talking about."

"No, I don't."

He shook his head, rolling his eyes. "Playing dumb are you? I didn't hound you because I like you. Plus you do my taxes for free. But enough is enough. Three months in arrears is a lot of money. I'm disappointed. I expected way more of you but seems like you're turning into one of those unethical lawyers. Trying to get by without paying. Stringing me along."

"But… " I was shocked at his outburst. I'd been nothing but kind to this man. Even searched out tax breaks that saved him oodles of money.

"No more buts. You have until seven o'clock tonight. Not a minute longer. If you don't come through, I'm calling the police to escort you out of here. I have tenants eager to move right in."

"But there really has been some kind of misunderstanding. Your files are wrong. Please, go check them again. You'll see."

"I'm not wrong. You are. Tonight at seven or you're gone." Without so much as a goodbye, he turned and left.

Imagine! The second time today I'd been threatened to be taken away, first by security guards, and now the police. As if I needed more stress. But I wasn't going to worry about it. He'd check, see he'd erred and be back apologizing. I knew I'd paid and I already had too much to think about as it was.

"What a big, old grump," I said to Sadie after shutting the door. She uttered a few barks in response and then dragged over a ball. Her favorite playmate was home and she wanted to party. Indulging her, we played fetch as I tossed it a few times, which was all it took to tire the tiny dog, who eventually curled up on her pillow and dozed off.

Finally having the chance to sit down, I expected full-out tears but soon realized I was still in too much shock, too confused about everything to even think. My mind couldn't seem to compute what happened and I needed an escape. Badly.

Once again, I called Jim. "Pick up, pick up." Damn. Still no answer.

Looking around, I saw my apartment was a mess due to my habit of changing clothes two or three times before I left in the morning, trying to find the best outfit that hid my extra pounds—especially my muffin top. Shirts, belts and jackets were strewn all over the living room and I'd never gotten around to cleaning. Feeling a desperate need to keep busy, I raced around tidying up, trying to kill time before Jim finished work. Wait until he heard about my being fired. He'd be all empathetic and make me feel better. I smiled, picturing him holding me in his arms, telling me everything would be okay. While folding up Aunt T's knitted throw cover, which I loved to snuggle up in when watching TV, I noticed the answering machine light flashing by the phone. That was odd. Most people either called me at work, emailed or texted. No one left messages on my landline anymore. Truly passé. I rarely even looked to see if the light was on. I quickly went over and hit the button, figuring it was a salesperson selling something.

About to hit delete, much to my surprise, I heard Jim's voice.

"Hey, Jess. Things aren't working out, so it's time we broke up. Have a nice life." Click, he hung up.

My heart skipped a beat.

"What the… ?"

Surely, I'd heard it wrong. Jim wouldn't do that to me, not to mention, you couldn't get dumped the same day you got fired. The fates wouldn't be that cruel. Would they?

I pressed the button repeatedly, playing it over and over. Had I heard it right? Was he serious? Was I really being dumped? No, that couldn't be. Surely, this was all a big mistake. That's right. I smiled. He was playing a joke on me. Silly guy. Probably trying to scare me, get me all riled up. Why just last week he said he loved how my face got all red, my voice stammered and it looked like smoke blew out of my ears, when I got mad after he'd borrowed my brand new Toronto Maple Leaf baseball cap and returned it splattered with mud. "Accidentally dropped it in a puddle," was his explanation. He laughed his guts out at my reaction. Yeah, he was just joking about breaking up. Ha, ha! What a kidder.

I glanced at my watch. Almost lunchtime. I quickly made a decision. I'd head over to his work, catch him and if he was free, we could grab some take-out and have a picnic at nearby Bayfront Park. That way I could take Sadie, who adored Jim. It'd be fun and just what I needed. I was sure he'd love my spontaneity; after all, he always said I was too much of a routine kind of gal, as he liked to fly by the seat of his pants. Today, I'd do just that. Fly. Hell, I had nothing else to do.

Sadie barked, as if reading my thoughts and agreeing.

"C'mon, girl. We're going for a drive."

I clipped on the leash, grabbed my purse and headed out, already feeling better at the prospect of surprising Jim. We bypassed the elevator and ran down the stairs. After allowing a brief potty break for Sadie in a patch of grass by the entrance, I herded her into my old, beat up Pontiac and we headed downtown to the Smith Insurance Company, where Jimmy worked. He was an agent there and a highly successful one. I couldn't wait to see him. This was just what I needed. A respite from all the chaos crowding my mind.

For once, the traffic was light and we made quick work getting there. I pulled into a lot on King Street across from the high-rise where the insurance company was housed. Leaving the windows partially opened, I grabbed a toy kept in my glove compartment and tossed it to Sadie, saying, "Have fun. I'll be back in a minute."

Jaywalking, not wanting to waste time waiting for lights, I entered the building as pride rippled through me. Jim told me tales of how hard he worked to get this job and I was amazed at his tenacity, applying every month for three years until they took him on. He loved it here.

The lobby was beautiful, sparkling clean with a massive, as well as elegant bronze fountain in the center of it all. I took a moment to toss in a penny for good luck. I needed it. My wish was that Kite would phone me and all would be forgiven and eventually forgotten. Conjuring up his sneering face, I thought *fat chance of that,* but I could always hope.

I'd only been here once before and for the life of me, I couldn't remember what floor Jim was on, so I checked the glassed-in information board and headed up the stairs to the fifth floor. I remembered his office was the second one on the right so I went straight there. Great! The door was open. I burst in, a huge smile on my face.

"Surprise!"

I stopped in my tracks or more like skidded would be accurate.

A stone-faced blonde sat behind Jim's desk.

"Excuse me?" she said, looking up from a pile of papers she was reading.

"Oh, sorry. I'm here to see Jim Lewis. I must have gotten the wrong office."

The lady raised her eyebrows. "No, you have the right one. It used to be Mr. Lewis's office. He hasn't worked here in quite a while."

*What?*

"Of course he works here."

"No, he doesn't."

"But he talks about the office and his work all the time. Did they move him somewhere else in the company? He said he got a promotion recently."

She started to look uncomfortable as she shifted in her seat. Her expression now was bordering on pity. For me. My heart started to pound.

"Is there some kind of problem?"

I turned to find a distinguished looking, brown-suited man walking up behind me.

"Yes. I'm looking for Jim Lewis."

"He left here a while back."

"That's what I told her," said the blonde.

I looked back and forth between them, noting their serious expressions. Nope. They weren't joking. He really didn't work here. What was going on?

"Did he take a job elsewhere?" I asked.

"We are not at liberty to discuss this," said the man. "Please leave."

"Well then, sorry to bother you," I said, having no alternative but to go.

My head was reeling as I walked back down the stairs. Had he changed jobs and I'd forgotten?

"Hey, lady."

I looked up to see the blonde running down the steps after me.

She was huffing and puffing as she gasped out, "He got fired."

"What?"

"I finally remember where I've seen you. He had a picture of you on his desk. You're his girlfriend, right?"

I nodded.

She looked around as if making sure no one was listening. "He was caught stealing petty cash. And it wasn't the first time."

My Jim? Stealing?

"No way. He wouldn't do that."

"Well, he did."

"Er… thanks for telling me." I didn't know what else to say.

"Figured you should know." She then dashed back up the stairs, obviously not wanting to spend any more time with me. She'd probably been told to keep it confidential and took a chance telling me.

Something was dreadfully out of whack.

Jim would never do such a thing. There had to be a logical explanation. I trusted him one hundred percent and knew he'd have reasons for what happened. I just needed to find him to learn the truth.

Getting back in the car, Sadie and I headed straight to Jim's apartment. He'd clear everything up. This was all just some kind of big misunderstanding like his fake "break up" message on my machine. I was sure I'd get a good laugh out of it when I found out his reasons.

His apartment complex was up the Hamilton Mountain, about fifteen minutes away. I couldn't cross my fingers hoping he was in, since I was driving, so I crossed my toes. We needed to talk. Badly.

Arriving at the building, I circled it three times before a parking spot became available. It was down the road, a fair distance from the apartment but I didn't care. I jumped out, opened the car door for Sadie, hurried her down the street and into the lobby. I was practically dragging her as she'd picked up some sniffs along the way and wanted to explore.

"Later, girl," I said, as I went immediately to the phone to dial up to the apartment. I'd been here several times and knew the number, so didn't have to waste time looking it up.

No answer.

Dammit! I tried again.

"Come on. Come on."

Still no answer.

Getting frantic, I saw a young girl come out of the elevator and head towards me. I grabbed the door as she walked through. Luckily, she paid no attention, for her cell phone rang a Lady GaGa tune and she was rustling through her knapsack looking for it. I hurried in, hit the button for the elevator, got in and pushed for the sixth floor, breathing a sigh of relief that I'd made it.

Jim was probably holed away, dozing off and on while watching T.V., waiting for me to discover his break-up prank. He was a sound sleeper and probably didn't hear my buzzing up or his phone. Yeah, that was it. It didn't explain the job change but I was sure he'd have an explanation for that as well.

When the doors finally opened, I hurried to apartment number six twenty-eight and banged on the door.

"Open up, Jim. It's Jessie."

No answer.

I rang the doorbell.

Nothing.

Knocked again. This time louder. No answer.

"Jim. I'm here. Let me in."

"Hey, lady."

I turned to see a middle-aged man peering out from his opened door, wearing what looked like black silk pajamas, beer can in one hand.

I decided on the spot that silk and a beer gut didn't go well together.

"Yes?" I answered, impatiently.

"Could you keep the noise down? Some of us work the night shift and like to sleep during the day."

Yeah, he really looked like he was sleeping, chugging down that beer.

"Sorry," I said meekly. After all, he was a big guy, I didn't want to annoy him and I really was making a pretty big ruckus out here.

"By the way, if you're looking for that guy who lives there, he's gone."

"Gone? What do you mean?"

"Moved out this morning."

"Oh, you must be mistaken."

"Nope. Helped him carry down a sofa. Loaded it into a silver truck along with the rest of his furniture. Said he was headed out west somewhere."

Jim owned a silver truck.

"Out west?"

"Yep!" His eyes squinted as he flicked his eyes up and down. "Hey, you're his girlfriend, aren't you? Saw him throw a picture in the garbage. Liked the frame so fished it out after he left. Here, wait a sec." He went into his apartment and returned with the framed photo. He held it up.

It was the one I'd given Jim on our two-month anniversary. The very one he kept on his desk at work. We were on the Maid of the Mist ship in Niagara Falls, yellow raincoats on, soaking wet with our arms around each other, Jim leaning in for a kiss. Using my camera, a fellow tourist took the picture and I thought we looked blissfully in love. Or… in hindsight, at least I did. He'd actually thrown it away? Pain sliced through me. For real?

"But what about his job?" I asked, struggling to put the pieces together.

"Job? That guy hasn't worked in ages. Always blaring his music, night and day." He stared at me, a wary expression on his face. "He didn't tell you he was leaving?"

"No," I said, feeling my eyes getting all misty.

"Here, lady. Don't cry or anything. Take the damn picture." He thrust it in my hands.

"Eddie, where are you?" trilled a giggling female voice from inside his apartment. "I need you."

"Gotta go," he said as he quickly shut the door in my face. I didn't blame him. Who'd want to take part in this drama? Especially dressed in silk pajamas with a female who needed you? Obviously, he had other plans.

I stared at the picture.

In a court of law, all the evidence looked bad and Jim would be convicted, but I adored this guy and after all, relationships were built on trust. I didn't want to be so quick to doubt him. I knew one last person I could ask.

Hugging the picture in one hand, still wanting to believe my Jim was just misunderstood by everyone, I led Sadie back down the elevator to the lobby and rang for the landlord. If he or she were anything like Parletta, they would know what was going on with their tenant, his comings and goings, what he was doing as well as where he worked. Maybe he'd be able to clue me in as to where he was.

A few minutes passed before a tall, stocky man arrived.

"You the lady who buzzed me?" he asked.

"Yes."

"Well, what do you want?" he said, impatiently, tapping one foot hard on the tiled floor.

Were all landlords in a hurry?

"I'm trying to find Jim Lewis."

"You know him?"

"Kinda." By the wary look on his face, I wasn't sure if I should admit it or not.

"Well he's trash. Pure trash. Skipped out on rent money."

My heart jumped a beat.

"So he's really gone?"

"Yep. Saw him packing his truck and when I approached, he hightailed out of the parking lot, skidding like a maniac. Hey!" He peered at me. "You family or something? Wouldn't like to pay his arrears account would you? Help a poor landlord out?"

Yeah, right.

"Sorry but no."

"Figured it was worth a shot."

"But what about his job?"

"What job?"

*Crap!*

"Did he at least leave a forwarding address?" I asked. A girl could hope, couldn't she?

"Not on your life." His cell phone rang and when he answered, I could hear a female voice chattering away.

"Yeah, yeah," he grunted. "I'll be there."

He hung up quickly, rolling his eyes. "Gotta go. Toilet overflowed on the ninth floor."

Pausing for a moment, he stared at me for a bit and

much to my surprise a flash of compassion rippled across his face. “Hey, if you’re his girlfriend, you’re better off without that piece of garbage. Daughter just broke up with a lowlife like him.” He pointed to the picture, which I still clutched. “Take my advice, he’s a loser. Too darn many of them around.”

With that final statement, he turned and left. Talking to him was like putting the final piece of the puzzle in place.

Truth stared me in the face and it wasn’t pretty.

## *Three*

For the second time today, my legs started shaking so badly I needed to sit. I dragged myself over and plopped down on one of the chairs in the lobby. Partially hidden by a large fern, it afforded me a bit of privacy. Sadie jumped up on my lap and I buried my face in her fur.

I finally grasped that it was all true.

Jim really did break up with me, had been pretending to have a job and now he'd skipped town.

*He'd also stolen from me.*

Every Sunday night like clockwork, he came over to my apartment, I'd make his favorite pasta dish and we'd watch movies. On the last Sunday of each month, I'd go to the bank and take out a wad of money, then spend the afternoon organizing my finances by laying a series of envelopes out on my coffee table. One for rent, one for student loan repayments, one for food and one for social activities.

I then counted out the necessary bills and slipped them in their rightful places. I dealt in cash as much as I could, not wanting to spend money buying and using checks, as well as not wanting to ring up my credit card. I'd been doing this since university, proud of the way I kept my finances in order. Jim, a die-hard Visa user, teased me, thinking it was a waste of time and just plain silly. Schoolgirlish.

Concentrating so hard I was getting another headache, I remembered that the last three months when he left for the night, he'd picked up the rent envelope and offered to stick it in the gray metal box attached to Mr. Parletta's door. He said something like "It'll save you time in the morning." I figured he was being sweet since I was always rushing around getting ready, as well as taking Sadie out for her potty break. I thought nothing of it.

*Now I knew.*

He was pocketing my money. That was why he never gave me that overdue notice.

Parletta was right. I really was behind in rent.

I banged my hand against my forehead. Stupid, stupid, stupid. What an idiot I was. That was probably why Jim left. By reading the notice, he would know the deadline was yesterday and I'd find out everything today.

A wave of sadness washed over me. Next to the day my father left, this was just about the worst day of my life.

Having no alternative but to head home, this time I allowed Sadie the chance to check out the area in front of the apartment building. She deserved it after patiently following me around, and the fact that she pooped on his lawn was a fitting act of revenge and statement of how I felt. I was up to my eyeballs in crap. Jim's stinky doo-doo.

Eventually we got in the car and drove back down the mountain, but the closer I got to my apartment, the edgier I felt. Mr. Parletta would probably see me arriving and be after me for the money. I just couldn't deal with that now, at least without fortification, so I decided to pull into the neighborhood Mac's Milk. Junk food was definitely on order at a time like this. Leaving Sadie once more in the car, I headed in.

"Well, if it isn't Ms. White. Good to see you," said the smiling sales clerk behind the counter, reaching out to shake my hand. "I remember how much you like chocolate. Bet you heard our chocolate bars are on sale."

I stared at the young guy, not recognizing him.

"It's me. Joey."

"Not Joey McAdams?"

"Sure is. Don't blame you for not knowing. Got ridda my Mohawk, then had my hair all chopped off," he said proudly.

I remembered his case well. He'd been caught one too many times smoking up at a nightclub he frequented. Facing a jail term finally knocked some sense into him, and with his promise to go to rehab, I managed to get him probation with a hundred hours of community service.

"What happened?" Not only did he used to have a Mohawk but also dyed it bright red. Said it fit in with his punk rock star image.

"*You* happened. Saved me from jail. Decided to straighten up, go back to school and get a job. Just started working here a few days ago."

"Really? Still playing in your band?"

"Of course. Going to a practice right after work."

"So everything's going well?"

"Couldn't be better."

He was right. He looked the healthiest and happiest I'd ever seen. I was glad to know he'd pulled his act together.

"Hey, I was gonna track you down to say thanks and catch you up on what's going on," he added.

Not wanting to tell him I was fired, and noting a lineup of customers behind me, I quickly said, "I see you're busy. I'll talk to you in a minute." I headed over to a large bin holding a mound of chocolate bars and grabbed a few, okay, five, as well as picked up a couple of homemade dog cookies courtesy of Danny's Dog Delights, a local dog lover who'd perfected the making of the ultimate canine biscuit. This way Sadie could join me in my eating fest. It only seemed fair.

I headed back to the cash register and after ringing in my order and putting everything in a bag, a cheery Joey said, "Good to get these bars when they're cheap. It'll save you lots of money and you can freeze them and take them out when you need them."

I didn't have the heart to tell him I'd be eating them all in one sitting. "Good idea." I smiled. "You look great, by the way. Hope you stay that way."

"Now you sound like my mama." He grinned. "But I'm gonna make it this time."

"I'm counting on it."

~ * ~

I decided on the spur of the moment to head to Lake Ontario. Maybe walking by the water would calm me down and help me sort things out in some kind of logical manner. I didn't remember ever feeling this messed up before. Usually I was focused and following a strategic game plan.

After a short ten-minute drive, I pulled into the parking lot at Hutch's Restaurant, famous for their fish and chips and views of the lake. Hmmmm… maybe I'd pick some up for the ride home but right now I needed some exercise. Stuffing my treats in one pocket and Sadie's in the other, we headed to the walkway that wound down along the water.

It was a beautiful trail and on this sunny May afternoon, it was literally gleaming with sunshine, but unfortunately I could appreciate none of its offerings today. I had my life to sort out. Hell, I didn't even know which crisis to focus on but decided the subject of Jim had to be buried for a good long while. It was way too painful.

Grabbing a chocolate bar, I made quick work of the wrapper and stuffed half of it in my mouth as I tried to summon up the rational part of my brain to help figure out a plan of action, but all I could think about were the thousands of all nighters I'd pulled over the years. All that studying. All those moot courts and practicing in front of a mirror, anticipating trying cases before a judge. Becoming a lawyer had been hard work, years of dedication, and I'd only been called to the bar such a short time ago. I'd been on fire to help people, to change the world, to make a difference.

Enthused, I'd even looked into working at Legal Aid or getting involved with Lawyers without Borders until I took stock of the thousands of dollars of student loans I owed. I needed a higher paying job to get rid of them. When word got out that the coveted firm of Kite, Packer and Sims was looking for a lawyer, I applied and scored an interview. The biggest bonus was that it was back in my hometown, Hamilton, Steeltown, land of the Tigercats. The city's football team's cheer rang out in my head—*Oskie Wee Wee, Oskie Waa Waa.* I was a black, gold and white fan all the way and was thrilled that I got hired, especially since the salary was generous and Kite promised I could take on pro bono cases. The perfect job for me. Now I had a way to pay my bills and still help those less fortunate.

I sighed, thinking about my first day at work. It had been such an exciting one. Months before, I'd gone on a health kick and painstakingly dieted off thirty excess pounds that had found their way to my hips over the years, courtesy of eating bags of chocolate chip cookies while studying. I'd saved like crazy to buy a black Armani suit, white silk blouse and Jimmy Choo shoes. The whole outfit cost a bloody fortune but I wanted to make a good impression and it turned out I loved working there. Emma and John had fast become my allies and I felt I'd landed in heaven.

So how had it all turned to hell? Because I was too nice? Because I wanted to help people?

"Damn it," I said out loud, stopping in my tracks.

"Watch it, lady," said a scowling power walker, who almost plowed into me.

"Sorry," I muttered, as I led Sadie over to a bench where we could sit. She was quite content to hang out on my lap, chewing on a treat while I still tried to make sense of this insane day.

*Do nice girls ever win? Do they always have to finish last?*

That old saying was certainly not a mistruth in my case. It was fact and I was living proof. It was just that I liked helping others, especially when it came to the law, but I guess I did carry things too far. I'd spend my days working for paying customers and evenings and weekends helping those who couldn't pay for a lawyer. I was always trying to care for others. Attempting to fix them. Always the person who went the extra mile and gave even if it left me exhausted. Always prided myself on being kind.

I'd heard a phrase once about how our greatest strength could also be our greatest weakness. Kite certainly thought so. Kindness was a bust in his eyes. I guess he never meant it when he said I could take on pro bono cases. He obviously wanted total concentration on making money.

Damn! Should I have done what Kite said? Got rid of those clients? Should I have compromised? I shook my head in frustration.

*Forget that. No way.*

However, somehow my stand for justice left me feeling empty. My pastor, Father O'Malley at St. Peter's, would think I was a saintly girl for sticking up for what I believed in. But would the good Reverend let me take a cut of his collections every Sunday because I was so kind? To pay the rent? *Yeah, right.* I knew the answer to that. No way.

Sadie barked and jumped down, wanting to get on with her walk. She spotted another dog down the path and pulled on the leash to visit. The young couple, holding hands and looking madly in love, graciously stopped and allowed a happy Sadie to greet their black lab.

"Beautiful day isn't it?" said the guy, leaning over to land a kiss on his loved one's cheek.

"Guess so," I answered, abruptly pulling Sadie away. Seeing two people that happy to be with each other made me want to puke.

I looked around. Everyone seemed ecstatic, enjoying the sunny day without a care in the world.

*I didn't belong here.*

I headed back, stopping for a second to let Sadie do her business. Gazing out at the water, I realized I had to think about what to do with my apartment. I couldn't put it off any longer.

Adding up in my head what money I had, I figured I could cash my last paycheck and along with my few meager savings, be able to pay Parletta the last bit of rent. But I couldn`t continue there. No job equaled no money and I couldn't afford it.

Could I stay with my best friend Maggie? Nope. Wouldn't work. She had her mother living with her. Emma's? No. She had a tiny one-bedroom apartment. There was no room for another person.

What could I do?

Anger raged inside me. I'd trusted Jim and look where it got me.

Thoughts of him peeked out from my bruised heart. *Don't think about him*. I needed to keep my wits about me to figure out my next step.

Sadie barked with excitement, pulling me out of my thoughts as she ran toward a flock of seagulls being fed scraps of bread by an older, white haired man sitting on a bench. He looked up and grinned.

"I'm retired, you know. Have nothing to do but sit and feed the birds. It's a great life."

"Well, I might be joining you. I just got fired," I said, surprised to be confiding in a total stranger. It was just that he looked so peaceful, a far cry from how I felt.

"Ahhh… you're young. You'll find another job."

"Hope so."

"Don't worry, you will. Life is all about ups and downs."

I wish I had his faith.

The squawking birds captured his attention again, so Sadie and I kept on going, making sure we avoided a pack of rollerbladers racing by.

"You're welcome to join me any time," yelled the man to my back.

"I just might take you up on that," I said, turning and waving goodbye, hoping that one day I could sit feeding birds, feeling totally content. At the moment it seemed like an impossible goal.

On my third chocolate bar by now, we took off to the car. I was on overload and tired of thinking about all this stuff. It was way too much, and besides, I couldn't postpone any longer what I had to do. Time was ticking by and my lawyer's ruling was in. There was only one answer to my predicament. I had no alternative.

I gently placed a tired Sadie on a blanket in the backseat of my car, and picked up my cell phone.

Heart pounding, I dialed a familiar number.

## *Four*

"Get down from that tree."

I peered through the branches at my mother standing below, hands on her hips, huge scowl on her face.

Yep, you got it. I was back home.

Back in the suburbs of east mountain Hamilton. It ripped me apart to do this, but I had no choice. Fortunately, she was here when I'd called from the beach. Bearing two orders of Hutch's fish and chips I'd arrived—what was that old saying?—with my tail between my legs, asking if I could take over my old bedroom again. Luckily, I didn't have to use tears, dramatics or threats as she said yes immediately and then left for a meeting. Typical. She was always rushing off to something.

Regressing by the minute, I headed up here for some private time, which was where I always went as a child, wanting my space. How quickly we humans revert to our kiddie ways when faced with enormous trauma.

"Did you not hear me the first time? Get down from there," she yelled again.

"No way. I'm not budging," I bellowed, wishing her meeting had lasted longer.

I patted the branch I was resting on. Good old Olive Oak, my best bud. Get it? Bud as in tree bud? I named her after Popeye's girlfriend, my favorite cartoon in the whole world, oddly enough, spinach being my favorite vegetable.

When I was little, Olive and I hung out all the time. Whenever I had problems, I climbed her and she soothed me with her quiet yet mighty strength. Not like my mother. Hazel bombed as a parental figure; hence as a teen, I started calling her by her first name, as if she were just some random adult figure planted into my life. At times, I felt she was. So… from here on, I plan to refer to her as Hazel. That would make me much more comfortable when talking about her as I never thought she deserved the title Mom, and still didn't. Yeah, she was letting me move home and I should be grateful but I was always bitter when it came to her. Stay tuned to find out why.

"You look like an idiot up there. A grown woman your age engaging in such child's play."

"Big fat hairy deal."

"What will the neighbors think?"

"I. Don't. Care." Who gave a hot damn what others thought? Rolling my eyes, I felt like I was six again, which was how old I was when I first made it all the way up here.

I really didn't think Hazel was actually mad, as this was a game we used to play when I was little. After all, I had caught her up on this very same limb once.

"Just wanted to see what you liked about it," was her response, when I'd climbed up, only to realize she'd taken my spot. I often wondered when I wasn't around, if she came here from time to time herself, also seeking the wisdom of this aged tree. She never grounded or chastised me when I eventually got down, so I figured she understood there were times I needed to be up here. Or at least I thought she did, but for some reason she always put on a show about it. Maybe for any neighbors walking by who saw me up here? Or did a thread of responsibility for her child manage to kick in? At least for a short while? Was she worried I'd fall and break something? Hmmm… somehow I doubted that.

As per the ritual, Hazel finally shook her head muttering, "kids today," let out a huge exasperated groan, stomped her foot, turned around, and literally marched back into the house. Watching her go, I took a good look at what she wore. When I'd talked to her earlier, she'd been sitting and I couldn't see her clothes.

Unbelievable!

She was worried about what the neighbors thought about me, while she strutted around in mauve sneakers with a long purple muumuu billowing out all around her? She looked like a giant eggplant, or at the very least, a small tent. Why she persisted in always wearing these huge dresses, brightly colored and reminding me of different hues of vegetables and fruits, I'd never know. To this day, I still couldn't determine her body shape since it was always hidden inside yards of material. She could be fat, she could be thin. Who knew? She was also eccentric in the fact that her long, white hair fell to her waist and was often tied back in a messy French twist with paintbrushes sticking out of it. Unusual for a woman her age or any age. Odd as hell.

As you may have gathered, Hazel and I had a complex relationship, to say the least.

I knew she kinda loved me, or at least I thought she did, but it was hard fathoming, as she was so busy criticizing and trying to bend me to her will. To what *she* thought was good for me. Too bad, she never stopped to consult me. Compliments, hugs, soothing words of comfort when I was hurt, were just not her way. Like today. After I'd poured my heart out to her about my problems she simply asked, 'What do you want?' No concern about how I was feeling or even a hug of empathy. It reminded me of the time I fell off my skateboard and skinned both my knees. Blood was everywhere. She handed me a roll of paper towels and walked away.

Her cool, critical behavior spelled out continual disapproval and left me struggling to please her, hoping for an occasional word of encouragement. Fat chance of that ever happening and as an adult, I found myself trying to win people over as if the whole world was made up of Hazels whom I had to please. Add that to the fear of abandonment stemming from my father having left me when I was ten, and I was quite frankly, a mess. At least he had been a source of encouragement during the short time he hung around.

In moments of introspection, I figured my chronic niceness stemmed from my parent's breakup and consequently the development of low self-esteem. I constantly feared being ignored, chastised or ditched. That was it in a nutshell. Not everyone had two troubled parents. Unfortunately, I did.

Oh, by the way, did I mention that Hazel is a world famous artist? It might be an important point to know in the whole scheme of my development. Hazel Hul paintings sell for hundreds of thousands of dollars these days. Abstract landscapes are her forte as she is adept at creating brilliant colors that dance and shimmy across her canvases. Most kids would be proud of this. I wasn't. I was just plain bitter, but who wouldn't be, taking second place behind a bunch of paintings? They were her first priority. Always.

*Stop!*

I knew what I was doing. Focusing on my bad relationship with my parents to avoid thinking of my current problems.

That is why I was up here. Had to be here. I was clinging to a tried and true lifeline attempting to make sense of everything that'd happened. I had three strikes in one day. In baseball terms, I was out. I dug my last chocolate bar out of my pocket, made quick work of the wrapper and bit into it.

Head spinning, still not wanting to think about my own life, I looked around, searching for more distractions. Just couldn't help it. There were only so many traumas I could dwell on at one time and I was in overload.

One big advantage of hanging around with Olive was that I got the best view ever of the backyard. It was beautiful. At least two acres of green space, it was like living in a park, and in the middle of it all, stood Hazel's old painting studio, a bit run down and in need of a new roof, but still delightful looking as I took in its rich brown color with white trim. It was like a giant gingerbread house, like the one I'd seen in a picture book discovered by the fairy tale siblings Hansel and Gretel on their trek through the woods. It had always been forbidden territory for me as it was the place where Hazel would enter and not return for hours at a time. In the depths of my imagination she turned into that mean old witch the children found living in the cookie house as she was often cranky and mean when she came back home, mostly dissatisfied about how a painting turned out. She didn't use it anymore as she had a larger one with better light downtown right next to her private gallery. This building had become a storage room but I still never entered it, feeling jealous, as it had stolen away Hazel for most of my childhood.

I didn't need any more bad memories right about now, so I turned my attention to the main house, which was actually quite charming. Really homey-looking. How deceiving its exterior was with its white wood and green trim—kinda cottagey with my bedroom window looking out at Olive. Ahhhhh… Olive. Good old Olive. I caressed the branch I was sitting on. She never let me down. I remembered whispering good night to her before heading to bed; and sometimes I'd pretend that my favorite tree reached out its branches and lulled me to sleep with a sweet song. God forbid that Hazel would ever do that.

Okay, I had pretty deep, horrendous feelings about returning home. Everywhere I looked seemed to summon up heartache. Damn it, I didn't want to be here. It was an okay place to visit once in a while, but hadn't been home to me in years, and now I had no choice.

I banged my head against the tree. Life sucked. It could

change in a moment and not for the good, in this case.

When would I ever find a balance between caring for people and caring for myself? Right now, watching out for others won, as I was always last on my list. Yeah, it was nice to be kind but is it really, if it hurt me? Repeatedly? When it left me with nothing?

No wonder I was clinging to this old oak tree. It was the only constant in my life. A life that was crumbling away.

Tears flowed freely now, the ones I'd brushed away at the office and couldn't summon up at home. I couldn't avoid it any longer.

*What was I going to do?*

Hadn't a clue. No idea whatsoever. Would any other law firm hire me, when they found out I'd been fired? Doubt it.

The only thing I knew was that I was going to pack up my belongings shortly. My apartment had come furnished, so there was little to move. I glanced at my watch. Two hours left until the deadline my landlord gave me.

The clanking noise of a window opening startled me, but not as much as the loud voice yelling, "What in hell are you doing in that tree? Have you lost your mind?"

Quickly wiping my tears, I ducked my head under a branch to see who was talking. I looked around, unable to tell the direction of the voice. Was someone visiting Hazel and saw me out here?

"Don't pretend you can't see me." This time the voice was curt and obviously frustrated.

Finally figuring it out, I looked over at the house next door, realizing it was my neighbor. Hazel told me some guy moved in three weeks ago; however, she'd left out an important point. He was absolutely gorgeous. You know the kind—sexy cowboy personified. Except for the hair color, he looked a lot like Jim. *Don't think about him.*

I stared, taking in his capful of rich auburn hair, my exact favorite shade of sunset, a bit on the longish side, grass green plaid flannel shirt and sky blue eyes. All his features united to inspire heart-skittering thoughts, as they were just plain beautiful. Or handsome, in male terms. Looking at him was like gazing upon a masterpiece, rich with delightful treasures that infused the senses. Whew! When did I become so poetic? Or artistic?

So far, his face and shoulders were all I could see, but I was pretty sure the rest of him was just as magnificent. But hey, what was I thinking? I shook my head. Who cared! Hell, I'd just got dumped and all men were on my crap list at the moment. Who needed them? I looked away.

"You haven't answered me yet. What are you doing in that tree? Are you stuck? Do I need to call an ambulance? The fire department?"

I leaned out on the branch as his voice sounded frantic. On closer look, he seemed worried as well as angry. His forehead looked tense with those indented stress lines and his lips were pursed together. I instantly felt bad that I'd bothered him, but hey, *wait a sec!*

*How dare he?*

"No ambulance and it's absolutely none of your business what I'm doing up here," I said in my best frosty voice, grabbing on tighter to Olive for reassurance.

I wasn't on his property and he needn't concern

himself. I could do whatever I wanted. I had to set him straight. Show him who was boss. The nerve of him interfering in my precious visit with my Olive

"It is my business if you're looking in my window," he bellowed.

"I'm doing no such thing."

"How do I know that?"

"I've got better things to do than look at you."

"Who are you? A voyeur? Stalker?"

"Nope. Just go back in your room and leave me alone."

With a loud, "Damn idiot!," he slammed the window.

"Don't flatter yourself that I'm looking at you," I yelled back.

I could hear the glass rattle and I was sure the windowpane would splinter into tiny little pieces. I was hoping, anyway. It'd look good on him for losing his cool as he was the one who was the real idiot here, with his brilliant red face, flushed with anger.

Without warning, a loud belly laugh emerged and I started to giggle. I laughed so hard I had to cling to Olive or I'd lose my perch and fall. I guess it was pretty funny seeing someone in a tree outside your window. But big deal. He'd have to get used to it. And what was he doing anyway that he didn't want me to see?

A bark from the base of the tree drew my attention.

"All right, all right, Sadie. Yeah, I know. Time's up. I'm getting down."

My ever-patient dog stared up at me. She'd been out on the front porch snoozing in the afternoon sun, but must have heard the commotion and, protective as usual, was making sure I was okay. She barked again, this time much more high pitched and demanding, signaling she wanted me down in a hurry. She was used to my climbing escapades, but had a limit. By now, she'd be hungry and wanting food.

I slid down, moving my foot from branch to branch until I reached the ground safely. Sadie jumped up, resting her paws on my calves until I scooped her up in my arms.

"Hope you don't mind me moving home." She cocked her head as if trying to understand what I was saying. "Don't you worry, only temporarily. Look on the bright side. You'll have this huge back yard to play in." She licked my face as if understanding my words and squirmed to get down; to run across the yard to chase a squirrel, trying to befriend him, was my guess. Luckily the yard was fenced in so Sadie could romp all she wanted.

A cold, eerie feeling iced up and down my spine. I whipped my head back up to the window. I could make out Red's face. Red! Not an original nickname, but it was the perfect description of him, with his face still bright, raging with hues of anger. Not to mention the auburn hair looking like a ball of crackling fire. So… Red, it was.

Annoyed at his gawking, I waved, making it known that I knew he was spying, called Sadie's name and the two of us walked in through the patio door to the kitchen. I was tired of being screened by a total stranger.

"About time. Want some soup?" asked Hazel.

I glanced at the steaming green concoction she was spooning into her mouth.

"Ahhh… no thanks. Any cookies around?" To hell with my diet. I needed more junk food. The chocolate bars were just an entrée.

"You know I don't keep that kind of stuff in my house."

Hazel was one of those health conscious fanatics. She may or may not have a weight problem, as I said, who could tell under that dress, but she was always on the lookout for vitamin-enriched food. Especially kale. She loved it while I abhorred all green leafy vegetables. I'd have to make a trip to the grocery store soon, if I was going to eat at all.

"Hey, who's the new neighbor?" I tried to sound nonchalant, even though I was really curious, as I poured food into Sadie's bowl. Fortunately, I always kept extra in my car, for times like these when she'd be hungry and we'd be far away from home.

"Nice guy. Brian's his name. He's just renting the place from the Petersons while they're away on some kind of business."

"Nice, huh?" Wasn't a description I would use. Angry, nasty, rude was more apt.

"Sure is. He helped me when my car wouldn't start one day. Drove me to the art supply store and arranged for a friend of his to take a look at it."

"Really? What does he do? Model or something?"

"Well, he's certainly good looking enough to do that. Not sure what he does for a living, though."

Typical. If it didn't concern her, she wasn't interested.

I glanced at my watch. Not much time left to move out of my apartment and I certainly didn't want to be escorted out by the police. It would be the final indignity. I looked over at Sadie who had chomped down all her food and chased it with swigs from her water bowl; and was looking quite content as she licked her lips in satisfaction.

"Ready to go, girl?"

She wagged her tail hard, understanding that the word "go" meant something exciting.

"Atta girl. Now get your leash."

The small dog quickly ran over and grabbed it off a hook near the door, prancing back, looking thrilled with her accomplishment. She should be. It took endless practice sessions to teach her that.

"Good girl," I crooned, rewarding her with a pat on the head. I took the proffered leash dropped at my feet and clipped it on. "Let's get going and pack up our stuff. Might as well get it over with."

"Want me to go with you?" asked Hazel.

That was a surprise. Usually she had no time for such acts of kindness, as she was off in her world of art, thinking of her next masterpiece.

"No, thanks. There's not much there."

I needed to do it alone. To say goodbye.

She looked deflated so I added, "You've helped already by letting me move in. Thanks. 'Preciate it." I thought about hugging her but nah, forget that. Intimacy was never a part of our relationship.

Startled, she raised her eyebrows at my gratitude.

Whether I survived living back here or not was a whole other problem, but for right now, I was just plain grateful to have a place to stay. So Hazel was champ in my eyes.

At least for the moment.

## *Five*

So that was it! A done deal. The second time today I'd packed up my meager belongings in two boxes and walked away from a life I loved. This was not fun. In the least.

A knock at the door startled me. I wasn't expecting anyone and sure hoped it wasn't Parletta back to give me another lecture about boys. He was happy to get the money but when I told him about Jim not handing over the warning notice, as well as stealing from me, he took a father's stand and went on about "nice girls like you being given a raw deal". The word nice came up repeatedly, and yes, I wanted people to think that about me, but today it just didn't cut it for it had gotten me nowhere. At the moment the word nice was synonymous with being ripped off.

Parletta was also really pissed when I told him I had to move out because I couldn't afford the rent and my newly developed cynical side figured it was probably because I did his taxes for free. I promised to continue doing them and he decided to give me a huge break, because he really did have tenants anxious to move right away. He let me out of my lease so I didn't have to cough up more money.

"For a smart girl like you, you sure are naïve," was his parting comment.

Yes, I'd been totally wrong about Jim, but I didn't need it pointed out to me by my landlord. No one knew more than me how I'd been duped.

I snuck up to the peephole to take a look. Oh my goodness! It was Maggie! I quickly unlocked the door.

"Need any help?" she said with a grin.

Touched, my only response was a bear hug where I held on for dear life. Good old salt of the earth Maggie. Having her around was like wearing a cozy, fuzzy pair of slippers, comforting and warm. The fact we'd been through so much together was a giant plus as we had shared history under our belt. First dance, first boyfriend, first kiss, first job.

"How did you know I was here?" I asked, puzzled, finally letting her go. Normally, I'd still be at work.

"Your mom."

"She called you?"

"Yep. Sounded worried, too. Even got my name right for a change."

"Really?"

Chock another one up for Hazel. A huge surprise.

I'd known Maggie since kindergarten and we always chuckled at how Hazel called her everything but her real name. She could recite off every paint hue going, even obscure ones, but connecting a name to the right person escaped her. It stunned me that she was concerned enough that she actually attempted to send in reinforcements, especially since I'd rejected her help.

"Figured you needed some support so I raced over."

Her short blonde hair was a wet, frizzy halo around her face, not the smart looking bob she wore at work, which meant she came right here after a shower.

That was what I loved about Maggie. She didn't care how she looked, in fact, just did the minimum, like fixed her hair and wore decent clothes under her long white medical jacket, to at least appear professional while with patients. But when she got home, it was sweatpants, jeans and usually T-shirts with silly slogans written across them. As I took in her scruffy Levis, both knees ripped and ragged, and her maroon and grey McMaster U sweatshirt, arms cut off at the elbows, it was hard to believe she was a pediatrician. A popular one, even. She looked more like a young waif on a street corner asking for handouts.

Sadie gave a delighted bark as she ran to greet Maggie, who was a sucker for all dogs, having two golden retrievers herself. She always had treats on hand and quickly pulled one out for my dog. I watched as Sadie grabbed the biscuit, ate it in one bite, and then peeked behind Maggie's legs looking for her friends. Did a look of disappointment really cross her face when she couldn't see them, or had I imagined it?

"Sorry, Jody and Rupert aren't here," said Maggie.

Sadie whimpered and skulked away to pout until Maggie threw her another treat to appease her.

"So." Maggie grinned, centering her attention on me again. "You didn't answer. Can I help?"

"Nope. No need. Just dragged down my last box to the car. Only had two of them, since this place came furnished. Threw my clothes in a bunch of garbage bags, so I'm all ready to roll."

"What are you doing just standing here, then?" Maggie said, wrinkling up her nose as if there was a bad smell.

"Er… saying goodbye. I really liked it here."

"Hard to believe." Maggie sounded doubtful.

I looked around the room.

Okay, the building was on Barton Street, right near the General Hospital, a rough part of town where sirens blared all night, but it was home to me. My own badly needed space and I loved it. It was tiny, with a faded, lumpy sofa bed, a worn brown armchair and a scuffed wooden coffee table. A tiny kitchen area was off to the right encompassing a dirty looking off-white stove and fridge. Old age had set in as rust appeared in patches here and there.

Yeah, it was kinda gross looking, dingy as hell, and at times, I got claustrophobic in my own living room, but the beauty of it was that it had been all mine. An escape from work, Hazel and all sorts of craziness. I could come home, curl up with Sadie and a good book, and leave everyone and everything behind until I re-surfaced the next day. I was really going to miss it.

"You doing okay?" Maggie asked.

"I'm fine," I lied.

"Let me know when you're able to talk about it."

That was the great thing about having a best friend. She knew not to push, knowing I'd eventually tell her everything when I was ready

"I will."

"Has Emma called to say when she'd be by?" asked Maggie.

"Emma? No. Why would she?" I glanced at my watch. "She'd be still at work. Tuesday, she starts around noon and keeps going until about eight."

"I'm here," shouted a voice from the doorway. "Left early to help out as well."

I turned to see Emma come waltzing in, dressed in a bright blue mini skirt and red blouse. She looked years younger than her actual thirty-two and would fit right in surfing for johns down on King Street. All she needed was bright red lipstick, not the pale pink she was wearing.

Man, I could never figure out her choice of dress. Downright gaudy, when she was rich as hell and could afford the best. Her grandfather left her millions when he passed away, yet she dressed in bargains straight off the rack at Zellers, her favorite store. No designer clothes for her. Money hadn't changed her a bit and I envied her life as much as Maggie's. Everyone seemed to have it together, and knew what they were doing, except me.

Hearing giggling, I pulled out of my fog.

"There she goes again," said Maggie.

"Wonder what planet she's on now?" chimed in Emma.

"What?" I asked. I knew they found it equally funny and annoying that I went off into trances from time to time, my thoughts flying around like gusts of wind, always thinking of about ten things at the same time. But I didn't share in their amusement. This was a traumatic day for me and if I wanted to roll around in my gloomy thoughts, so be it. But then again. They were here to help so I shouldn't be too pissed.

"Sorry," I muttered. "Did you say something?"

"I asked if you need any help," said Emma.

"Did Hazel call you too?"

"Nope. Maggie did. I've been phoning and texting you like

crazy but you never answered. I'm worried sick about you."

"Sorry. It's hard to talk about it."

I noticed Maggie giving her a warning look as she said, "Yeah, she doesn't need us. It's all done."

Ignoring her, Emma said, "But I can give you the money so you can stay."

"Thanks, but no."

Emma rolled her eyes. "Trying to be tough, I see."

"You got it," said Maggie. "Miss Independent. Always has been."

"Well then, c'mon. Let's go out for a drink. It'll get your mind off stuff," said Emma. "I'm buying. And I won't take no for an answer."

"Fine with me," I said.

Grateful for the support, I decided to go the path of least resistance. It was easier than arguing and a nice cold beer would go down well at the moment. Besides, I needed some cheering up.

The two of them grabbed the garbage bags filled with my clothes and took off, mumbling something about leaving me alone for a bit to say my goodbyes for the last time.

For a few minutes, I looked around the place I'd called home for the past year. I sighed deeply and decided I'd wallowed enough, saluted and with a heavy heart, joined my friends by the car.

After placing everything in my trunk, they hightailed it over to Jake's Bar, in downtown Hess Village while I went to Hazel's to drop off Sadie. She was snoring away in my back seat, obviously tired out from all the crap going on today. When I pulled into Hazel's, I carried Sadie in and gently placed her on her doggy bed in my old bedroom. She didn't even open her eyes. Deciding I could bring in my belongings later, I got back in my car and headed downtown to meet my friends. It crossed my mind that Hazel wasn't there; I guessed she was still painting away at her studio. Good! I didn't have to make small talk and could get away quicker.

Jake's was one of those bars that reminded you of the sitcom *Cheers* and a place the three of us frequented quite a bit. In fact, we had a standing date to get together every Wednesday night at seven o'clock. No excuses were accepted and no boyfriends were allowed. It was and always would be a ladies night out. Those were the rules and we'd made a pact promising to obey them.

Since this was a trendy part of town with popular nightclubs lining the cobblestone street, it was hard to find parking but I lucked out after circling twice, and inched my way into a spot on King Street. Throwing money in the meter and realizing I'd kept my friends waiting, I hurried up the small incline toward the black arch with the green sign heralding Hess Village in shiny gold letters. I loved it here and Jake's was like a second home.

Maggie and Emma stood by the front door; I waved as I sped up. A flashing red welcome sign beckoned us in and even though it was a weeknight, the place was packed, teaming with mostly singles out to socialize.

"Well if it isn't Blondie, Brownie and Streaks," shouted out Jake.

Okay, so it wasn't really like Cheers where "everyone knew your name", but Jake did have nicknames for us—centered on our hair color, in Emma's case her often colored strands. Not original but cute, nonetheless. He always remembered what we drank, and threw out those made up names to everyone as his way of being friendly. Fortunately, he didn't offend anyone. We all accepted it as his own peculiar brand of humor especially since he was always here for us whenever we needed him, be it for booze or advice. Not only was he the owner but the bartender, and I figured when it hit closing he just curled up on one on the stools and went to sleep, not trusting his baby to anyone else.

We looked around, realized every table was full, even on the patio, so we pulled out stools and sat at the bar.

"The usual?" Jake asked.

"Sure thing," Maggie answered for all of us.

"New tattoo?" I asked, pointing to the eagle on his forearm.

"Got it done today," he said proudly.

"Surprised you have room for another," said Emma. "What's that? Number fifteen now?"

"Sixteen. Everyone has some kind of addiction," he answered. "I'm not unique in that."

Yep. Mine was food.

He quickly slid over a light beer for me, scotch for Maggie and a piña colada for Emma, which said a lot about our personalities. I was just plain boring, Maggie was no nonsense hardball, and Emma was sweet.

"How's Jim?" asked Maggie, taking a sip of her scotch. Judging by the blissful look in her eyes, it obviously hit the spot.

"History." I hated to ruin her moment, but truth was in order. I never lied to my closest friend. What would be the point? Maggie knew me well enough to discern my facial expressions anyway.

"What?" echoed Maggie and Emma.

I took a sip, and then responded with a simple, "He dumped me." No use being gentle about it. I was a bonafide dumpee.

"When?" asked Maggie.

"Today."

"No way," she said, leaning over to give me a hug.

"Way," I said, but I didn't really want to elaborate. It was too painful and saying it aloud made it even more real. "I'm okay," I whispered to Maggie. She pulled away but gave me a long searching look. Of course she didn't believe me and she was right not to. I lied.

Emma still looked shocked as she too leaned in for a hug.

"Actually, he even stole my rent money," I added, figuring I'd get it all out on the table.

"The bastard," said Emma.

"You're going to charge him, right?" asked Maggie.

"Yeah. You're not going to just let him get away with this, are you?" chimed in Emma.

"Well, it gets worse. Guess I should also tell you he skipped town without leaving a forwarding address."

Maggie looked floored. "You see. Having a boyfriend is nothing but a pain. That's why I don't have one."

"Well, I disagree. My Joseph is a sweetie," said Emma.

"You're just lucky," I said.

"Are you really okay?" asked Maggie. "What a hell of a day you've had."

"Bit shaken up. Just chalk it up to experience. After all, I'd only been dating Jim for six months."

"But you saw him almost every day," exclaimed

Maggie. "That made you closer, like you'd been going out for years."

"Just say it. I'm a fool with bad taste in men."

"Not a fool. Naïve, maybe," said Emma. "I never liked that guy. He had shifty eyes."

"Or better yet. You're too trusting," added Maggie. "Or, maybe just a touch of being a fool." She grinned.

I grinned back. "I'm more than a touch of being a fool. I'm a downright idiot. Now, can we not talk about it? Remember, I'm trying to forget about things for a while."

"Excuse me, but may I have this dance?"

All three of us looked up at a tall, cute guy standing there, but he only had eyes for Emma. Didn't blame him. Maggie was her usual messy self; I was covered with grime and dust from packing, as well as cleaning, while Emma looked like she'd stepped out of a fashion catalogue. A weird one, mind you but she looked gorgeous. Having some guy panting by her side was nothing new for her as she was always being hit on.

"No, thank you," she said, smiling. "I'm taken."

He looked disappointed. "Well, thought I'd try."

He didn't even glance our way before heading on over to play pool.

We all stayed quiet for a bit, sipping our drinks, lost in thought. Maggie looked pensive, probably worried about one of her patients, while Emma was enjoying the music, tapping her toes along with the beat, giving me a headache. I caught them sneaking looks here and there, as if making sure I wasn't crying or anything. I wasn't but decided I'd have to get out of here soon. My mood was too down to be in such an upbeat, party kind of atmosphere. I should have known better.

"You're not going to wallow are you? You get right back out there and hunt down another job," said Maggie, turning to stare me in the eyes. "First things first. You can look for another guy later."

"I agree. Don't let your termination affect you," said Emma.

At least termination was a nicer word than fired. Didn't jolt me as much.

"I'll try," I said, "at least about the job. As for boyfriends, who needs them?" But my stomach felt as if I was carrying around a huge rock, as sadness took over again.

"Another round, ladies?" asked Jake.

"None for me," said Emma.

"Me neither," added Maggie.

"Aw, why not? Count me in," I said.

"Well, I'm driving you home then," said Emma.

"I'll drink to that," I responded, taking a big gulp, finishing off my beer, getting ready for the next one.

"You're not getting away with saying so little. You need to talk about Jim at some point," said a sympathetic Maggie. "Not to mention the issue of your job and moving back home."

"I know, I know," I answered. "Just not tonight. I'm beat."

For now, alcohol and friendship was what I needed as I welcomed another drink.

Dulled pain didn't hurt as much.

## *Six*

Slowly coming out of my eating/depression binge, I sensed eyes glaring at me. Peeking out from under the covers, I sneered at my Barbie dolls perched on shelves across from the bottom of my bed. Damn perfect females mocking me with their damn perfect little lives. Perfect bodies, too. I bet they'd never get fired.

I picked up a pop can and whipped it at them, knocking two of them on the floor. Who cared? That was where they belonged. Silly things anyway, which was why I'd left them there all these years. Who could ever measure up to Barbie? No wonder Ken left her. Or were they back together? I wasn't quite up on the latest Barbie trends.

Frustration hit me hard. Again. I was so damn angry.

During the past couple of weeks, I'd spent my days blanketing the city with resumes only to be shunned every single time. Twice I'd scored interviews but the people doing the screening looked at me with eyebrows raised when I told them I'd worked at Kite's. I refrained from using the word fired but obviously they would have checked it out and of course, I never heard back. I kept calling one firm that was openly looking for lawyers, until the receptionist told me to stop. Pushing for more of an explanation, she whispered, "Kite's spreading the word not to hire you. You don't have a chance. Give it up."

So give it up, I did. I was an outcast. A 'has-been' lawyer, only six months out in the work force. Damn him!

On top of all this, I had no idea where Jim was, and I still hoped for explanations and a return of my money. I'd texted, emailed and called but he never picked up or answered. I even tracked down a couple of his friends but they claimed not to know where he was. Either they knew and weren't telling or really were ignorant of his whereabouts. I tried to pretend I was still his girlfriend hoping they didn't know he dumped me, claiming it was urgent, but no one bought it. "Get real," one guy said. "We know he broke up with you. Just leave him alone." Yeah, like I was the bad guy in this situation.

I'd officially hit rock bottom. Lower than I'd ever dropped before.

A lotta people would drink or do drugs. Not me. I headed to the grocery store, filled five bags full of treats, locked myself in the bedroom and ate until I couldn't stuff another particle of food down. Sure, I knew I was covering up my feelings with junk, but I couldn't help it. Life sucked. Big-time.

But right now, as I looked around, even I couldn't take the filth in my room. Nor the smell. My bed was littered with potato chip bags, chocolate bar wrappers and empty boxes of donuts, while the floor had soda cans strewn across it. Little pools of pop dribbled out, leaving rivulets of color all over the rug. I wrinkled up my nose as I sniffed eau de chocolate, spicy chip dip and sweat. I sniffed my armpits. Okay, that was just plain gross, but I was trying to be honest here. *When in hell had I taken my last shower?* I couldn't even remember.

Suddenly feeling nauseous, I fumbled around on my night table, latched onto a bottle of Pepto Bismol and quickly slurped down a mouthful, hoping to soothe the fire in my belly. Fat and salt raced through my body and threatened to explode in one gigantic hurl. I checked to see if my garbage can was near the bed. Good, it was. Just in case.

"What a pigsty," I said out loud, although no one was here to listen, except my loyal dog curled up near my feet.

Hearing my voice, Sadie shot off the bed and headed out the door. Where was she going? Was she abandoning me like everyone else?

I leaned back on the pillows, perched against the headboard.

*What had I done to myself?*

No sooner did I sink into self-introspection than I was just as quickly pulled out of it by Sadie running back into the room like a whirlwind, leash in her mouth, tail wagging madly. She put her paws up on the side of the bed.

"Okay, Sadie. I get the hint." I laughed for the first time in days. She looked so darn cute and here I'd been ignoring her, except for the times I took her out for potty breaks. I guess when she heard my voice she figured she'd give it a try. It worked. It was hard to say no to her.

Slowly, I eased out of bed.

First, I needed a shower badly. Even I couldn't stand the stink of me. I headed into the washroom turning the water on as hot as I could stand it and wiped away days of grime and chocolate stains, emerging squeaky clean. I glanced at the scale. Should I or shouldn't I? Awww, what the hell. Deciding to face the damage, I jumped on and was disgusted to find I had indeed gained weight. Crap! All that dieting in the past for nothing. Eleven pounds of extra fat had piled on, mainly around my midsection, which resulted in my having to leave the top button undone on my pants. Damn it! Thank goodness, I could put on a long T-shirt, which would cover my rapidly growing muffin top.

I stared at myself in the mirror. My eyes still had a sad, haunted look and dark circles stood out beneath them, showcasing my pathetic state. My face, framed by wet locks, looked puffy and pale as I tried to comb my hair into some semblance of a style, but it wouldn't co-operate and I finally gave up. Frustrated, I was tempted to pick up the scissors and cut it all off, but it had taken so long to grow it past my shoulders I was able to reel in that thought. I picked up my hair dryer and decided to extend the effort to dry it, hoping that would give it added bounce. Didn't work, but to be honest, I did feel better. Definitely more awake.

Finally ready, I tied my lackluster hair back into a tight ponytail. Clean, dry and almost free of the effects of my binge, except for my larger stomach, I clipped Sadie's leash on and headed out.

The day was warm and the sun blinding as I led my prancing dog down the sidewalk. She was so excited she even managed to thrust me into a lighter mood and I actually started feeling a little better. It was good to be getting some exercise for a change with a healthy dose of vitamin D on the side.

As we turned down the next street over from ours, Sadie barked her delight and ran up to a beautiful black lab puppy. I pulled her away; after all not everyone liked their dogs mixing with others, but the lady on the end of the leash smiled and said, "It's okay. Jasmine loves other animals."

"How old?" I asked.

"Seven months."

"She's beautiful."

"Yes, she is. Not mine though. She belongs to my mother who lives down the road. Fell and broke her leg so that ended her daily walks. At least for a while. I pop over during my lunch hour from work to take her out."

I laughed as Sadie put her paws up on Jasmine's face, as if leaning in for a kiss.

"By the way. Caroline Miller is my name. Your dog's pretty playful."

"Jessie White's mine. Yeah, Sadie loves to make friends. Always wanted a brother or sister." I couldn't believe I actually smiled. Seemed like forever since I'd done that.

"I think I've walked by your house before. Unless there's another dog who looks like yours and hangs out on a veranda. A big white one over on Winterberry Avenue?"

"That'd be it."

A puzzled look crossed her face.

"But isn't that Hazel Hul's house? My mother has one of her paintings and said she lives there. That's why I took note of it as I went by. Figured the dog was hers. Are you related?"

"Yep."

"Really?"

She looked at me, eyes squinting, as if deep in thought.

"Hey, you wouldn't be able to do me a favor, would you?"

"What?" A bit wary, I stepped back. Many the time I'd been asked or rather used was a more apt description, to convince my mother to donate a painting to various charities.

"Would you be able to walk Jasmine? You know the saying. A tired pup is a happy pup. If she doesn't get out every day, she's a little hellion at home. I'd pay you good money. I don't have time to do it, what with working and taking care of my two children. Not to mention my husband."

I looked at her closely, and noticed how stressed she appeared. Hair falling out of her scrunchie, eyebrows squeezed together, with even darker circles than mine under her eyes.

"Sure, why not." Hell, I had nothing else to do and I really should be walking Sadie every day anyway. This would force me to get out of the house.

"How about I take you over to meet her now?"

She was a quick negotiator. Probably wanting to seal the deal before I decided against it.

"Okay."

We walked back to her mother's. She lived in a tiny white bungalow, bordering on cutesy, with a flowery wreath on the door and what appeared to be almost twenty garden gnomes situated throughout the flowerbed.

I followed her as she opened the door and led me into the living room, where a small grey haired lady sat, leg in a cast, watching *Oprah*.

"Mother, I've found you a dog walker and guess what? She knows Hazel Hul."

I watched the lady beam as she reached down to pet Sadie.

"Really? Well, if you look over in the dining room, you'll see my Hul painting. I was lucky to pick it up at an auction. Expensive, but worth it."

*Oh, no! It couldn't be.*

I moved closer.

*It was.*

The very painting my mother was working on the day my father left. The day he slipped away in the middle of the night, leaving me a note.

*A damn note.*

Too much the coward to talk to me directly, he wrote on a piece of scrap paper which, I was embarrassed to admit, I still had tucked away in my wallet, blurred with tears. I closed my eyes and felt I was ten again, picturing the words he'd written.

*My darling daughter,*

*Please remember that I love you with all my heart, but I must go away. It is for the best.*

*Love, Daddy*

The best for whom? Because it sure as hell wasn't the best for me. In fact, it was the worst day of my life.

I remembered running to his room and he wasn't there.

I looked in his closet, everything was gone and when I took off to find Hazel, she ignored me and kept right on painting.

*She couldn't even spend some time with me? Helping me cope?*

"Are you okay?"

Opening my eyes, I saw Caroline staring at me. *Get a hold of yourself.* I quickly snapped out of my flashback.

"I'm fine. I just love this painting and I'm glad it found a good home."

*Yeah, right.*

"How are you related?" asked her mother.

"Daughter."

"Well, my goodness." She looked flustered as she patted down her hair. "Glad to meet you." She reached out her hand for a shake.

"Jessie said she could walk Jasmine every day."

"Oh, could you?" She looked delighted. "I've been feeling so guilty and poor Caroline here has no time."

"Sure I could. No problem." As long as I didn't have to look at that painting and have old memories stirred up every day. But I knew how to fix that. I could just drop Jasmine off and scoot, claiming stuff to do.

"I can pay you twenty dollars a day. Would that be okay?" asked Caroline.

Twenty dollars! A hundred and forty dollars a week! That was more than okay. It was a goldmine. The most money I'd seen in ages. At least this way, I could make my student loan payment at the end of the month and stave off bankruptcy. Not a good place to be as a lawyer.

Realizing Caroline was staring at me looking nervous

about her offer, I quickly said, "More than okay. I can be here tomorrow at ten. Would that work?"

"Perfect."

As I let myself out of the house I practically floated on air all the way home.

*I had a job.*

A small one but it paid me something. I felt so good I even decided to clean up my room and worked for two straight hours, finally getting everything neat and tidy. The pop stains were hard to get off the rug but eventually gave in, although my right hand hurt from scrubbing. I even picked up my fallen Barbies, dusted them off, fixed their hair and placed them carefully back on the shelf. "Sorry," I mouthed, feeling guilty when faced again with their beautiful, serene expressions. I then dumped my bedclothes in the washing machine and, feeling happy, headed back out to pay Olive a visit, wanting to share my good news.

After climbing up, I noticed my neighbor had left his window wide open. He seemed to be home often but I knew his car was away at the moment, so I was free to snoop. Curious, I leaned over to see what he was hiding. Shading my eyes with my hand, I could make out a computer sitting on a desk, a T.V., a great big old green easy chair with a bowl of what looked like popcorn kernels on one of the armrests. That was it. What did he do? Surf the net and watch movies all day? Not only did he look like Jim, but probably was a lazy lout like him. *Don't think about Jim.* I was finally feeling kinda good for a change and any thoughts of him would ruin my mood.

I leaned back and rested against the trunk, glancing

down at my footrest—a pair of two by fours nailed together. The beginnings of a tree house my father attempted to make with me. He wasn't very handy, so nothing much had been done and then of course he left. I bent over to see if our initials were still carved on one of the slats. Sure enough, they were. J & D 4ever, it read. Hah! That sure didn't last.

Hmmmm… a thought surfaced as my brain whirred away.

Maybe I could finish the tree house. As a kid, I always wanted one and maybe I could fulfill that long ago dream. Hell, I had nothing else to do and it would at least give me something to think about and keep my mind off my current problems.

Excited for the first time in ages, I climbed down and trotted off to Dad's tool shed where I remembered he kept the wood for the tree house stored. A big padlock secured the door. I went back in the house, searching for and finding a ring of keys hanging on the hooks, which Hazel used for her purse and coat. It took a bit to locate the right one but soon I did. Fighting off the cobwebs, I took a step into the dim interior and back a few years in time. Tears surfaced when I saw my smaller tool belt hanging beside my dad's larger one on a rack off to the side. I could still remember the day he gave it to me, eyes full of pride, declaring us carpentry partners.

*Enough of this.*

I wasn't going to allow sentimentality over a father who abandoned me to ruin the first excited moment I had in ages. I wiped away my tears.

Locating the small stack of lumber, I was disappointed

to find the boards rotten and unfit to be used. What did I expect? They'd been lying there for ages.

Frustrated, I walked out of the toolshed and it was then I noticed it. Like a godsend. A big pile of lumber on the neighbor's side leaning up against the fence shared by the two properties. Divine providence, for sure.

Almost as if in a trance, I marched right over and grabbed a couple of two by fours. It occurred to me to ask the neighbor to borrow them but I needed them now and didn't want to deal with his arrogance. Besides, it looked like he was gone for the day. It also occurred to me that I was stealing but in the state of mind I was in at the moment, I just didn't give a damn. Too bad. As I mentioned, I was feeling happy for a change and didn't want to risk sinking back into depression. He wouldn't notice anyway as I'd just taken a few.

Leaning them against the tree, I went back to the shed to grab my father's hammer and some nails. I dusted off my tool belt; it didn't fit. I hesitated then wrapped my father's around me and climbed back up Olive, managing to pull the planks up as well. After placing them where I thought they should go, I'd just started nailing when a loud voice yelled out, "Oh no! Not you again."

Startled, I swung around to see who was talking, quickly lost my balance and fell. I tried grabbing on to a few branches to save myself, but had no luck.

I hit the ground. Hard.

Everything went dark for a second, but then… wait a sec. Something wet was on my face.

I opened my eyes to find two tongues feverishly licking me. One was Sadie's and the other was from a big bruiser of a Great Dane. Hence, the huge tongue that practically wiped my face right off.

"Squid, get back." The Dane moved away.

"What the hell?" I sat up.

"Take it easy."

I looked to see a man squatting down beside me. Oh great. Red was here. He must have arrived home and I never noticed.

Even with a spinning head, I discovered that hormones wait for nothing as I managed to sneak a look and take a quick inventory. I'd only seen his head and shoulders before. Yep, he was handsome all over and yep my heart was racing. From attraction or the fall?

Embarrassed, I was pissed to be seen in such an unflattering position. I moved my legs and arms. Good. Nothing was broken. I quickly pulled down my T-shirt. Oh, damn! Had he seen my unbuttoned jeans and rolls of fat?

"Did you have to startle me?" I lashed out, preparing to scoot out of there as quickly as possible.

"Do you have to sit in a tree?"

"Yes."

"You're crazy, you know. What twenty something woman climbs trees?" He leaned back and looked at me quizzically.

"This one does."

"Really. A woman your age doing this kind of thing. What were you? A tomboy as a kid and haven't grown out of it? A wannabe lumberjack?" He shook his head. "It was all your fault, you know."

"Was not." I knew I sounded like a little kid, but that was how he made me feel. Like a two year old standing up to the bully. "I was minding my own business and you just had to interfere."

"You can see right inside my window."

"So?"

"You're invading my privacy."

"Like I said… so? I'm on my property, not yours."

I struggled to get up, lost my balance and was heading south again when two strong arms righted me. A shudder raced through me. Oh, no. I was actually having a reaction to this guy? Like, as in being really attracted to him? *Crap! I was,* I thought as I felt my face flush.

Staring into his eyes, all I could think about was, man, this guy was hot. Too bad, he was such an asshole.

Reigning in some sanity, I pushed away fast, hoping he hadn't noticed the blush on my face. After all, I'd succumbed to good looks in guys before and discovered they certainly weren't a guarantee of character and this guy was certainly no Prince Charming. Lazy cretin.

Avoiding his help, this time I got up slowly as a round of barking sounded out and I turned to see Sadie and the Dane racing around the yard, obviously enjoying each other's company. I didn't realize he had a dog. Double crap. That might create a problem, as Sadie loved to socialize. I sure as hell hoped I wouldn't have to discourage her from visiting every day, as she'd be wanting Red's dog Squid, to come out and play. That would be such a pain. Sadie was usually a good judge of character. How could Red have such a nice dog, when he was such a creep?

Anger surfaced. He'd caused my fall and all I knew at that moment, was that I had to get away. Right now, he reminded me of Kite. In control and thinking he was always right.

"C'mon, Sadie, let's go," I called, feeling a bit bad for breaking up her fun. "Come and get a treat."

The word 'treat' was her undoing. She stopped in her tracks, took one long lingering look at the Dane, then turned and followed me. No way was she giving up a morsel of salmon.

"You forgot this."

I turned around to see Red holding the tool belt. I went over and snatched it back. I then remembered about the wood, looked up and gave a sigh of relief that the two planks remained up there, snuggled among the branches.

"By the way. You're doing it wrong," said Red.

"What?"

"The platform won't be safe if you nail the boards the way you've got them. Try them the other way."

Did I really see the makings of a grin on his face?

"What in tarnation do you know?" I said, as I turned and kept on walking.

I didn't look back again at Red, nor did I say goodbye. I was making a point—a 'don't mess with me point'. I didn't need any more complications in my life and relationships weren't even on my 'to do' list. Even friendships with neighbors.

At least that was what my head thought. From the way my pulse was still racing, I think my heart was on another track. Hopefully, I'd get it back in line. I had no time for daydreaming about men with rich auburn hair and nice butts. Gorgeous locks or not, he was cranky and full of himself. Look how he sounded off, giving me advice.

Confidant that his way was the only way. Arrogant SOB. That was enough to send him out of my radar.

I shrugged my shoulders and pushed thoughts of Red back to the far recesses of my mind. The space where cobwebs and dust hung out, right next to files of my father. No way was I wasting time thinking about him since I had more important things to think about. Like how not to go into debt and how to get my independence back. I didn't need a green eyed, red haired know-it-all distracting me.

## *Seven*

Excited about my new construction project, I headed there right after I walked the dogs. I snuck next door, grabbed a few more planks and almost made it back to my yard when I heard a door slam, and a loud voice boomed out, "Just where do you think you're going with that wood?"

*Busted.*

Red stomped over and stood right in front of me.

"What wood?" I tried to act nonchalant as I sashayed on by him.

"You're stealing. You know that, don't you?"

"I am not." I tried to add just the right amount of dignity to my voice. "That fence was not built properly. It's on my property. We own about three feet on the other side of it, so technically it's my wood."

It was a ridiculous lie, but just couldn't help myself.

For some reason, Red pushed all my buttons and brought out the 'un-nice' side of me. It actually gave me a rush. He was just too handsome and arrogant for his own good; and after all, since being nice got me nowhere, taking a walk on the mean side was something I was giving a try. At least towards my neighbor.

Sure, I was stealing but I'd planned on buying some more and replacing it before the Petersons moved back. They'd never even know I borrowed any, unless of course Red ratted me out. But who would they believe? Neighbors who'd been here forever or a newcomer? I rest my case.

Ignoring him, I scrambled up the tree, pulling the wood up with me. I was quite proud of myself. I'd managed to build the base and yes, Red was right. When I nailed the planks the way he suggested, it worked better but I certainly wouldn't tell him that. Wouldn't give him the satisfaction. Now I was working on some walls. This was turning out to be great therapy as it gave me something to do and a real feeling of accomplishment. Of course, it also gave me the avenue to spy on my neighbor, for I still wondered what he was afraid I'd be seeing. Was he doing something illegal? So far, all I'd discovered was that he liked Seinfeld re-runs and, as well as popcorn, ate pretzels and drank beer during CSI Miami. Hmmmm… I could really get into this voyeur thing.

"It'll never work that way."

I looked down to see Red yelling up at me.

"What?"

"If you fasten that first piece of wood to that branch," he pointed to one to the left, "it'll anchor it more."

"Get lost. I don't need your help."

I might just enjoy being mean as I watched him shake his head, mutter "you'll see", and walk away.

Jim's face flashed before me. I couldn't help it. He liked to tell me what to do as well.

I'd been avoiding thinking about my ex, because it hurt too much and I still couldn't fathom that I'd been dumped and in such a callous, cold-hearted way. I conjured up his smiling face on the last day I saw him. He'd been telling me a silly story about his work. Obviously, a fake one.

Good old fun loving Jim. My first serious boyfriend, as I'd been too busy studying and training Sadie to get into the whole dating scene. He won me over, making me laugh for hours on end; and somehow all my problems seemed to slip away when I was with him. He was also quite the charmer but I guess I'd be charming too if I was scamming money off people. A wave of bitterness washed over me. Men! Horrid things. I needed to think of something else. Like dogs for instance. That was a happier subject.

Much to my surprise, Sadie and Jasmine attracted a lot of attention on our walks. People stopped to ask about them and when I told them I was a dog walker, many of them wanted to know if I could help them or a friend. Right now, I was walking eight dogs a day. Cash was flowing in and I could afford to give my mother a small amount of rent, buy some food and pay at least the monthly interest on my loan. It was better than nothing and I was enjoying the fresh air out with my animal charges. A few pounds of blubber even managed to melt off my waistline.

Feeling good for a change, I started positioning the first piece of lumber. What the hell, I'd try it Red's way.

"Works well, don't you think?"

I looked over to see Red leaning out the window, a huge grin on his face.

"Maybe." I still wasn't going to give in and agree.

My cellphone rang, saving me from having to hear any more advice from Mr. Know-it-all.

"Jessie, here."

I listened to a chattering Maggie for about a minute.

"Okay. I'll be right over."

"Going somewhere?" asked Red.

"None of your business," I yelled, as I shimmied down the tree, scooped up my dog, put her in the house, then raced out the door to my car.

Maggie said she was finished work for the day, and asked me to come over, as she had something important to tell me. Something urgent.

That got me moving. Fast. When Maggie used the word urgent, it meant serious business.

On the drive over, I envisioned all kinds of tragedies—like she'd gotten into a car accident, or found out she had cancer, or was declaring bankruptcy, or something really horrid.

I pounded my fist on the steering wheel when I had to stop for a red light. *Would I ever get there?*

Her office was in the north end of the city, a block away from McMaster University, and it took me thirty minutes, in the evening rush hour traffic. When I squealed into the parking lot beside the red brick bungalow that housed her clinic, I noted her gray Chevy was there, all in one piece, so she certainly hadn't been in any accident.

I jumped out of my car and ran up the tulip-lined walkway. More tulips marched across the front of the house, each multi-colored blossom spaced apart precisely to the inch. Maggie had planted them herself and her attention to detail was to be applauded, but then, that was how she ended up one of the best pediatricians around. *Stop!* Enough of this. What was I doing reflecting on flowers of all things, when a crisis might be going on? Avoidance, I guess. Scared to find out if something tragic had happened, not knowing if I could deal with any more. But I'd stalled long enough and needed to get my butt in gear.

"What's wrong?" I shouted, as I raced into the office.

"I'm in here," answered Maggie.

Following her voice, I was startled to see her sitting calmly at her desk, sipping a coffee, looking like she had all the time in the world. What was more surprising was that Emma was there as well. Dressed in a bright cherry pantsuit with a long flowing grape scarf tied around her neck, she sprawled on a small couch. Her outfit was the colors of my favorite popsicles and I salivated on cue.

Both women were smiling at me.

"What's going on?" I eyed the two of them suspiciously. "If this is some kind of emergency, why are you guys sitting here sporting grins?" I plopped down beside Emma, as Maggie's personal space was small. Just large enough to hold a desk, file cabinet, couch and bookshelf.

Emma got up, poured me a cup of coffee, handed it over and sat back down. She still wore that mysterious smile.

"What's up?" I asked again, this time louder, annoyed that I'd raced over, obsessed with all sorts of horrible thoughts, only to find them engaging in a coffee party.

"Patience, Jessica," said Maggie, as she rolled her chair over and shut the door with a bang. "You'll see."

"What?" I muttered. This didn't sound good, especially since Maggie used my full name—Jessica not Jessie. She only did that during serious times or angry moments. Today she sounded frustrated. But the both of them still kept smiling away.

"Well, you won't answer our calls or the door when we pop over," admonished Emma. "So we pretended there was a tragedy to get your attention."

"That's just plain cruel. I could have gotten into an accident trying to get here fast." I was getting pissed by the second. Agitated, too. "I'm just not ready to talk about things and besides, I've been busy or out."

"Sorry about getting you here under false pretenses," said Maggie. "Just felt we had no alternative. Next time take our calls. Answer the door." She didn't look too sorry, as her eyes flicked to the left of the door.

I looked over and it was then I noticed the glass pot on a small table tucked back in a corner. I got up to take a look, having a sneaking suspicion I knew what was going on. Yep, just as I thought. A candle, matches, notepad and pen sat side by side beside the pot.

I turned to stare at the both of them. "Is this what I think it is?"

"Sure is," said Emma, as she got up and pulled the table closer to where they were all sitting.

"We're staging an intervention," added Maggie.

"No way," I said.

Years ago, Maggie and I used to get together every Thursday night to watch the latest *Friends* episode. It was an evening of pig-outs on junk food and laughing hysterically at the antics of Monica, Phoebe, Chandler,

Rachel and Ross. One episode had the three women creating a "boyfriend bonfire", where they burned mementoes from old loves, in order to move on in their lives. Of course, the silliness escalated and their apartment caught on fire, which, of course, meant gorgeous firemen showing up to put it out. The episode was hilarious and one night, when I was upset over a particularly difficult law course, Maggie reenacted her own version of the *Friends* episode. I was to write down all my worries and burn them, leaving the ashes in the pot where we'd bury them later. From time to time we re-enacted the "bonfire", whenever we felt the other had to move on after some kind of tragedy or problem. Like when Maggie witnessed her first autopsy and was horrified or I got messed up by another fight with Hazel. We hadn't done it in ages though, leaving it behind amidst our university nostalgia.

"Time to put all the crap that's happened to you in the past," said Maggie as she retrieved a paper bag out of her desk drawer. I imagined she'd brought junk food, in particular chocolate, as we never did this without some munchies on hand. Hunger pains growled as I opened the bag she plopped down on her desk. But what the hell?

"Celery? Carrots? What happened to brownies? Or chips and dip? Where are the cookies?"

"Heard you've had too much of that, lately," said Maggie.

"How do you know that?"

"Your mother."

What? Hazel again? Showing interest in my life? She actually called up Maggie again? Arranging for an intervention?

"She told you to do this?"

"Well, not exactly. I mean, no one knows about this silly thing we do except you and me. And, of course, now Emma. Your mom was worried and asked for our help. I decided it's time we resurrected the bonfire."

"This is my first intervention," said Emma, looking excited, sitting on the edge of her seat, obviously thrilled to be part of this.

"But I figured you were due one," added Maggie, as she swung her chair around her desk again so that Emma and I were on the one side, while she was on the other. The table sat in the middle. I was amazed at how adept she was at tooling around on that chair. Lots of practice, I surmised.

Maggie handed me the pad of paper and a pen.

"Now, get to it. Write," she said. She looked over at Emma explaining, "We first make a list of everything that's bugging us."

Things were actually going a bit better but I hadn't told them yet. I also hadn't told Hazel. I didn't know how to explain that after years of studying at university I was walking dogs for profit, as well as building a tree house. Fortunately, she hadn't noticed. I was sure they'd all think I was crazy.

Not knowing how to get out of this and also thinking it might be a good idea after all, I complied and started to write, stopping now and then to chew on a celery stick. I soon got right into the spirit of things, and everything and everyone that bugged me went on my list, including Red. As a matter of fact, I found myself writing his name down after about every third item. My list looked like this: being fired, having to move, Red, losing Jim, moving home,

Red. You get the gist. I continued on for a few pages, writing paragraphs about Kite. When I finished, I looked to see if it was complete and if there was anything else I could squeeze on the paper but as I scanned down the list I saw that I had written my neighbor's name way too many times. Sheesh. Didn't know he irked me that much. Guess he was like a red rash that continually itched and bugged the hell out of me.

Finished, I finally put my pen down, and Maggie immediately struck a match and lit the candle.

"Now burn it," she ordered.

Slowly sticking the paper over the flame and watching it catch fire and wither away, I had to admit, I felt pretty darn good. Like a huge weight being lifted off my shoulders. I'd forgotten how cathartic this exercise was. A real cleansing.

"Now, repeat after me," said Maggie. "I promise to leave the past behind. To be free, move on and begin again."

As I said the words, I hoped this ritual act of consciously choosing to get rid of problems would help me get my life in some kind of order. Any kind of order would help at this point.

"Group hug," said Emma, jumping up, obviously caught up in the excitement and probably wanting to add her imprint to the scene. Maggie and I joined her and I found myself squeezing their shoulders tightly, grateful for the support. What would I ever do without them?

Feeling pretty good, surrounded by people who cared, a rush of confidence infused me. At that moment, I somehow believed I could conquer the world. To hell with

Kite, Jim and Red. I could and would survive. Hey, speaking of Red, it still puzzled me that his name obviously churned around my mind so much. Hopefully that would lessen, now that the paper with my list of issues was a pile of ashes, which I quickly swept into the pot. We certainly didn't want the arrival of firefighters. Cute or not, we weren't trying to replicate the T.V. show that closely.

"Now, it's my turn," said Emma, looking all excited as she leaned over the arm of the chair, gathered up a knapsack, and opened it. It was full of paper. A shadow of worry crossed her face as she looked back and forth between Maggie and me, then centered just on me.

"I thought I'd join in, unless of course you mind? After all, this is your moment. I can do it another time."

"Are you kidding? Go for it. I won't feel so centered out."

"The more the merrier," said a reassuring Maggie.

"But what is that?" I asked, curious, as I pointed to the paper.

"Old love letters from four former beaus." Emma grinned. "Time to get rid of them."

Leave it to Emma to have inspired guys to write mushy letters. I hadn't so much as even a romantic email from Jim and here she had a whole sack of letters. I had to admit that a twinge of envy settled in as she dumped them on the fire. When the flame grew higher, Maggie got up and retrieved a fire extinguisher, just in case; but luckily it settled down quickly.

Emma clapped her hands in excitement, exclaiming, "Goodbye to Jake, John, Fred and Harold. Hey!" She turned to us, "Another group hug." Her eyes were shining, obviously enjoying the whole experience.

As we wrapped our arms around her, I thought, *nothing like getting rid of old baggage.*

"Now, Jessie," said Maggie finally pushing away and watching for my reaction. "After burying these ashes out back, we're all going to your place."

"Pardon?"

"Your mother invited us for supper. She has a surprise for you."

"What is it?"

"It wouldn't be a surprise if I told you. Besides, I don't know."

Well, this was certainly odd.

# *Eight*

Back at Hazel's, I walked into the kitchen and right into the arms of my most favorite person in the whole world, Aunt T—my inspiration, my muse, the mother I always wanted. She'd been off gallivanting overseas and I'd missed her like crazy. Used to be, I'd know the exact minute she'd get home but this time I'd totally forgotten, having been wrapped up in my own stuff.

"Let's give them some time together," said Hazel, ushering Maggie and Emma into the living room.

I was surprised at her sensitivity.

"I'm so glad you're back," I said, hugging Aunt T, not wanting to ever let her go; craving the comfort she represented. "When did you get here?"

"Flew in this morning."

I pulled away and stared at her, hoping she wasn't just a product of my longing, but no, there she stood, in her red sweat pants and hoodie, her brown curls bouncing as she laughed at my reaction. Thank goodness. She was real.

It was always hard for me to believe this warm, caring woman came out of the same family as Hazel. When my father left, she was the one who took charge of me, loved me and made me feel important and special. She chauffeured me around, taught me to drive, attended parent/teacher interviews and school events. Sigh. All the stuff Dad used to do.

As I continued to stare, she whispered, "Yes, it's really me."

"How was France?"

"Lovely. But we can talk about that later, dear. Heard you've been troubled lately. How are you doing?"

"I got fired."

"I know."

"From Hazel, right?"

"Yes."

"Have I disappointed you? It was kinda our dream together."

"Never. You're my pride and joy."

Good to know.

It was Aunt T's situation that piqued my interest in law school after her millionaire husband took off with his secretary and their money, and left her penniless. No lawyer wanted to go up against such a powerful man, but she finally found one with heart, who helped her get what she deserved. Seeing firsthand how a lawyer could change people's lives for the good spurred me on to pursue law for a career. Too bad that part of my life was a bust.

"You haven't answered. You know you don't have to put on an act for me. You doing okay?"

"Actually, a bit better," I answered honestly.

"A bit? You can do much better than that. Now that I'm back, I'm going to see you get whole again."

Good old Aunt T. As I clutched onto her, I wondered as I always did, what the T stood for. At first, I thought she meant Auntie but watched her sign her name once and saw it really was Aunt T. One day I was determined to find out, since she ignored my questions and Hazel wouldn't give away her secret either. Must be a story there somewhere, and I was sure, an interesting one.

"Okay if we come back in now?" asked Hazel from the doorway. "The roast is almost done."

"Sure, come on in," said Aunt T. "We can catch up later."

"A roast?" I was shocked. "Ms. Vegetarian health conscious cooked a roast?"

"No, I did," said Aunt T. "Your mother's just keeping track of time, and thank goodness, or it'll be burnt."

I sniffed delightedly.

"Chicken soup as well?" I asked.

"You bet."

Aunt T's soup was legendary, at least to me, and used to grace the table every time I had a hard day at school. How she always managed to know when that was I'd never figured out. Her fragrant broth was her answer to everything and it was guaranteed to cheer you up within minutes.

I peeked into the pot on the stove. She'd obviously cooked up a chicken and made it from scratch along with her homemade tea biscuits that graced the center of the table tucked in their basket, not to mention the roast. Since she only got back this morning, the fact she squeezed in the time to do this, knowing I would benefit from it, touched me. Life was always so much better when she was around.

“Are you going to join us, or just stand there and sniff?” asked Maggie. “I’m starved.”

“Just like the good old days, when you were always over for supper,” said Aunt T. “You were always starving then, too.”

“Only for your cooking,” said Maggie, as she grabbed a biscuit and slathered it with butter.

The meal was great fun. Delicious food and good conversation, and at one point I looked around the room, and felt fortunate to have such a terrific support system. Even Hazel appeared to be trying by making small talk between sips of something green and slimy instead of sitting there quietly like she usually did, lost in her world of paintings.

“So what are you planning to do now?” Aunt T watched me closely as she nurtured a cup of coffee. “What’s the next step?”

Surprise! I actually did have a plan. One I’d been tossing around for days. Should I or shouldn’t I tell them? Seconds passed.

“I have an announcement to make,” I finally said.

Lulled by how good I felt, I decided to just go for it, anxious to see what they thought.

Everyone stopped talking.

“Go on,” urged Aunt T.

“I’m thinking of opening up a business.”

“What kind?” asked Hazel.

“A dog day care.”

“What?” Four voices spoke up at once.

“You’re giving up law?” asked Emma, clearly shocked.

“No, law’s giving up me.” They all knew about my

rejection from various Hamilton firms.

I smiled at their surprised faces.

"Where?" asked Maggie.

"Er, right here. That is, Hazel, if I can use your old studio in the back yard."

"No problem. It's just sitting there empty."

Once again, she surprised me. For sure, I figured she'd freak out about my leaving law but to allow dogs to run around, possibly soiling her once sacred area was incredible. But it was good she did since I had no other alternative. I was counting on her letting me use it.

"I think it's a great idea," said Aunt T, always my best supporter.

"Now that I think about it, I second that," said Maggie. "You love animals. Hell, any dog you meet follows you around instantly. Sounds like a dream come true." She grinned. "At least for you."

"Is there a need for such a service?" asked Emma. "I've never heard of such a thing."

I didn't blame her for being skeptical. Taking care of dogs was quite a departure from defending clients.

I quickly explained about my dog-walking venture and how it had increased from one pet to eight.

"Seems like we need a place people can drop off their animals when they're gone for long hours, or something comes up, and they're not able to walk them. Not sure if I qualify but I'd like to give it a shot."

"So that's why you're never in when we call?" asked Maggie. "You're out walking dogs?"

"Right." I still didn't want to mention the hours I spent building the tree house.

"You've done a wonderful job with Sadie," said Aunt T. "I think four obedience and five agility classes, plus competing for three years qualifies you to take care of dogs, not to mention all the tricks Sadie performs. I bet you know more about those furry creatures than most trainers."

"Besides, you're smart, organized and on the ball. You'll make it work," said Hazel.

*Who was this woman and why couldn't she have been like this when I was younger?*

"What about zoning restrictions?" asked Emma.

"Always the good secretary." I smiled, knowing she was just looking out for me. "I already checked it out and there's no problem."

"It's been zoned already when I sold paintings out of my studio," added Hazel.

Aunt T stood up. "Well, come on. Let's take a look."

"Now?" My head jerked up.

"Well, you're done, aren't you?" We both looked at my empty bowl and plate.

"I guess."

"So, get a move on."

She grabbed my elbow, pulled me up, and ushered me out to the studio. Maggie, Emma and Hazel followed. Sadie as well.

When I got to the door, Hazel handed over the key. Much to my surprise, I hesitated. I wanted to go in, hell I needed the building for my livelihood, but was nervous all at the same time.

"Come on. Hop to it," urged Aunt T, giving me a little shove.

I opened the door and turned on the lights. Sadie

rushed by to explore and I moved aside to let everyone in.

Taking a deep breath, I entered behind them but all I could picture was Hazel and her paintings. She practically hid in here when Dad took off. Painful memories loomed out at me from the dusty corners. It was probably a mistake even to think of using it.

"Forget about that for now," whispered Aunt T.

Startled, I looked over and she winked. I forgot to mention she had an uncanny ability to read my mind. I nodded my agreement as I quickly tossed those thoughts away, tired by the minute of feeling gloomy and melancholic. It was time to move on and dog daycare seemed the perfect venue for me. I stood up tall, gathered control of myself and slowly perused the room.

It was full of boxes of stuff, which made maneuvering around difficult, but a tremor of excitement raced through me. The large room had lots of light, beautifully tiled floors, a washroom and a small kitchenette where Hazel used to make tea and meals when she worked through the night. It really was quite delightful, and I could summon up in my mind happy dogs running around playing with one another, and snoozing away in the corner.

Sadie grabbed hold of an old tennis ball she had sniffed out and ran over for me to throw it.

"You know, this place is perfect for a dog daycare, Sadie. What do you think?"

She barked, jumped up on her back legs and danced around, obviously giving her approval. Or at least that was how I interpreted it. She was probably just looking for the ball in my hand.

"You're just showing off." But I smiled at her antics as

I whipped the toy across the room.

"Do you think I can really do it?" I whispered to Aunt T.

"Of course. Why would you even doubt yourself? You always achieve whatever you put your mind to."

"We'll help you clean it up," announced Maggie, busy inspecting the floors.

"Sure will," added Emma. "It'll look good as new."

"Thanks, guys."

"Most of the boxes are old frames and stuff. We can store them in the basement," said Hazel. "Sort of forgotten I had all this tucked away in here."

Having their support meant a lot and I felt I could actually pull this off. It would be a job where being nice was an asset. One where I could pour out my kindness in making sure the dogs were happy and content. A job where I was my own boss and couldn't be fired. I mean, I could hardly fire myself. Seemed like the perfect one for me. At least for now. I'd have to sit down and really figure it all out, as well as look at some kind of financing, but if I started slowly and built wisely, it might just work.

After calling it a night and saying goodbye to my guests, I tried to get some sleep but just couldn't. Now that my plan was out there in the open, I was too excited. I needed to commune with the one thing that never failed to soothe me. Olive.

Grabbing a flashlight, I headed out to the back yard and climbed up.

*What the hell?*

I was shocked to see four walls constructed on the tree house. I reached out to touch them. Sturdy and solid.

I looked over at Red's house and I was sure I could make out his silhouette, standing at the window, watching. At first, I was pissed, thinking he had no right to do this, but it looked so damn good I just sat down and smiled. It was much better than what I could have managed.

Not bad, not bad at all.

Next! A roof!

## *Nine*

When I arrived back after walking Sadie and the rest of my furry charges, I was surprised to see the lights on in the studio and I could hear voices chattering away. I recognized Aunt T's car, as well as Maggie's and Emma's, parked in the laneway. I entered, just as Hazel said, "We're definitely going to have to put on a new roof. Now let's see what needs to be done in here." She had a tape measure in hand, pencil behind her ear, looking like a seasoned contractor, except, of course for her long flowing yellow dress that brought to mind bananas.

Maggie spied me at the door. "Surprise! Aunt T arranged for all of us to meet here today to clean up. Hope you don't mind."

"Figured we could at least get rid of all the cobwebs for you," said Aunt T, a knowing look on her face.

I was sure she also meant the cobwebs in my mind. I'd been dreading being alone here with all my memories. I figured this was her kick in the butt in case I gave up and quit. She'd united the troops and they were all here lending their expertise; and I admitted I was darn lucky. Hazel had a gift of setting everything up so it was pleasing to the eye, Maggie had an extensive aptitude for practicality, Emma was a pro at running an office with, of course, Aunt T being the drive behind all of us. I really had the best people rooting for me. Girl power to the highest degree.

"You really don't mind, do you?" asked Aunt T, a serious look on her face. "Figured that if I asked you'd be Miss Independent and say no. So I just did it anyway."

"Don't mind at all. In fact…"

A loud shriek from Emma interrupted me.

"Gross! There's a dead mouse back here."

Looking around to find her, I burst into laughter when I spotted her lying on the floor, duster in hand, sporting bright blue tights and a sequined green blouse, wiping underneath some cupboards. Those were her cleaning clothes?

"Need a hand?" I asked.

Emma scrambled up. "No, I can handle it." She grabbed a plastic pail, took the broom and swept the rodent in it, dropping it in the garbage. "Used to live on a farm and had to clean up many a barn. Just surprised me, that's all."

Eager to join in, I rolled up my sleeves and started helping Maggie carry boxes to the cellar. It took seven trips and on the last one, I grabbed my notebook on the way back as I'd been working on a "things to do" list.

"Eventually we'll need more space, possibly an addition," I said. "It's all in my plans." I waved my book where I'd filled twenty pages so far. "One room for small dogs and the other for big ones. Sometimes they mix, sometimes they don't. Just can't chance it."

"Well, if you ever have a lawsuit, you can defend yourself," said Maggie, with a grin.

I grinned back. "Guess I could."

"You'll also need a desk, chair, computer and telephone," chimed in Emma.

"And lots and lots of dog toys," said Aunt T, looking around, excitement in her eyes. I was sure she was just relieved that I'd made a decision and was moving forward. Hadn't even had a junk food fest in days, as I'd been too darn busy.

"Picked a name yet?" asked Maggie.

I hesitated, not sure about my choice, and then decided to just spill it.

"Kinda, but don't laugh. How about White's Waggles? After all, happy waggling tails is what I aim to create."

Total silence. Didn't they like it? Was it a stupid name?

Finally, Emma burst out with a round of applause, the others joining in.

"Great name," she exclaimed.

I relaxed at her praise, realizing that when your self-esteem is in the toilet, all pats on the back are welcomed.

"Perfect," said Maggie.

"I love it," said Aunt T.

"Not bad," added Hazel.

What? She wasn't going to criticize?

"Not bad" was big stuff from her. I expected to hear about how to improve on it, but she just kept on measuring the back wall, leaving the name suggestion alone.

That puzzled me. What was with Hazel's support all of a sudden? Granted, she showed no emotion when I asked her if I could move in, but I had to admit in hindsight, I did notice her eyes twinkling. I thought it was just the reflection of the light from the sun shining in the kitchen window, but maybe it wasn't. Maybe, she was glad to have me under the same roof again. That would be odd, though. Unless it was criticism from how I wore my hair to how I dressed, I rarely heard anything good come out of her mouth when it came to me. And boy, she was one to talk about clothes, with all her shapeless gowns on parade.

My curiosity was piqued and I'd been meaning to ask her what was going on, but was afraid my questions might stop it, and I really liked this nicer Hazel a whole lot. Better just to keep my mouth shut.

As we all continued to pitch in, wiping down the walls, gabbing away about anything and everything, I was getting more excited by the minute. A lot of people changed professions and maybe this was a better choice for me. It felt great being busy, figuring out what I needed. From time to time, I stopped and made more notes. I took endless measurements and my mind's eye was working overtime sorting out details.

Everyone jumped on board with their own ideas and as the morning rolled on, as grateful as I was for their support, they were starting to drive me crazy with their outlandish suggestions. What was that saying—too many cooks in the kitchen? Constantly interrupting my thoughts with their own agendas, which would obviously cost a bundle. I finally couldn't take it anymore and shouted out a loud "Stop!"

That certainly got their attention as I quickly said, "Most of it will have to come later. In case you've forgotten, I'm back home because I have no money. I'm going to start small and build slowly. I have no choice."

"Why not start big?" asked Hazel.. "I'll foot you a loan."

At least the offer of money didn't surprise me. She was very generous that way. She used to plead with me to let her pay for my education but I wanted to do it on my own terms, not wanting to be tied to her.

"Thank you, but no thanks. You're letting me stay at the house and use the building for free. You've done enough."

"Look at it as an investment," she said.

"Absolutely not. I have an appointment with the bank in," I glanced at my watch, "an hour. I'm asking for a loan," I announced proudly. I wasn't planning on telling them, in case I was rejected, but figured what the hell.

"But what will you use as collateral?" asked Maggie, looking worried. Having set up a practice, she knew all about those kinds of things.

"I'll think of something. Now, all three of you—don't get too carried away with grandiose ideas while I'm gone. Remember, little by little is my motto." But I was afraid my words were ignored as I looked at their glazed-over eyes. They were all in a renovating and organizing mood, which was starting to border on interference. Don't get me wrong, I appreciated their help, but sometimes they crossed the line. But right now, I needed to get to the house to change.

"Catch you guys later."

"Good luck," said Emma and Hazel at the same time. They looked at each other and laughed. I was hoping they found it amusing that they had spoken at the same time. In other words, I hoped they weren't laughing at me and my audacity to apply for a loan. After all, I really didn't have collateral and they all knew that.

"Hey, Jessie," called out Maggie.

Almost out the door, I stopped and turned around.

"Yes?"

"Do you mind if I bring over some extra stuff I've got lying around at home that I think you could use?"

"As long as it's extra and you're not forking out your own cash for stuff, no problem. Go ahead." After all, I knew she had superb taste.

"Good." From the twinkle in her eye, I figured she was up to something. What, I hadn't a clue and didn't have time to worry about it.

"But, hey, wait a sec. Shouldn't you be at work?" Puzzled, I looked at Emma. "The both of you?" Immersed in my own stuff, I actually forgot they had jobs. What were they doing here? I counted the days in my head. Yep. It was Monday. A workday.

"I'm taking a brief vacation while Dr. Hill covers for me," said Maggie. "You helped me set up my office. Time I reciprocated."

"Me too," said Emma. "I took some well-deserved time off."

And to think I was getting frustrated with their over-involvement. I couldn't believe they'd do this for me. Man, I was one lucky girl. Add in Aunt T and even Hazel and I had it made. Afraid I'd choke up with emotion, I glanced again at my watch and said, "Gotta go or I'll be late." With that, I raced out the door before warm fuzzy thoughts threatened to infuse me with sentimentality and I got all teary eyed.

After showering and getting ready, I looked down at my plain white shirt, black pantsuit, and black pumps. Unfortunately, my Armani suit didn't fit anymore because of my weight gain and my Jimmy Choos looked too dressy for my discount special. But I thought I looked okay. I'd even gathered my hair into a prim chignon, wanting to appear professional and in control.

Would I do?

*I was counting on it.*

Jumping into my Pontiac, always grateful that it even started, I switched gears and tried to think happy, positive thoughts all the way to the bank, hoping this would make it actually happen and money would soon be deposited in my account.

"I'll get this loan. I'll get this loan," I repeated over and over, like a mantra for meditative purposes, as I pulled into the parking lot. I was psyched and determined to secure some startup money, a definite need to get my business off the ground.

Clutching my briefcase, filled with papers full of stats and estimates, I raised my head high and marched into the CIBC as if I were a confidant millionaire, coming to check on my money. This was new territory, as I had never been in this financial institution before, but wanted to start fresh. My old bank knew how little money I actually had and wouldn't be impressed with my asking for more. In fact, I was sure they'd say a big fat no. Here, they might give me a chance. Or at least I hoped so.

I headed to the receptionist, a petite dark haired girl who handled a slew of phone calls efficiently, judging by her unfrazzled, "Please hold for a moment." While I waited, I checked out her nameplate and after a few moments, she put the receiver down and smiled up at me.

"May I help you?"

"Sure can." I smiled back. "Miss Samson, I'm here to see Mr. Davis, please," I said confidently and firmly, a far cry from the nervous wreck I really was. Damn my shaking legs.

"May I tell him who's here?"

"Jessica White. His four o'clock appointment. I'm a bit early." I glanced at my watch. Like, really early. It was only three-thirty.

She pointed to a chair. "No problem. Have a seat. There's coffee on that table over there, if you'd like some."

"Thank you." But caffeine was not what I needed right now. I was too wired as it was and didn't think I could even hold a cup without my hand shaking and spilling it all over my suit. That'd be a great professional first meeting. A messy, coffee-stained client asking for a few bucks. I was sure I'd win no brownie points for that look. So I tried to sit quietly, nervously shuffling my feet against my will, waiting for what seemed hours but in reality was probably only about five minutes, for I'd no sooner sat down then Miss Samson came right back, saying, "Mr. Davis can see you now."

Good! I was impressed. I hated making appointments and being kept waiting. The fact I was able to get in early was a bonus.

"Thank you," I replied, as goose bumps started to prickle along my arms. I was barely holding it together and I was sure the receptionist sensed that, as she reached out to shake my hand, saying softly, "By the way, Ms. White, you can call me Irene. And don't worry. Mr. Davis is really nice." She winked reassuringly. She probably dealt with a lot of customers nervous about asking for loans.

"Thank you and the name's Jessie." I was pleasantly surprised by her friendliness. Could it be an omen? A positive one? A loan-producing one?

She led me to a cubicle near the back. Once again, I forced myself to stand up straight, hold my head up high and ooze confidence, fake though it was. I really needed this loan. Badly. My one and only checking account had about a hundred measly bucks after paying bills. How pathetic was that?

"Your appointment is here," announced Irene, then she winked again as she walked away, saying softly, "Good luck." I smiled gratefully. I'd need all the luck in the world, to pull this off.

Mr. Davis had his back to me, rifling through files in a cabinet off to the side of his desk. I just stood there, waiting for him to acknowledge me, at the same time, admiring the view. Just couldn't help it. His suit strained against his muscles, showing off a well-built form and cute, round little butt. I wondered how old he was. He certainly worked out, that was for sure. I looked up and saw that he also had thick auburn hair.

Oh no!

*Was it who I thought it was?*

As he turned, I almost passed out on the spot.

Get out! It couldn't be.

"Not you," I burst out. "I can't believe it."

Of all people, it was Red.

Dammit!

Having only seen him in casual clothes, this time he was dressed in a smart looking midnight blue suit, blue shirt with a tie to match. He looked like he'd just stepped out of *GQ* magazine after a photo shoot. I blinked a few times trying to clear my vision. Had I stepped inside a nightmare? Was he a stalker? Was he following me? But then, why would he have an office in the bank? And… really, I would be the stalker, arriving at his place, not the other way round. Had I lost my mind?

But, man oh man, he looked good. Damn good! Smelled good too, as a wave of spicy cologne wafted by.

If I was meeting him anywhere else, I'd be drooling in the presence of this big hunk of masculinity, but here in a business-like environment, when I knew I needed him to do me a favor, I was just plain dumbstruck.

My self-esteem plummeted as I realized this wasn't looking good for my loan. Red hated me already; although I was sure I detected a hint of amusement in his eyes. He didn't look the least bit surprised, but I guess he would have recognized the address from the application I'd submitted a few days ago. He knew I'd be here, hence his state of complete serenity. He was in control. I definitely was not. I was a shaking mass of nerves.

"Please sit down, or would you prefer to have this meeting in a tree?" he drawled out dramatically with a hint of a smirk, obviously well aware of my shock. Especially since I was standing there beet red. My wide opened mouth was surely another clue. I shut it fast, trying to gather up some control.

"Very funny." I sat down, knees together, hands resting on them as I pulled myself together. Professional, bordering on prim and proper, the height of respectability, was my plan of attack. My need for money was too great. I had to get him to approve my application. I just had to or my new venture would be toast before it even began. I had to make nice or at least fake that I was.

"So tell me why this bank should grant you a loan?" he asked as he sat down as well, opening a file on his desk. He clasped his hands together and focused on me so intently I almost melted. I was also mad at myself. Imagine feeling an attraction for this guy. I must be sinking even lower than I usually did, when it came to my taste in men. Anyhow, who cared, I was done with dating. I was not interested in the least.

I shook my head, bringing myself back to the present. "Well, I want to open up a business."

"What kind of business?"

"A dog daycare."

He raised his eyebrows so high that I thought they'd hit the ceiling.

"You must mean child daycare."

"No. For dogs. When owners work long hours or bring home puppies and need someone to watch them while they're out."

He paused for a moment, looking startled as his eyebrows were now squeezed together, as if he thought I was crazy.

"I see." He looked down at the open file. "Hmmm… so you were a lawyer with Kite, Packer and Sims but left there about a month ago. Why, may I ask did you walk away from what you are trained to do?"

"I had no choice in the matter, sir. I was fired." I decided honesty was best. No sugarcoating or hiding the truth. I also figured by calling him sir, I was extending a measure of respect. Hopefully that would help him put that whole tree-climbing scenario out of his mind.

"Really." He grinned. "Now that doesn't surprise me. Was your boss upset about your penchant for tree houses?"

So much for hope.

"I'm not amused. In the least." Angry, I leaned forward. "Can you not just let the tree thing drop, for a moment? I'm here on serious business."

"Sorry." But he didn't look too sorry with a grin stretched across his face. "Why were you let go? Hope that's not too intrusive."

"No, I can answer. Too much pro bono work."

"Oh." He looked surprised at that. "Can you tell me more?"

I'd tell him anything to get what I needed.

"I was promised that I could represent pro bono cases. But word spread and I had folks lined up at the door, wanting my help, and I didn't turn anyone away. To make a long story short, Kite didn't like it and I'm gone."

"Hmmmm… ," he said. "Interesting." He seemed to think about that for a bit before saying, "Now how much do you need to open up this, er, dog care center?"

"About thirty thousand to start with."

"How do you plan to use it?"

"Mainly to put a new roof on my mother's studio out in the back yard, paint and numerous repairs inside."

"You're using your mother's backyard?"

He looked blown away. Was he worried it'd disturb him? I sure hoped not. That alone might hinder my bid for money.

"Yes."

"Have you had experience in dog daycares?"

"No, sir. But I'm a hard worker and I love dogs." Okay, that sounded trite, but it was the truth. But I kicked myself anyway. It was like saying I wanted to work at the Dairy Queen because I liked ice cream.

"What collateral do you have?"

"My car."

"That old green Pontiac?" Now, he looked astonished. "I'm surprised it's even drivable."

I'd forgotten he'd seen it.

"What do you mean? It's in mint condition." Yeah, right. Hell, it was on its last legs er wheels, so to speak.

"I'm sorry. That's not enough." He paused, and then delivered the verdict. "I did some checking up on you. With no collateral, no job and a bad credit rating due to late payments, I'm afraid I'll have to say no. Unless, of course, your mother, relative or a friend co-signed the loan. That would work."

"No thanks." I needed to do this on my own.

"Then, I'm sorry."

Surprisingly, I think he meant it, judging by how he looked at me, then flicked his eyes down. He did this several times. *Did he actually have a heart?*

Not knowing what else to say, I got up and walked out of the room, without speaking another word, also annoyed that now he knew my business. But in all honesty what bank would lend me cash? I was a poor risk. Even I knew that. It was stupid of me to even apply for one.

But double damn him, anyway. It just had to be Red who turned me down. The fates were definitely working against me.

I shook my head as I got back in my car and held my breath as it started. Thank goodness. It'd be really embarrassing if my "collateral" conked out in the bank parking lot. Fortunately, it purred away, or clunkered along was more like it as I tore out of that parking lot like a bullet, just as my inner bad ass emerged.

Next time I was in that tree, I was planning on throwing a rock through his window. That'd teach him to mess with me.

I smiled. Revenge could indeed be sweet. Hmmmm... it just might make me feel a whole lot better.

## *Ten*

"Life sucks," I moaned, as with one long swig, I drained my beer and crashed the mug down on the countertop. "Another, please."

"C'mon, Brownie. Can't be that bad," said Jake, sliding over a second mugful.

"Well, it is." I sighed dramatically, glad I'd headed here after my rejection from Red. I couldn't face going back to the studio and seeing everyone's sympathetic looks or hearing advice and offers of money. Beer would take the ache away; at least I was hoping it would. Chocolate bars would come later. I wondered if Mac's Milk still had them on sale?

"What's got your panties in a bunch?" asked Jake.

"That lousy saying, for one."

"Sorry. Guess it is kinda crude."

"Apology accepted." I drained the beer quickly. "More please."

"Jeez. Get hold of yourself, will ya?" He shook his head. "No more for you. That's two in approximately five friggin' minutes. You're cut off."

"One Piña Colada, please."

I knew that voice and turned to see Emma slide onto the stool beside me. A bright red Emma, as she was dressed head to toe in a pantsuit that made her look like a hothouse tomato. A slim, sexy one though. Maybe more of the plum variety. Sheesh! I hoped she wasn't going to start dressing like Hazel and begin wearing those long flowing, shapeless shifts. I'd found Emma drinking coffee with her a few mornings, gabbing away and I couldn't help but notice they were hitting it off. I didn't think I could take two of them running around in billowing tents that resembled fruits.

"How did you find me here?" I asked.

"Educated guess. Heard about the loan, or lack of it, from your mother."

I should have known. On the drive over, Hazel texted to get the scoop and I told her I'd been turned down by our neighbor. She must have let the whole lot of them know. Was she being mean and gossipy, ratting me out in her "I told you so" mode, or kind and actually worried? Hard to tell these days with this new version of Hazel making an appearance.

I sighed again, loud and long. "White's Waggles will have to wait. Doggy daycare is just not meant to be. At least until I have some money."

Jake handed over the piña colada to Emma and a large glass of water for me. Emma sipped her drink in silence, then said softly, "Don't give up so quickly."

"But I can't start a business without a cent. There's things I need."

She stared at me, her eyes intense. "You sure it's what

you really want to do?"

"Yes," I answered quickly, pounding my fist down on the bar. "I've thought long and hard and really want to give this a go. I'll have to figure out another way to make some quick dough. Maybe Jake needs another waitress, or something."

Emma set her drink down, rummaged around in her purse and pulled out a slip of paper.

"Take it."

"Take what?" I glanced down to see what she shoved in my hand. I held it up to the light.

Paper? This was no paper. I stared, astonished. It was a blank check with her signature on it. I handed it back.

"No way."

"Yes."

Since she refused to take it, I slapped it down in front of her.

"No."

"Please," said Emma. "It's no sweat off my back but would mean a lot to you. C'mon. You know I have a shitload of money in the bank. None of it I earned and I'd love to help."

"But I don't know when I could pay you back."

"Who cares? Never, as far I'm concerned." She turned her head away. "Anyway, money has certainly never brought me happiness."

"What?"

"You heard me."

"Emma, what's wrong?" She sounded desolate, certainly not like her usual happy self.

She slowly turned her head to face me and I peered closely, noticing her red eyes and a tear traveling down her cheek. She was obviously upset about something. What an idiot I was not to catch on quicker. I mean, how self-centered could I be?

I slid my arm around her. "What happened?"

More tears that gushed into full out sobs.

"Oh no. It's Joseph, isn't it?"

She nodded, pulled some Kleenex out of her purse and proceeded to blow her nose.

"Had to dump him," she finally gasped out.

"But I thought he was a great guy?"

"Me, too."

"For goodness sake. Don't keep me in the dark. What happened?"

Wiping the tears from her eyes, Emma muttered, "Found out he was, what's that word? A gigolo. Out for my money."

"But didn't he used to pay for all your dates? I remember you mentioning that once. That the two of you would fight over who coughed up the dough for a movie or dinner."

"Yeah, he did. At least at first, but lately he'd forget his wallet when we were out, even when we were shopping for stuff he needed. Like deodorant and shampoo for instance. Then he kept saying he had no money. I was beginning to get suspicious. To be safe, I even had a P.E. investigate him."

"P.E.?"

"Private eye."

"I know what it means. Just can't believe it. Really?" That was a surprise. She'd never breathed a word.

She sorta smiled. "I ain't no dummy. One night after drinking too much red wine, I stupidly told Joseph about my inheritance. He didn't look surprised and it turned out he knew. Someone told him. Who, I don't know and he wouldn't tell me. So my accountant suggested I check him out." She rolled her eyes. "Found out he has a history of mooching off women who have big bucks, wooing them, getting married and ripping them off. He has four divorces under his belt."

I was shocked. "Good going, Sherlock. Did you tell him you were on to him?"

"No way. Didn't want to get him angry. No telling what he'd do. Just simply gave him the old "it's not you, it's me" routine. I just wanted to get away from him." She sighed. "But to tell you the truth, it broke my heart since I'd been thinking he was the one."

"So sorry about that." I leaned over and gave her shoulders a squeeze. "But hey, join the club. That means all three of us are now single."

"I know." The loudness of her groans beat out mine.

"Hey, young lady. Would you like to play a game of pool with me?"

We both turned to see an older man standing there grinning. He had a shock of blond hair sticking out under his cowboy hat and looked a bit like Robert Redford in his earlier days. Of course, his blue eyes were only on Emma.

"No thanks."

"Awwwww… come on."

"Get lost," she snapped. "And I mean it."

"All right, all right. Don't have a conniption." He stomped away.

I was surprised at Emma's reaction as she rarely lost her cool, and kinda felt bad for the guy, but enough of that, she needed my support. I raised my glass of water. "Here's to being single and loving it."

She managed to muster up a weak smile. "I'll drink to that." After taking a sip, she said, "So will you make me happy and take the damn check?"

I shook my head. "Still can't."

She rolled her eyes. "I figured that. Hey, Jake, could you give us some coffee here?"

"Coming right up," he replied, and quickly plopped down two mugs of steaming black java.

"Something wrong with your drink, Streaks?" He pointed to the barely touched piña colada.

"No. Just decided I don't want it."

"Well, because you're such a good customer, I won't charge." He smiled as he took away the glass.

"Thanks, Jake," said Emma.

But I knew she'd leave him a large enough tip that would cover the cost.

"Now hurry up and gulp this down." She pushed the mug closer. "You need to be completely sober. We have a surprise for you," she said, obviously back in control with a now urgent tone of voice.

"You do?"

"Yes, I got sidetracked. I actually was sent out to find you." She glanced at her watch. "Your aunt'll be sending out smoke signals soon, if we don't get there."

"What is it?"

"Can't tell. Now get drinking. I promise, you'll like it."

Both of us concentrated on getting the necessary caffeine fix. Gulping down the last drop, I stood up; ready to go but not sure I was up to it.

"Hey," said Jake to Emma, as he came over to pick up the cups. "Make sure she doesn't drive. She gulped down a few drinks too many, too fast. Don't want to have to take her keys away."

"Don't worry. She's with me."

I didn't protest, knowing Jake was right.

Emma made short work of getting me home. For once, all the streetlights were in our favor and we made it in fifteen minutes, not the usual twenty-five. As she undid her seatbelt, I grabbed her arm.

"Promise me you'll call or come over whenever you need to talk?"

She smiled. "Thanks. I will. Now, c'mon, they're waiting for us."

Getting out of the car, she directed me to the studio.

I stopped dead in my tracks.

The first thing I noticed was a brightly colored sign over the door, proclaiming, "White's Waggles" in red and black, my favorite colors.

"What the… " I said, shocked.

"A Hazel Hul original," said Emma with a grin. "You can thank your aunt. She's been hard at work here all day, directing the bunch of us." She opened the door. "But you haven't seen anything yet."

"You mean there's more?"

"Oh, yeah. Much more. Now get in here."

I walked in the door to Maggie, Hazel and Aunt T standing there with huge smiles on their faces. Then Sadie raced over and I swung her up in my arms as she licked my face excitedly. I had only taken a few steps when I gasped. "Oh, my goodness." I clung tightly to my dog as wonder hit me hard.

The whole place had been transformed into a canine world. A big, beautiful space for furry animals. There were beds, big and small, lined up against one wall. A huge container holding water that dripped constantly into a large bowl sat in the center of the room, alongside a carton stuffed with every imaginable dog toy that existed. Two areas were roped off—one for rest and another for play. I couldn't figure out how they got it exactly the way I pictured it, until I saw my notebook lying on a chair opened at the sketch I'd drawn.

"We snooped," said Aunt T, following my eyes, looking a tad guilty.

"Yeah, we made her do it, cuz we knew you couldn't stay mad at your aunt," said Maggie. "At least for long. And we wanted to make it just the way you envisioned."

"That's okay," I answered. I was blown away. They did it with love, which was certainly all right in my books. I couldn't be mad at that.

I looked around again, this time more carefully. It was then I noticed that Hazel had outlined a stunning mural on the back wall with pictures of every kind of dog imaginable, but one of Sadie held center court. When I put my squirming dog down, she actually ran up to it and barked, probably figuring the animals were real and here to play.

"Not sure you'd like this but I thought my gift to you would be this mural. If it's okay, I can finish it or paint over it, if you don't want it," said Hazel.

She actually seemed kinda shy, as she shuffled her feet back and forth.

"No, I love it."

I was surprised to see the normally confident Hazel look relieved.

There was also a desk complete with a chair and a computer up and running, sitting next to a printer. I couldn't believe it and much to my shock tears rolled down my cheeks. This time, they were tears of joy as the realization hit me that I could do this. I could still open my dog daycare center. They had provided everything I needed to get started.

"I don't know what to say," I blubbered out.

"Don't say a thing," said Maggie. "Just know how much faith we have in you."

"But why would you do all this for me? You have your own busy lives to live."

"Remember those long nights when you helped paint my office?" asked Maggie.

"And you never minded if I took a longer than usual lunch," said Emma.

"Well, it's payback time," said Maggie.

"We want you to believe in yourself," added Aunt T, in her usual philosophical tone of voice. "At least as much as we do."

"This is just what you need to get you smiling again," said the nice Hazel.

"Group hug," shouted out Emma, breaking the awkward moment, as we all joined in. I was getting used to her touchy-feely ways and was quite enjoying the feeling of solidarity.

After a rough couple of weeks, it sure felt great to be in the arms of my friends and family.

*"Who needed a loan anyway?"* I thought. Damn that Red. He could just go to hell, for all I cared.

I could do this without him.

## *Eleven*

"Is there really more wood here, Sadie? Or am I imagining it?"

She cocked her head to one side as if trying to understand what I said, then ran off to sniff around the boards.

"Yep. Sure looks like it. That pile of lumber is definitely bigger."

*Had Red added to it?*

Was he setting a trap? Trying to catch me?

*Who cared!*

"Great! More for me to use." I refused to be intimidated.

Picking up a few two by fours, I headed back to Olive, almost expecting my neighbor to jump out and stop me. Fortunately, nothing happened.

I was so close to fulfilling my childhood dream that I was planning to get right to work, hoping to finish the tree house before my business took up all my time. Yesterday, I'd even painted everything a beautiful chocolate brown so that it blended right in among the oak leaves.

Struggling up the tree with my load, I noticed

something looked different. Took me a bit to realize the slats I'd nailed to make part of the roof had been re-arranged. A wood nymph perhaps? Sneaking up here to help me?

Oh, who was I trying to kid? Red had hit again. What was he trying to do? Show me that he was a better builder?

I was tempted to rip it all down and go back to my way, but it really did look better and like the walls, was sturdier, so I decided to keep his work and fashioned the rest of the roof the same way. I'd just pretend that it really was a wood nymph that'd helped. Yeah, that would make me feel better.

Smiling, even whistling, I finished it off, but eerily enough, I kept feeling eyes on me. Several times, I turned towards Red's window, expecting him to be there but nope, he wasn't. I was sure he was sneaking peeks from time to time. Damn him, anyway.

After positioning, hammering and finishing up the roof, I slathered on a coat of paint, then slid down and ran back inside the house to grab the rug I'd purchased the other day, along with a new notebook and pen. I unrolled the rug across the floor, and was amazed at how perfect it looked with its multi-colored leaf motif. Cheery and bright, it fit right in. I placed the pen and notebook in a small wooden box I'd brought up yesterday and contentment rippled through me. It was done. A place of retreat, rain or shine, where I could also record my thoughts and ideas. Stretching out on the floor, I stayed put for a bit, enjoying the feeling of a task completed. But I couldn't stay long. I had a lot of other work to do.

The next job on my agenda was to head over to the studio, eager to do more cleaning and fixing stuff, especially screwing in those handles that were hanging loose off the cabinets. Once again, I sucked in a sharp breath when I glimpsed the sign—White's Waggles. It looked just as beautiful as it did the first night.

Entering the studio still gave me a thrill as I envisioned what it would be like when opening day arrived.

"Soon, there'll be all sorts of dogs running around," I said to Sadie, who was busy inspecting the new toys, probably deciding which one to break in first.

"Here, girl." I pulled out one of her tug toys that I kept in my back pocket for emergency reasons, figuring she'd find the new ones hard to resist and have them scattered all over the room in no time. I threw it across the room and she scampered to retrieve.

"Those toys aren't yours," I said sternly. "But you can play with your own." When she returned with it, I whipped it again, back and forth, back and forth until she plopped herself down for a nap, worn out from the running.

"So what do you think?" I asked out loud, once again talking to my dog. She often proved to be my best sounding board, as she agreed with everything I said. The perfect listener.

This time, I noticed her drooping eyes were completely shut, but I kept right on gabbing, so excited about everything that I felt the need to speak the words out loud, to somehow make them more real.

"It's looking better every day. Soon we'll be open for business."

I grew more ecstatic at this venture by the minute, and promptly got to work sweeping, wiping and fixing. After a solid hour of work, I sat down for a second and breathed in the anticipation of success.

Looking around, I was still amazed at how much my friends and family helped. Being on the receiving end was new to me as usually I was the one doing the helping. It was a humbling experience and resulted in my sadness slowly ebbing away. Keeping busy made me almost forget about being fired; and thoughts of my breakup with Jim were not as painful. What did I lose out on anyway? A cheapskate who conned money out of me, knowing darn well he'd never repay me? Who needed a man like that? Who needed any man, for that matter? It took me long enough to realize an important fact, namely, that I could make it on my own. Hadn't had a serious boyfriend before him and I could survive without one now.

Looking with pride down the length of the room, I noticed paint cans off to one side by the mural. Hazel was getting ready to add color to her work. I walked over and took a look. A few more dogs were penciled in.

I still found it hard to believe she took the time to do this.

*Something was up but I hadn't figured out what.*

Did she feel sorry for me and want to boost my ego? Had she come down with some horrid disease and figured it was time to forge a bond with her only child? Now, that was an awful thought. Or… was there a man in her life making her happy? Was that why she stayed out late sometimes? I figured she'd been engrossed in her paintings and wanted to keep working while the inspiration struck. But then again, occasionally she said she'd been out with friends. Was she hiding something? Could she really have a boyfriend? For real?

I shook my head. Couldn't be that. *"No man can make you happy,"* was her motto. I couldn't even remember her ever being out on a date or showing the least bit of interest in having a relationship. She never even reacted when some attractive older man walked by, so immersed in her mind's eye of her next painting.

"No way," I said out loud to a now snoring Sadie. "It couldn't be a man."

"Pardon?"

I turned to see Hazel walk in the door.

"Er, nothing."

"Talking to the dog again? You can't fool me." She smiled as she headed to the mural and got right to work. As usual, no casual conversation on her side, but that was okay with me.

I had to admit that being around her while she finished the mural, was unnerving. Something I was definitely not used to.

Grabbing a rag, I started dusting, but for some reason I couldn't keep my eyes off of Hazel. I'd never seen her at work before, as I was always banished from the room with an "I can't concentrate when you're around." I was amazed at her exquisite dexterity with a brush, as I watched her create a golden retriever out of a penciled outline, making the dog come to life, almost as if real and ready to jump out of the wall.

As much as I was delighted at what she was doing, unbidden and unwanted memories walked across my mind, stirring up old, buried feelings.

I always felt jealous of her paintings, as they'd stolen Hazel away for most of my childhood. It was like her art pieces were her children and they were demanding, requiring endless attention to detail, soaking up her time and effort. She was obsessed with them. I mean, who else had a mother who would stop her vehicle right in the middle of an intersection, regardless of a line-up of cars, to sketch something that caught her eye? Or cut up vegetables and rub them all over the canvas, to get the exact hue she wanted. Or show up at parent/teacher night, covered in paint, even splattered on her face? I could never forget the time she shook hands with Miss Garrison, my eighth grade teacher, and left grape stains on her hands. A weird shade, as well. Who knew what my mother combined to get this color but all I knew was that Miss Garrison's right hand was purple for close to a month.

A tear slid down my cheek. She had hurt me repeatedly and now she was being kind? Nicer? Did she think this would make up for all the pain she'd caused in the past?

*Could it?*

I shook my head. I just didn't know.

My thoughts were interrupted, gladly, I might add, by the arrival of Emma, a plastic bag dangling from her wrist and carrying two trays of Tim Hortons' coffee.

"Howdy," she said cheerily, laughing at my surprised expression. "We're all here again to finish up the cleaning; that is, if you don't mind."

"Of course not." Hell, I'd even welcome a visit from Kite if it kept my mind off of old hurtful memories.

As she pulled off her jean jacket, I stared at her T-shirt—white with 'White's Waggles' printed across it in red and black, to match the sign. She then dug around in the bag and pulled out a gold, gift-wrapped parcel, complete with a gold bow.

"For you," she said, handing it over.

"Nice shirt," I said with a grin, as I took the gift and just stood there holding it. "Can't take this, though. Whatever it is. You've given me too much as it is."

"You have to," she said. "I had it specially made for you. Go on, open it."

I slowly removed the tape from the paper, pushed it aside and smiled as I discovered the same T-shirt. Two of them. A smaller one for Sadie.

"Figured it'd get us all more in the mood." She grabbed her bag, pulled out another shirt, walked over and handed it to Hazel who quickly slid it on. She then went right back to her painting without saying a word. I was surprised she was so calm. As a kid, if I interrupted her, she'd scream, "Get away from me."

*Don't think about that, now.*

"But, Emma. I can't pay you for these," I said softly, although it felt so good to have her here and I thought the shirts were a brilliant touch.

"Pay me? They're a gift. Now, put on that T-shirt and let's get to work," she ordered. She went over, knelt down and pulled the shirt over Sadie's head. "Sorry, girl. You can go right back to sleep. Just want to get you dressed like the rest of the team here." Sadie glanced down for a second at what she had on, but quickly laid her head back on her paws, continuing her snooze.

I was wearing a bulky sweatshirt and pulling it off would make my hair stand up like a scarecrow, so I took off to the washroom to save anyone having to witness me like that. I exchanged my top for Emma's gift and as I preened in front of the mirror, once again I thought about just how close White's Waggles was to becoming a reality. Soon, really soon. I couldn't wait.

"Hey, are you going to spend all day in there?" yelled Emma. "There's stuff to be done."

"Coming right out," I answered as I patted my hair in place, secured it with a barrette and grabbed hold of the doorknob, just as Aunt T walked in, sporting a White's Waggles T-shirt and carrying paint cans and brushes.

"Nothing like a coat of paint to spruce things up," she said with a grin. "And don't worry, its forest green, just like you mentioned in your notebook."

Blown away, I couldn't say a word so I hugged her, picked up a roller and with three of us at work painting and drinking coffee; the room was finished in record time. As I stood back to admire the clean look of the walls, I could hear someone at the door.

"Well, the posters advertising the grand opening are plastered all over Hamilton. I even handed out a bunch to people on the street," said an excited Maggie as she bounded in waving a newspaper in one hand, a bottle of red wine in the other. "The ad came out today in the Spectator. I think the offer of free dog biscuits will be a hit. We're all set. Ready for business. A true milestone. Now, let's have a drink to toast future success." She clanked the bottle on the desk, then took off back to her car and brought back a box containing four wine glasses.

"But it's only ten in the morning," I protested.

"This is all too exciting not to raise a glass and toast," said Aunt T. Obviously, she seemed to know what Maggie was bringing, as she also took off to her car and came back with a cake spelling out "Congratulations, Jessie" on it. Once again, I knew she was piling on a liberal dose of support to keep me upbeat and positive. You just gotta love her.

"Oh my goodness." I giggled. "Are you trying to get me drunk?"

But I was moved by their thoughtfulness.

"Who says anything about getting drunk? We still have stuff to do. But one glass is okay," said Emma.

"All right. Just one, half full, please."

"But first." Emma grabbed another package from her bag. "You have to put this on, Maggie."

I laughed as Maggie opened it up. The parcel contained another White's Waggles T-shirt, which she quickly threw on over her blouse and strutted up and down the studio as if a model on a runway.

"I'll wear this with pride, not to mention the free advertising," said Maggie, as she got to work opening up folding chairs. She then poured us all a drink and raising our glasses, she made a toast. "To White's Waggles. Long may it live."

"To White's Waggles," we all chimed in, clinking our glasses and taking sips as per a traditional toast.

"To being single and loving it," added Maggie as once again we clinked and drank. Lately we'd been including that in our Wednesday evening toasts. Even Hazel and Aunt T joined in, both being single as well.

The light died in Emma's eyes. I quickly said, "You still okay about Joseph?"

"Never better," she answered and we all clinked again.

But I knew she was lying. She had that grief-stricken look whenever the subject of guys came up.

"Men! They're good for nothing," I said loudly, hamming it up. Maybe if we all said it enough times, we'd believe it, or at least Emma and I would. The rest seemed to embrace being manless. I took a big long sip this time. Really, a huge gulp, then spit most of it out when a knock and a loud booming voice reverberated from the doorway, startling me.

"Thought you were running a dog daycare, not a bar?"

Damn. As I grabbed a paper towel and tried to wipe the spit off my face, I looked over to see Red standing there. How embarrassing. The businesswoman who'd wanted a loan a few days ago with wine slobber all over the place. A human fountain.

*Had he heard my comment about men?* I wished Maggie had shut the door and locked it. That would have kept the riff raff out.

I jumped up, trying to appear composed and sophisticated but when I looked down at myself, I was sure he wouldn't buy it, not with wet, red stains streaking down my T-shirt.

"We're celebrating," I said, snottily I might add. "But once again. None of your business. I'm on my own property."

"I think he's kidding, Jessie," said Maggie, giving me an odd look.

"What's next? Tree climbing?" he asked.

Everyone started to laugh, as they all knew my habits. I

also saw that his eyes were twinkling and he was trying to fight off a grin.

"What are you doing here?" I asked. "Coming to gloat about how you refused my loan?"

His eyes flicked around the room then came to rest on mine. I wasn't sure, but I thought he looked impressed. Or at least that might be why he raised his eyebrows. Who knew? Maybe he had a nervous tic.

"Thought I'd offer to do the roof myself," he said gruffly, his eyes avoiding mine. "That is, if it's okay with you."

He was offering to help? Really? No way. I didn't believe him.

"So you think you could do it better than me?"

"No doubt whatsoever." This time his eyes held mine and he was full out smiling. We both knew I was talking about the tree house.

"What's the angle?" I finally asked, knowing darn well I couldn't fix a roof.

"No angle."

"She'll take your help," said Maggie and Emma at the same time.

I gave them a dirty look. "I can't afford to pay you. For labor or supplies."

"I can," piped up all four of them.

"No way," I said sternly.

"I have a pile of shingles I won't be using and a few friends who'll work for a case of beer," insisted Red. "It's free."

"I'll get the booze," said Maggie.

"I'll get the munchies," said Emma. "And by the way,

you haven't even introduced us."

"Oh. This here's Red, er Brian. This is Emma, Maggie, my Aunt T and of course you know my mother."

"Red, huh! How original," he said, before shaking everyone's hands.

Betrayers. They all looked like they were about to drool over him. Hazel and Aunt T as well.

"So, what's your answer? Is it a go?"

"There has to be a catch somewhere." I stared at him, willing him to reveal his ulterior motive.

"No catch."

His stare never wavered. I tried to outlast him, but blinked several times before saying, "Okay, then. But I'm not a charity case. I'll pay you back." I swallowed my pride and accepted his offer. I really needed that new roof.

"Not necessary, but if you want." He shrugged his shoulders. "I'll be here bright and early Saturday morning, if that's okay."

"Fine."

He started to leave, then looked back saying, "Sure you don't mind that a man's doing the work?"

"What?"

"Judging by the toasts and clinking of glasses as I came in, you think we're good for nothing." He looked serious but again there was that twinkle in his eyes.

"Oh, just joking around." But I could feel my face redden.

"Thought I'd make sure." With that, he left.

Sheesh! I was burning up with embarrassment.

"That's the loan officer?" asked Emma, dramatically fanning her face.

I nodded.

"Hot stuff."

"Hot bod, too," said Maggie. "He's also your neighbor?"

"Yes. You really think he's attractive?" I did, too. But no way was I letting on that little piece of information. I'd never hear the end of it.

"Are you kidding?" asked Emma. "He's downright delicious. Eye candy for sure."

"Well, I don't see it," I said.

"Are you blind?" asked Maggie. "Wouldn't throw him out of my bed."

"Has anyone ever been in your bed?" asked Emma.

Maggie rolled her eyes. "No comment."

"No need for ridicule," I said. "That guy's nothing but a big pain in the butt."

"But he's doing free work for you. Can't be that bad of a guy," said Maggie.

"Well, he is and it's not free. I'll pay him eventually."

"How about we all go into the kitchen and I'll make us some sandwiches before we get back to work. We can have the cake for dessert. Alcohol with no food in our bellies is dangerous," interjected Aunt T, probably trying to stave off any more arguing about Red.

"Just one rule. I don't want to talk about my neighbor any more," I said.

"Me thinks the lady does protest too much," said Maggie.

"No Shakespeare talk either."

"Well, I'm up for food," said Emma. "Any more booze and I'll be convincing you all to join me while I egg

Joseph's house, or something even more evil. Like slash his tires."

"Could be fun to do that," said Maggie. "Booze or not, I'm game anytime you want. The ultimate revenge thing might knock some sense into him. Prevent him from going after someone else."

"Yeah, great thing for a respectable pediatrician to be caught doing," I said. "Come on. Off to Hazel's kitchen we go."

"It's your kitchen, too," said Hazel in a soft voice. But I ignored her. No way. It was hers and my stay here was temporary. I was still hoping to find my own place, at some point.

As we walked over, all I could think about was—*why in the world would Red help out?*

Didn't make sense.

Didn't make sense at all, but what was that saying? Don't look a gift horse in the mouth? Even though he was a pain in the butt, Red was proving useful.

Maybe, just maybe, I wouldn't throw that rock in his window after all. At least I'd think about it.

## *Twelve*

"What the hell?"

Loud noises dive-bombed my sleep and without thinking, I screamed at the top of my lungs, "If you're a burglar, better run before I sic my dog on you."

I looked down at Sadie snoring away. Yeah, right. *She'd sure scare someone away.* She hadn't even heard the commotion and knowing her temperament, she'd probably run off with the intruder.

Wait a sec! If someone was breaking in, shouldn't I be doing something? Like calling 911? But then again, why would he or she be making so much noise? Or was it just a stupid burglar? Like one of those robbers who steals something but accidentally drops his wallet at the scene, directing the police to his home.

Groggy and half-asleep, I tried to listen carefully. Hmmmm… sounded like loud thuds, barking and male voices shouting back and forth. I was pissed. Was it workmen fixing roads again? Didn't they know others slept around here? Or couldn't they at least come back later?

Rubbing my tired eyes, I finally swung my legs out of

bed, stood up and grasped hold of the windowsill to look out in the back yard. I realized part of the reason I was hearing so much outside noise was I'd forgotten to close the window and the screen was no barrier to keeping things quiet.

I shook my head trying to clear it out, as I was still in foggy sleep mode. No suspicious characters milling around dressed in black, wearing ski masks to conceal their identities, but what looked like a team of men carrying large bundles of something black and dropping them on blue tarps. Red's dog was running around letting out a bark every once in a while, as if directing them. How odd!

Hearing a loud clearing of the throat, I looked straight down to find one of the guys staring up at me. Underneath a Toronto Blue Jays' baseball cap, I caught sight of sunset hair. Red! With his arms crossed, he looked annoyed. I guess he'd heard my loud complaint and warning. Sure scared him, huh!

"We're out here doing the roof," he said. "What did you think was happening? I told you we'd be coming."

"But it's," I looked at my watch. "Oh, 10:30." Oops, I'd slept in. What an idiot I was. Here he was trying to help me and I was being an old crab. I also probably looked a mess, as I glanced down at the faded Tiger-Cat T-shirt I'd worn to bed. I reached up to pat my hair into some kind of order, as I was sure it looked like a typhoon had swept through.

"Not everyone snoozes their life away, you know," he added.

"Oh, sorry. Late night last night."

His eyes narrowed. "Drinking more wine?"

*What was it to him?*

"Of course not." This time it was my turn to sound indignant. Once again, it was none of his business.

I wanted to say more but made an attempt to stifle my sharp tongue. After all, it wouldn't pay to engage in a verbal war, especially since Red was doing me a huge favor. I really needed this roof done so I had to play nice and not frustrate him. So what if he was the reason I'd gone to bed so darn late? I'd been up trying to figure out my finances, trying to determine just where I stood. So far, I was drowning in bright red ink, with bills to pay and not enough money to pay them. Damn him for not giving me that loan.

But back to the task at hand. *Remember—play nice, Jessie.*

"Er… would you guys like some coffee?" Hopefully that would help endear myself, at least a little bit, as the other workers were starting to look up and stare. I was sure they'd never seen a real, live, ugly old witch before and I was probably scaring them. I needed to get away from the window and stop giving everyone a private screening of my bedroom apparel. La Senza, it definitely wasn't. Coffee was the least I could do.

"That'd be nice," he answered as, surprise, a grin flitted across his face. It changed his whole appearance instantly, softening him into a sweet 'aw shucks' kinda guy.

Man, but he was pretty darn breathtaking as I took in his jean cutoffs and black T-shirt, the sleeves ripped out. Maggie was right. He was definitely eye candy. Too bad he didn't have a great personality to go along with it, instead of an arrogant, snobby one. But, hey, he did smile. At least a bit. That was a beginning, even though I was sure he was silently laughing at me, not with me.

Realizing I was just standing there, staring at him, I quickly scrambled away from the window frame and threw on jeans and a clean T-shirt, hoping he hadn't noticed me checking him out. Running down to the kitchen, I stopped in my tracks. Something was different. I looked around. Hazel wasn't there.

That was odd. Usually on a Saturday, she'd be reading the newspaper and drinking coffee by the gallon, caffeine being her one vice in her otherwise health conscious world.

Worried, I ran back upstairs and checked her bed. Nope. Hadn't been slept in. I quickly grabbed my phone to see if she'd called. Sure enough, there was a message saying she was staying overnight with a friend. I guess I'd slept through the ring. What friend, I hadn't a clue. Didn't even know she had close friends besides her paintings. They seemed to be all she needed. Once again, I thought—did she have a boyfriend? That was hard to think about since she'd always been such a loner but then again, she'd never stayed out all night before. Or at least while I'd been home. But it was also none of my business. She had every right to date.

I shook my head free of such thoughts as I had Red to think of, and quickly tore off back to the kitchen, and got the coffee going. Searching through my stash of junk food, I pulled out a box of oatmeal muffins I'd picked up the day before. Arranging mugs, plates and goodies on a tray, I added the coffee pot and headed out to be greeted by a loud, dramatic—"Thank goodness." A tall, sandy haired guy came towards me. He was dressed in blue overalls, red plaid shirt and big, brown heavy work boots.

He tipped his baseball hat and said, "You're an angel. Coffee is just what I need. Slept in and didn't have time to get some this morning." He grabbed a steaming cup and took a sip, then uttered a loud sigh of contentment. "Name's Dave, by the way. And you must be Jessie."

"Nice to meet you and thanks for helping. 'Preciate it."

"No problem. Me and Brian go way back."

Brian? Who was that? I wracked my foggy, sleep deprived brain.

"Your neighbor," he added, obviously cluing into my blank look.

Oh right, Red.

"Really? Brian's from Hamilton?" I jumped in, trying not to appear like an idiot.

"Yep. Went to Bentwood High together."

"Hey, no revealing my secrets," said Red, as he strolled over. He actually had another smile on his face as he picked up a mug. Two smiles in one day? Call up Guinness. A record was set.

"Come on and join us," he yelled to the other men. As they came over, he said, "This here's Mike and Jeb."

"Hi," I said, reaching out to shake their hands. "Thanks for helping."

"No problem," said Mike, reaching for a muffin. "After all, Brian is the first person to help us build our decks or whatever else we need done."

"Yep. He helped do my roof so I'm glad to help him

back. First bit of exercise I've had in months," said Jeb, a husky blond.

"Well, you should get away from that computer of yours sometimes," teased Dave.

"Hey. Someone's gotta keep an eye on the stock market."

"Jeb's a stockbroker," said Mike, keeping me in the loop.

I noticed Red stayed quiet. His eyes stared off as if deep in thought. Finally, he gulped his coffee down quickly, how he could do that with such hot liquid I couldn't tell, and then walked away saying, "Gotta check something. Be right back."

"He's a perfectionist," said Mike. "Always has to double and triple check his work."

"Two steps ahead of everyone," added Jeb.

"Did all of you go to the same high school?" I asked, curious to get more info now that Red wasn't around. I hated to admit it, but he intrigued me.

"Yep," said Dave. He seemed like the designated spokesperson. "Sure did. All played football together, too. Old Brian there was the quarterback."

"Best player in the state. Recruited for football scholarships in five colleges," added Mike.

"But oh no, he had to turn them all down and head to Harvard to study architecture," added Jeb, but there was pride in his voice.

"Architecture? But he's a loan officer," I said.

"You don't know?" asked Dave, looking quizzical.

"Know what?"

"Brian's a renowned architect. We're real proud of

him. His work is all over Canada and the U.S. and he's in big demand. Even designed a building over in Dubai. He's just home because his dad is sick," said Dave. "Don't know how you did it, but you lucked out having the best around doing your roof. He loves getting involved in every part of building. Heck, he's made the laying of shingles an art form."

What? So he really did know what he was doing when he made suggestions about my tree house?

"But why is he working in a bank?"

"A bank? Didn't know that. I swear that guy's a workaholic," said Dave. "He grew up doing summer jobs there, all through university. Guess he's helping out." He shook his head, looking worried. "He's been acting strange since he discovered his fiancée cheated on him." He stopped for a moment before saying quietly, "Here he comes. Reckon he won't like us talking about him."

A hush went through the group.

"Wanted to make sure I had the right number of shingles," said Red. He looked around and then grabbed a muffin, oblivious to the fact he'd been the topic of discussion. Or maybe he had a suspicion, as his eyebrows rose a fraction when he looked at me.

My mind was twirling as I watched Sadie playing off to the side with Squid.

I was having my roof put on by a famous architect? Who also helped build my tree house and had even worked in Dubai? And… he also had a fiancée? Who cheated? Were they still together? And I still didn't get the whole bank scenario. Okay, he worked there during university, but what was he doing there now? And how come he had so many days off? He obviously wasn't there every day because his car was in the driveway most of the time. Man, this was confusing.

"C'mon guys. Back to work. Coffee break's over."

Thank goodness he interrupted my thoughts. A headache threatened.

"You're a hard boss to work for," complained Jeb.

"Awwww... you're just soft from all that typing stuff you do," said Mike.

"Better than working with cars," fired back Jeb.

"Hah! Say that the next time you bring your Ford to my garage," said Mike.

Jeb pretended to be annoyed, but it was obviously all said in good humor. The guys seemed close.

"Can I help?" I asked, figuring I could at least do that. Pay my way, so to speak.

Red started to shake his head no, then stopped and looked at me for a long while.

"Well, okay. You can toss the scraps we throw off the roof into those boxes." He pointed to a bunch, stacked up against the house.

"Okay, I'll do that."

Judging by a flare of compassion in his eyes, I was sure he didn't need nor want my help but figured I needed to feel involved for my pride's sake. Who needed pity, but I couldn't very well renege on my offer. I also couldn't stop staring at his butt when he climbed up the ladder to the roof. It was a damn fine piece of work. Good architecture going on there, that was for sure.

But just what was his story? If I had to come up with a description, the word complex came to mind. A famous architect, traveling and working the world, but obviously a home oriented guy as well, especially if he took time off to see his father, not to mention he also had the same friends since high school. And he might be engaged as well?

"Daydreaming, are you?"

I looked up to see a curious Red staring at me.

"What?"

"I asked three times if you could toss up a bottle of water for Dave. He's apparently dying of thirst."

"Oh, sorry." I quickly ran over, got one and climbed up, handing it over.

"No problem."

At least he was a good sport about it but as our hands touched, an electric jolt raced through me. Startled, I jumped and then sneezed, trying to hide my reaction. Luckily, I didn't fall off the ladder.

"Damn allergies," I said, rubbing my eyes, pretending to be having some kind of reaction, as I climbed back down.

Sheesh! Jim never elicited any response like that from me. It was an odd feeling. As if my mind was going in one direction while my body was headed the other way. Somehow, against my will, I found myself attracted to Red and as a matter of fact, my heart still seemed to be racing to the beat of the nail gun he was using.

Crap! Who needed this?

Wanting to get my mind off my neighbor, I was just about to make an excuse to get away, when a car pulled up and out popped Maggie and Emma. Thank goodness. An escape!

"Excuse me," I said, as I quickly headed over to greet them.

"Told you we'd be here to help," said Emma, all decked out in purple overalls and a bright yellow T-shirt. Maggie had on her usual scruffy jeans with a green plaid shirt, hair stuffed up under a Hamilton Bulldogs' cap. Emma looked like a fashion plate, while Maggie and I looked like part of the crew. Hell, I couldn't even fit into most of my clothes after that last eating binge. I was wearing my fat ones that I'd almost given away when I'd hit my lowest weight in years. Thank goodness, I didn't.

"Used to help my daddy shingle," continued Emma, obviously in a gay mood, as she strutted right over to inspect their work. "Hi, guys," she said cheerily, waving her hand.

Dave, Jeb and Mike looked blown away by her vibrancy, not to mention her display of bright colors topped by orange and black hair piled high on her head.

Maggie headed over, carrying a large platter. "Made some sandwiches and snacks." She then leaned over to whisper, "How come your face is so flushed? Not getting sick, are you?"

"No, I'm okay. You don't have to play doctor with me. Come on. Let's put this stuff in the kitchen." I quickly changed the subject, since I didn't want her to know the reason I was red was from being in my neighbor's close proximity. Hell, I was still trying to get over Jim. I shouldn't be reacting to another guy so soon.

"There's more in the trunk," said Maggie.

"Can't believe you did all this," I said as I grabbed three bags of snacks from the trunk. "I was just going to order pizza."

"Said we'd do it," said Maggie.

I jumped back as I heard pounding footsteps and looked to see Dave rushing over.

"Well, let me help you, little lady," he said, as he took the tray from Maggie, nodding at her cap. "You a Bulldogs' fan, too?"

"Never miss a game," she said.

I was actually surprised Maggie didn't tell him to get lost. She was a huge advocate of women's rights and didn't take too kindly to men folk helping her out if she could do it herself. Especially calling her "little lady". I'd heard her chastise guys for trying to hold a door for her. Surely she'd set him straight. But I literally gasped in shock as tough cookie Maggie, instead of protesting, actually giggled and directed him to the kitchen. They set off, talking about hockey. Weird as anything.

I gathered up the rest and started to follow with my own load, just as the two of them came rushing back out the door. Dave led a flushed Maggie over to inspect their work and I couldn't help but notice that he bypassed me as I struggled with a bunch of bags. I guess chivalry was dead when it came to me. Go figure! As I looked over to see Mike and Jeb fawn over Emma, I decided that Wednesday night needed to come soon, to reaffirm our love for being single. Who needed these hard working, sweat stained cowboy types anyway? I certainly didn't, even though it was hard work keeping my eyes from glancing over at my very cute neighbor. *Stop that.* I turned and headed in.

After unloading the groceries on the table, I joined the group again. Watching Red, just couldn't help myself, I picked up on the fact that he was getting agitated as he looked over, a scowl on his face, obviously noticing the lessening of work as the men fussed around with their guests. He glanced at his watch, then said loudly, "Just a bit more before we break for lunch, please."

"Er, sorry, boss," said Dave, respectfully. Not the least bit sarcastic.

Much to my surprise, they all jumped to do his bidding, while Maggie, Emma and I wandered around trying to help by dumping waste materials in boxes and handing up bottles of water. I kept away from Red although I still found myself watching him. A few times he even caught me and grinned, so after that I made sure I stayed on the opposite side of the studio at all times. As far away from him as I could.

Around noon, we broke for lunch amid sighs of pleasure from the guys when they saw the feast Maggie and Emma had prepared. When I added the booze, they looked like they'd died and gone to heaven, although I noticed they weren't gulping the pints down and asking for another. Fine by me. Certainly didn't need a bunch of drunk workers around.

As I assisted everyone in filling his or her plates, playing the role of proper hostess, I still noted that Maggie seemed to be hitting it off with Dave. Big-time. From the bits and pieces I could gather from their conversation, it turned out he had custody of a young son and was fascinated that my friend was a pediatrician, not to mention by their obvious shared liking of the Bulldogs. They were currently engaged in an intense discussion about children and their ailments. I also noticed Red stayed far away from me and refused to drink even one beer. Good! My heart needed a rest from the chaos he set off inside me when he was too near.

Mostly, we were entertained by Emma's stories, all during lunch. She always had something interesting happening to her and her latest was about her car being hit by a kid on a tricycle. She was threatened a lawsuit by the boy's mother, just for having her vehicle parked in her own parking spot where the child plowed into it. How ludicrous, but Emma seemed to attract drama. Weird things really did happen to her but it made for entertaining conversation. Good icebreakers.

Noticing the sandwiches were going fast, I ran in to get some more goodies and almost tripped over Emma when I started to head out again. She must have been following right behind.

"You free for supper tonight?" she asked.

It was then I noticed how tired she looked and that heavy make-up was caked over the black marks under her eyes.

"Are you kidding? After all you've done to help me? Of course."

"Good. Maggie's joining us, too."

"Need company, huh?" She looked worried about something. Was Joseph bothering her?

"It'd be nice."

She gathered up a platter of cookies and headed back out. I followed, wondering what the problem was but soon got busy passing around dessert.

After gulping down a couple of cookies, Red jumped up and climbed back up on the roof. His friends joined him and before I knew it, it was six o'clock and everything was done.

"Thank you so much," I said. "I really appreciate all you did."

"No problem," said Red, as he started to pack up. I'd considered asking them to stay for supper earlier in the day, but now had plans with Maggie and Emma.

As I watched Red walk away, I still struggled on how to pay him back. It might be quite a while before I had any spare cash hanging around.

Maybe I could offer to cut his lawn or do his laundry. Nope! That'd be kinda gross. Especially if I had to wash his underwear.

Better yet! I could offer free daycare for his dog. Maybe, but Squid seemed happiest when his master was around, which was actually quite a bit.

I'd have to come up with something.

*This was a huge gesture of kindness from an absolute stranger.*

## *Thirteen*

Since all three of us had Irish blood, Emma insisted we go to Dooley's Irish Pub clear across town. It'd been receiving rave reviews and we'd talked about trying it out at some point. I volunteered to drive as a way of thanking them for all their help. It was the least I could do.

The Pub was situated in a community called Ancaster, formerly a little town, now under the auspices of Hamilton. I'd forgotten what a swanky area it was, as we drove by what seemed to be mansion after mansion. Finally finding the restaurant, I quickly parked in the lot behind the building and we walked around to the front door

Green curtains were strung across the large window and the name Dooley's was painted in green on the black door. It looked warm and inviting, and walking in we were immediately immersed in the magical land of Eire favoring, of course, Irish décor and food. Naturally, Irish stew was the number one special written on the black chalkboard sitting beside the cash register, but the second dish looked intriguing—cabbage and corned beef pizza, guaranteed to whet the appetite of good old pizza lovers like me. Curious, I continued to look around, noting that the tablecloths were sprinkled with shiny green paper cutouts of shamrocks, Oh Danny Boy was playing softly in the background and there were a few Irish dancers performing on a small stage off to the right. The atmosphere was fun and lively.

Maggie picked out a corner booth and I slid in beside her while Emma sat across from us. The restaurant host brought us glasses filled with ice water and left us alone to look at the menu, saying that our waitress would be with us shortly. I read with delight all the new dishes I'd love to try.

"First let's have a glass of wine," said Emma. "We have to celebrate the new roof." She beckoned over the waitress and placed her order. Red merlot for all.

Discreetly, I reached down into my purse, flipped open my wallet and snuck a peek. Good. I had a couple of twenties, courtesy of rolling all the change in my piggy bank. Enough to pay for my dinner, at least. In fact, I should pay everyone's meal for helping out but just couldn't afford it. One day, I hoped.

"Hey, guys. What do you make of this?" asked Emma. "Do you remember me telling you about the housekeeper who took care of my Grandpa?"

"Sure do," said Maggie.

"Yep," I said.

"Well her son, Drew Fitzgerald wants to pay me a visit. Isn't that kind of odd?"

"Have you met him before?" I asked.

"No. Didn't even know she had a son. He's a lawyer." She paused for a second before saying, "Do you think he's going to contest the will?"

So that was what had got her in a tizzy.

"Why would he do that?" I asked. "You're the only remaining relative and besides your grandpa had a will."

"Yeah, but we weren't close. Josh suspects her son is trying to get more money for his mother, which of course would benefit him, by claiming she deserves more than the generous sum of money left her."

Good old Josh Stein, Emma's financial advisor. I'd met him once and sized him up as the ultimate gold-digger. I swear money signs literally flashed in his eyes whenever he looked at Emma. I figured he was the one after her money so planted scare tactics to keep her tied to him. But Emma adored him, so I kept my mouth shut.

"Did you set up a time?" asked Maggie. "Or did you refuse the invitation?"

"I decided to meet him just to see what's up. Figured it's better to know my possible enemies. It's not for a while though." Another pause. "Would you look into it for me?"

It took a bit to realize she meant me.

"What?" I asked.

"Well you're a lawyer. Can you check it out? See if he stands a chance and what loopholes he could possibly find? Just so I'll be prepared?"

"Here are your drinks, ladies," said the waitress.

Good. Saved by the wine.

"To White's Waggles," said Maggie, raising her glass.

"To White's Waggles," Emma and I reiterated, clinking our glasses.

After taking a swig, Emma said, "So will you? Check into it?"

Not so saved. I was about to say no, not wanting to do anything "lawyerly" that would remind me of what I'd lost, but the woeful look on her face did me in.

"Of course I will."

Poor Emma. Ever since she received that inheritance she'd received requests for money so many times she'd lost count. No wonder she was suspicious.

"So how's it going with the two of you anyway?" asked Maggie, probably sensing my discomfort and changing the topic. "How are you both doing without Joseph and Jim?"

"Getting better," I answered. "Rarely think about him anymore."

"Wish I could say the same," said Emma. "But I'm improving. Instead of fifty times a day, I'm down to thirty."

"Told you, you're better off without a guy," said Maggie, as she raised her glass. "Here's to the single life. Long may it live."

We clinked and sipped.

How ironic at the very moment all of us were embracing not being hitched to anyone, Emma whispered, "Look who's here." Before I could even turn my head, she smiled and waved.

Oh, no! It was Red, Dave, Mike and Jeb at the door. What made it even worse, was Maggie yelled out, "Care to join us?" Looking at her face, I was sure I detected a glint in her eye. I bet she arranged this and didn't tell me for fear I wouldn't come. She was right. I wouldn't.

Crap! I certainly didn't want to deal with my neighbor right now and all the feelings he stirred up, but judging by the way Dave's face lit up at Maggie's suggestion, I guess it was a sure thing. Dammit. They were joining us. I watched as he conferred with the others, noting Red did not seem too pleased, shrugging his shoulders with a resigned look on his face, and then they all headed our way. The waitress arrived as well saying, "Can I help you?"

"Yes," said Dave. "We're going to join these lovely ladies. Can you move us all to a larger table, please?"

"Sure can," said the waitress with a giggle and a blush, obviously affected by all the testosterone. Dave alone oozed enough charm for all of them. She pointed to a large table nearby. "You can sit there."

After we got situated in our new space, the waitress handed the guys menus and said she'd be back in a jiffy. To add to my frustration, Red was across from me. He didn't choose the seat. It was all that was left after the other guys sat down.

Maggie and Dave immediately started in on another conversation about children and their ailments, Emma was talking to Jeb and Mike about home repairs while Red and I sat in silence. Usually I was a gabber by nature but for the life of me I was tongue-tied and couldn't think of anything to say and he didn't speak at all. In fact, he looked grateful when the waitress came back and the conversation swung around the table about ordering the pizza. It was a group decision to try the cabbage and meat special and while we waited for the pies to appear, I couldn't take it anymore and said, "Thanks again for doing the roof."

"Just glad to get rid of those extra shingles."

"Sure appreciate it though," I said, wondering who in hell had spare shingles lying around? And just the right amount to do my roof?

Silence stretched out again and I tried to ignore it by listening in on Maggie and Emma's conversations, while searching for a topic to discuss with Red. Surely, there was something we had in common that we could talk about. Damn. Couldn't think of a thing. So I laughed along with the others at Emma's monologue about getting stuck in the elevator with an older man eating garlic cloves out of a paper bag as if they were peanuts.

When the pizza finally arrived, Red looked visibly happy as if thrilled he now had an excuse not to talk. Or maybe he was just hungry, but man, this guy lacked social skills. He could at least make some effort. It shouldn't all be up to me. But I had to admit I was also grateful that, with my mouth full, I wasn't tempted or expected to make small talk either. Luckily Maggie began sharing humorous anecdotes from work, which prompted Dave, Mike and Jeb to join in.

This helped us all get through dinner and Emma was beginning to look less stressed, so that was a good thing.

After we'd eaten our way through three large pizzas, Emma said, "Hey, let's all go to Jake's for a drink. Heard there's a great jazz band playing there tonight."

"I'm in," said Maggie.

"Me too," added Dave. "And I'm sure Jeb and Mike will come. They never turn down a night out."

"You betcha," said Jeb. "Mike and I have been trying to get together for ages so I certainly don't want the night to end yet."

"I'll go," said Mike.

"What about you, Brian? You in?"

"Yeah, Jessie," said Emma. "Are you coming?"

"No, thank you," said Red and I at the exact same time.

"Well," said Dave. "I'll give you a lift home then join you guys at Jake's."

"Jesse's got her car here," said Maggie. "How about we all go with you guys and she can drive Brian home. They live right next door to each other."

What was wrong with her? Couldn't she pick up on the evil vibes I was sending her? Now I had no choice but to say, "Sure, I can drive you home."

"Okay," he said, but didn't look too pleased. I guess he felt he had no choice either.

"Pssst… Jessie," hissed Maggie. "Isn't that Jim standing by the door?"

"No way," I said, as I turned around to look.

A tall blond man slowly perused the room, as if searching for someone. Was it Jim? For real?

"Jessie," he called out, noticing me and practically running over.

Man, it really was him. His hair was a bit longer, he'd grown a beard but I'd know those eyes anywhere with their big fringed girly lashes. Lashes I'd die for.

"Parletta said you'd moved back home. Paid you a visit and your mother told me where you were." He widened his arms. "How about a great big hug for your honey bunny." He smiled, fully expecting me to comply.

Honey bunny? Confused, I froze, not knowing what to do, feeling six pairs of eyes on me.

Damn! I should never have left that note for Hazel,

telling her where I was. But she knew I'd been looking for him and probably figured I could finally get the money he owed.

"What's the matter? Not glad to see me?" He pouted, looking genuinely hurt. "I've missed you sooo much."

When I still didn't move, he looked around, then said, "How about we go over there in the lobby. At least we'll have a bit of privacy."

"Don't do it," said Maggie, grabbing my arm.

Her voice pulled me out of my trance.

"Have to," I said, shrugging her arm off. The money he'd scammed would sure come in handy right about now.

Somehow, I managed to get up. Jim grabbed my hand, but I shook it free and followed him to an isolated area where a few chairs had been set up to accommodate extra diners waiting to be seated. Fortunately, no one was there.

"I realized I can't live without you," said Jim. "Surely you feel the same?"

"Get real." At last, I found my voice. "You stole from me."

"But I needed it." He never batted an eyelash. Like, the fact he needed it would make it all right.

"It's called stealing. A felony."

"Awwwww... baby, c'mon. We all have failings."

"And another thing. What happened to your job?"

He shrugged his shoulders. "They were horrible people to work for."

"Yeah, you stole from them too. And by the way, I'd like my money back."

"Sweetie!" He looked insulted. "You know I don't have any lying around."

"How would I know that? You lied to me about everything."

"A few small white ones. What's the big deal, anyway?" He looked indignant. "Why are you making such a fuss about nothing? We're a couple. We should be sharing everything. Money included. Now, c'mon and give me a kiss."

He moved closer but I backed away, staring at him in amazement. He just brushed off stealing and lying as if it were nothing.

Still looking hurt, he said, "Why are acting like this? Don't you wanna get back with me? We're good together, baby."

Oh, no. Not the lopsided smile. He looked so damn cute when he did that, knowing it always undid me every single time.

My heart softened a tad.

Did I want to get back together? Could I forgive him?

Considering the circumstances, of course the answer should be no but as I stared at him, I couldn't help but feel attraction. Man, he was gorgeous. A beautiful face, tall with muscles of steel. Wrapped in his hugs always felt comforting, soothing not to mention exciting as hell. I was not a good-looking girl by beauty's standards and I'd always been in awe that this gorgeous hunk of guy wanted to be with me. How about that for bad self-esteem?

*Was the stealing and lying really so bad?*

As if sensing my weakening, Jim put his arms around me. Ashamedly, I did the same. I gazed up into his eyes.

*Could we work this out?*

Leaning down for a kiss, he murmured, "You're too darn nice for me to ever let you go again."

*Nice?*

I pushed away.

It was being "nice" that got me in trouble in the first place. What was I thinking? This guy was nothing but trouble. How could I even consider taking him back? *Had I lost my mind?*

I looked around and spotted a glass of wine on a nearby table.

"Excuse me," I muttered, and much to the astonishment of the woman obviously enjoying a bottle of wine with a date, I picked it up and threw it in Jim's face.

"Get lost, jerk. Instead of trying to get me back, you should fear a lawsuit."

I could feel my lips turning up into a grin as he stood there, dripping red wine, a stunned expression in his eyes. I knew at that moment it was completely over. Through. Done. I'd never get that money back anyway. Jim had now been relegated to a past mistake. It was onward and upward from here on in.

"So here's where you've gotten to, sweetie." An arm wrapped around me and a kiss landed on my head. "I've been looking all over for you."

Shocked, I looked up to see Red, sporting the most dazzling smile I'd ever seen. He leaned in for another kiss. This time, right on my mouth. My heart raced so fast, I wondered if there was a defibrillator around, just in case I went into cardiac arrest.

"Just play along," he whispered, as he raised his head.

Turning to walk away, Red kept his arm around me and I caught Jim's shocked expression out of the corner of my eye. I had to admit I enjoyed that immensely.

Still shaken by Red's kiss, I never said a word as we settled the bill and all of us went to our cars. I was startled when my neighbor got in the passenger seat but then remembered I was to take him home.

"Be back in a second," I said, suddenly remembering something I had to do.

Racing into the restaurant again, I headed to the table where I'd borrowed the wine.

"So sorry for ruining your evening," I said, pulling out a twenty. "Here, this should cover it."

"Are you kidding? Keep your money," said the woman. "That was awesome. I wished I could have done that to the last guy who treated me like dirt."

The man she was with didn't look too happy and eagerly grabbed the cash I offered. Hoped she dumped him soon.

Getting back in the car, I turned the radio on, not wanting to cope with small talk. At least with music blaring I could focus on the tunes. Rude, yes. But I was tired and in survival mode. Jim's appearance had really upset me, but not as much as Red's kiss and having him nearby disturbed me even more. Luckily, the drive home went by fast, thank goodness for the Beatles, and soon I pulled into my laneway.

Red jumped out to open my door before I even had the keys out of the ignition saying, "I'll walk you to the door."

"No need to," I said, as I slowly got out.

We both stared at each other for an awkward moment and I sorta thought his gaze dropped to my lips, but before I was sure about that, he muttered, "Okay", turned and walked away.

Watching him go, I had one last thing to say.

"What did you do that for?" I yelled.

He stopped in his tracks.

"Do what?"

"At the restaurant. Why did you get involved?"

"Thought I could help." He turned to face me.

"I was handling it okay."

"I know."

"I don't need to be saved by a man."

"I know that, too."

"Just wanted to make sure you do."

As I walked into the house, guilt surfaced.

Having Jim think I had a boyfriend helped a lot. That way, he'd leave me alone because I knew for sure, he had too much of an ego to beg, thinking he was every woman's fantasy.

Red did help. A lot.

But somehow, I couldn't bring myself to thank him.

I'd built walls for a reason and I wasn't about to let them down.

## *Fourteen*

Today was the day. The grand opening of White's Waggles. After weeks of intense preparation, it was finally here.

Excited, I jumped out of bed and raced for a shower, dressed in two seconds flat, and headed out to the studio. Sadie followed behind, probably confused about what was going on, and what I was in a dither about.

I had only been in the room for about ten minutes, when in walked Emma. Not expecting her, I watched in surprise as without a word, she pulled her laptop out of its case, plopped it on the desk, plugged it in, powered it up, then grabbed a nameplate from her purse and set it down. It read—*Emma Blake*—receptionist.

She looked at me and grinned. "Gave two weeks' notice and quit Kite's. I'm all yours. That is, if you'll have me."

"What?" Stunned, that was the only word I could get out.

"I'm here to help," she added.

Finally finding my voice, I said, "But, Emma. It could be years before you get a salary."

"Like I care. I'll finally be working in a job I'll enjoy. After all," she pointed her finger, "you need someone to keep you organized. You can't do it all by yourself."

She was right about that as, speaking honestly, I was nervous. I couldn't afford to bring employees on board and wasn't sure I could keep on top of everything that had to be done.

"But I can't ask you to do this."

"Who needs asking? I volunteered." She sat down, planting her two feet on the floor. "Get used to it. I ain't moving. Deal?"

I reached out for a handshake, which turned into a hug as I whispered, "Deal." I was a lucky girl.

The phone rang, cutting into our warm, fuzzy moment, and Emma picked it up. "Good morning. White's Waggles at your service."

Happily, I realized she already sounded like she'd been here for years. Her input would be invaluable as running an office was her forte, but I also couldn't help but notice that she kept looking anxiously at the door from time to time.

Was she expecting someone? She could hardly sit still in her chair; and come to think it, I'd never seen her this agitated. She seemed as nervous as I was, as once again I glanced over the room. Everything seemed in order, shiny, clean with trays of delicious doggy treats lining a table we'd borrowed from Hazel.

"What's up?" I asked, when she finished with the call.

She waved me away as she picked up the phone again and, after a minute, I heard her say, "Yes, of course we have room for little Gloria. You may bring her to us right now, if you'd like."

I smiled, relief settling in. More recruits. When we first started advertising, I'd been upset that we had no bookings. Lots of inquiries, but no one committing. But much to my surprise, the phone soon started ringing off the hook with interested customers and now we had several arriving soon.

Glancing at my watch, I realized our first dog would be here in thirty minutes. Anxiety wound through me, as I ran around making sure everything was ready for about the tenth time this morning, my dog following, as if checking out things as well.

"Hey, Sadie. Are you all set to meet Gloria?"

She happily wagged her tail, as I reached down to pet her, knowing she didn't understand, but once again, loved how she agreed with me. Cathartic for my insecure personality.

"I'm looking for Jessica White," said a voice from the doorway.

I looked over.

"Oh my goodness. Joey McAdams."

He walked over, carrying a huge bag. "I'm just on my way to work but have a present for you." He opened the parcel so I could take a peek. "Homemade dog biscuits from Danny's Dog Delights."

Sadie could sniff out one of these biscuits in five seconds flat and raced over. Joey pulled one out and gave it to her.

Smiling he added, "A friend of yours came into the store with a poster and when we got talking, I discovered it was your business. I remembered you bought some for your dog." He leaned over and whispered, "There's also a stash of chocolate bars at the bottom of the bag. Just for you."

Laughing, I whispered back, "Thanks. Just what I need." I quickly added the dog treats to the trays and shoved the chocolate in a drawer for later. Eyeing how good the cookies looked I added, "Every dog who tastes these will be back for more. You've just raised the ante here."

"Well you helped me a lot." He looked around. "This place looks awesome. I'll have to bring my dog over for a visit."

"Anytime," I said. "What breed do you have?"

"German Shepherd. Er, are you not a lawyer anymore?" he asked, looking confused.

"Just taking a break."

"Oh." But he still looked puzzled as he glanced at his watch. "Better get going or I'll be late."

"Hey, thanks again. I really appreciate it."

"No problem."

I was hoping his act of kindness was a good omen of greater things to come.

"Here they are," said Emma, a great big huge smile on her face. "Only five minutes late but they made it."

"Who?" I looked over, wondering what she meant. As far as I knew, only one dog was arriving shortly. The rest were coming later. Who qualified as 'they'?

Startled, I was surprised to see Carl Jacobs and Sam Allen enter the room. I hadn't seen them in ages.

Carl had called the law firm when I first arrived and luckily it was Emma who spoke to him. She arranged for the two of us to meet, and at his panicky urging I picked up his friend Sam, as a pro bono case. Both were retired from Stelco, the big steel company that employed a slew of Hamiltonians, but unfortunately Sam had massive gambling issues. Carl, a recovered gambler, became his sponsor at Gamblers Anonymous, but one fateful night, Sam snuck away to Fallsview Casino in Niagara Falls, lost a ton of money, and got into a spat with a security guard when he accused an employee of fixing the card games. A huge fistfight ensued, police were called, and Carl bailed him out of jail. Sam had no money as he'd repeatedly spent it at casinos, hence my entry into the picture where I managed to get him off with community service and a commitment to keep attending a support group.

"Great to see you," I said, but I was puzzled. It sounded like Emma had invited them or at least, she seemed to know they were coming.

Were they visiting? Checking the place out? Did they have dogs? Had they missed hanging at my office and wanted another place with free coffee and pastries? I glanced back at the side counter by the fridge. Yep. We still had some coffee and donuts, which they were welcomed to.

But much to my surprise, they both hung their coats up on a rack I'd installed at the front door and when they turned around they had on White's Waggles T-shirts. Emma must have provided them. Something was up.

Carl walked over to me and shook my hand. "Congrats on the new business venture. And surprise! We're here to help. Sam and I can take the animals out walking for exercise and potty breaks. Give ya some time to do other stuff."

I was shocked yet relieved at their offer. Along with Emma, they were godsends.

"But I can't pay you."

"Couldn't pay you either. But that never stopped ya from helping us," said Sam.

"Yeah, and besides. Us retired folks got lots of time on our hands. Walking dogs will keep us fit, too," added Carl, patting his well-developed paunch. "Doctor says I need to get rid of this."

"And we won't be late again. Got lost getting here. Carl turned right when I told him to turn left. But now we know where we're going we'll be here every morning lickety split," said Sam.

"Won't happen again. Thought I knew this area but guess I don't," added Carl.

Aunt T used to spout out that saying about 'being kind and it will return to you tenfold', but this was the first time it ever happened to me. Here I was down on my luck, and everyone was showing up to help. Even former clients. I reached over to give each a hug as Emma beamed in the background. I gave her the thumbs up, knowing she'd set the whole thing up.

"Thanks, guys."

"Is this the doggy daycare?"

A tiny, white-haired woman marched in, holding a tiny, white poodle. Both of them sported a red ribbon in their hair. All those articles written about how often dogs look like their owners were definitely true in this case. They could pass as twins. Of course, I was exaggerating, but you know what I mean.

"Sure is," I answered. "So this is Gloria?"

"What a cutie," said Sam, as he leaned over for a pet and was greeted by growling and bared teeth.

"Oh, don't worry. She won't bite. She's a sweetie and just excited about being here. Aren't you, baby?" she cooed as she gazed at her poodle adoringly.

This dog was no sweetie. The tiny fur ball continued to lock eyes with Sam, seemingly about to lunge at his throat as he took another step back.

"Hi Gloria," I said, in my most soothing but firm voice, trying to calm down the poodle while at the same time, show her who was boss. I was sure she sensed her mistress was leaving and was upset or maybe she was glad to have the freedom to run wild. Hopefully not. Anyway, I had to set the boundaries so she'd know I was in charge.

"You're going to have a good old time here today," I added, as much to my surprise, Gloria jumped into my arms and started licking my face. I grabbed on tight so she wouldn't fall. That was all I needed. A dog to break a leg on my first day.

"Well, my heavens. I've never seen Gloria take to anyone so quickly. By the way, my name's Gladys." Beaming, she reached out to shake my hand.

"Jessie. Glad to meet you and don't worry, we'll take good care of your dog." Gladys and Gloria. Hmmmm… even the names were similar. I'd have to struggle to remember in order to keep them straight.

"Good. Trouble is, she barks all day when I'm at work. Superintendent of my apartment building says I have to get rid of her if I can't get her to stop. Can't help it if she misses me. But then I saw your ad, and knew it was the perfect solution." Her eyes brightened as she lifted her dog's head up so she could look into her eyes. "Now you'll never be alone during the day, ever again," she said softly. Gloria rewarded her with a lick.

"We'll take good care of her," I said.

As luck had it, Sadie ran over to me looking up, as if saying, "Can I play, Mommy?" She always had a knack of being in the right place at the right time. Gloria barked and squirmed to get down, so I put her on the floor and the two dogs happily sniffed each other, then took off playing tag. The tiny poodle seemed to love this game as she'd slow down for Sadie to catch up, then speed up like a whirlwind.

"Look it. She's got friends already. She doesn't even care that I'm leaving," said a sad looking Gladys. "But at least I'm glad she seems to like it here."

"Well, you don't have to worry about her when you're gone," I said.

"You're right." But I thought I detected a tear as she turned and left quickly. I knew it was harder on her than Gloria. The poodle was having a blast.

"This here's Sparky."

I stifled a giggle as a big bruiser of a man walked over to me, carrying a tiny puppy cradled in his arms.

"Hello, Sparky," I crooned to the small black lab and was rewarded with a wiggling tail.

"Name's Bill. You sure you'll take good care of him? He's just a pup and too young to be left alone." He looked worried and sounded nervous.

"I promise," I said, as I lifted the dog away from his owner.

"Be back in a minute. I left his food out in the car."

"You'll be okay, Sparky," I said softly, trying to console the puppy as he whimpered his protest at being away from his owner, however the pup perked up when I put him down to greet Sadie and Gloria.

"Here you go." Bill handed me a huge box filled with enough kibble for a good two years, five toys on top of a small dog bed that looked so comfortable, I wanted to lie down in it myself.

"You are coming back for Sparky, right?" I asked.

"Of course." He sounded indignant but then broke into a smile. "Oh, I get it. I overdid the food part." His face turned red.

"A bit. But it's good to see how much you care about your pet."

"Sure do. Rocky, my yellow lab, passed away a few months ago and I miss him like the dickens. Got this one here to keep me company."

"Sorry to hear about your other dog but looks like Sparky adores you," I said as the pup ran up to greet his owner.

"Sure does. Just worried 'bout leaving him. I've been on holiday and spent every minute with him."

"He'll be fine. Now, scoot. You'll be late for work."

"Can I phone later to see how he's doing?"

"Of course. Emma at the front desk will give you a card with the number on it."

As he turned to leave, I saw him glance back twice. It was actually quite sweet to see this big tough guy so in love with his little scrap of a pet. Sparky, however, never even noticed he was leaving, as he'd joined his dog friends again and they were all busy exploring the new chew toys.

Soon after he left, Emma ushered over another dog. A great big golden retriever, a bit on the heavy side.

"This here's Goldilocks," whispered Emma.

Her owner was trailing behind, looking flustered. "Already late for work," she muttered. "Hope you don't mind a pregnant dog. 'Fraid to leave her alone."

"How pregnant is she?" I asked.

"Don't worry. Her due date's a while yet. Gotta go. See ya."

"Wait," I called. "Our large dog section is not finished yet." Actually, it hadn't even begun.

"Don't worry. Goldie loves little dogs." Then she took off out the door before I could say another word.

Emma shrugged her shoulders. "Sorry. She told me her dog was a miniature golden doodle."

"Well, she's certainly not that. But hopefully she's right and Goldie loves little dogs. I guess she was desperate, having to work and watch over a pregnant retriever. Can't say I blame her," I said, but I sighed with relief when I noticed the other three dogs running over to greet Gloria, who wagged her tail in apparent joy. Looked like it might work out.

"What's the owner's name?" I asked, realizing she hadn't stayed long enough for me to find out.

"Jill," answered Emma, as she turned to welcome more pets.

Six more dogs arrived and that was it—a full house. Several of them hadn't booked ahead of time but took a chance and dropped in. They got lucky and so did we.

Thrilled to be back working, I got busy watching over my little charges, feeding them and making sure they knew where the water bowl, beds and toys were. Carl and Sam, pooper-scoopers and bags in hand, helped by walking them and taking them for regular potty breaks. They also took charge of the puppy Sparky who would play for short periods then fall asleep. I smiled as Sam sang the wee dog a lullaby and his whimpers turned to snores. The dog's, I meant, not Sam.

I was keeping my eyes on everyone and everything and it seemed I lucked out. No big dogfights and nothing too out of the ordinary. A few minor scraps as the dogs got used to each other, some occasional growling, but nothing serious that time and familiarity didn't fix. I even got right down on the floor and we all played chase the ball and I couldn't believe how much fun it was. I could hardly call it work, as I was having the time of my life with all my new furry friends, but was a bit surprised when I heard a loud woof and a scratching at the door.

"What's that?" asked Emmy, doing a count to make sure we hadn't lost one.

"I don't know but I'll soon find out."

Not sure what to expect, I opened the door slowly, and there sat Red's dog Squid, wagging his tale like crazy. I looked behind him. No Red. He'd be a great ad for the business—a dog arriving by himself to join in the merriment.

"Woof!" he barked out again, as if to say, "can I come in?"

A long chain was dangling at his feet, attached to a stake that had obviously been screwed into the ground. No doubt about it, he'd made a run for it. He'd probably heard all the barks and felt left out of the dog party.

Gloria, Sadie, Goldie and Sparky ran over. Squid wagged his tail and started to whimper.

Oh, what the hell. I unhooked the chain from his collar and the big dog happily bounced around with the others. What was even funnier was that Gloria took a particular liking to Squid and followed him around everywhere he went. It was so darn cute seeing the big huge dog bond with the tiny, little poodle. Squid even intervened between two dogs fighting it out over a chew toy. He was a definite asset as he was kind of like a nanny. Different breed, but a lot like big, old lovable Nana in the story of Peter Pan. But I'd better return him soon.

Just as I was about to run over to Red's house to tell him where his dog was, the door abruptly opened and in he walked. It definitely felt a bit awkward, as I hadn't talked to him since the night at the restaurant.

"Have you seen…?" He stopped in his tracks. "What in the world?" He stared at his dog lying on the floor; Gloria sprawled fast asleep on his back, while Sadie cuddled beside him, licking his nose. Hard to believe, but Red's face turned the color of his hair.

"Sorry about this. I thought he was tied securely." He shook his head. "No wonder he was so darn quiet when I got home. He wasn't there. When I went to get him, I noticed he'd taken off with his chain, as well."

"No problem. Always room for one more. He's welcome here anytime. As you can see, the other dogs love him."

"Squid, come here," commanded Red.

I smiled as his dog just completely ignored him.

"I mean it, boy. Come here," he said again.

This time his dog looked at him, then turned his head away. His new dog friends won out over his master. Red sighed in frustration.

"Hey, why don't you just leave him here?" I asked. "He's obviously having a blast and the other dogs adore him. Look, the rest of them are even crawling all over him now." I pointed as the other dogs, obviously tired from their tug of war game, curled up beside and on him. Squid was like a real live doggy bed, warm and comfortable.

He hesitated for a minute, then said, "You don't mind? I'll pay."

"No way. It's the least I can do after you putting the roof on."

He glanced at his watch. "Well, if it's really okay, I've got some stuff to get done."

"Don't mind at all. Now, shoo."

After Red left, Emma and I had a bit of down time as the dogs took naps. Six o'clock rolled around so fast I could hardly believe I'd put in a full day's work. After all the dogs were sent home with their owners, and just as I was about to walk Squid over to Red's, Aunt T, Maggie and Hazel showed up with another cake, one of Aunt T's famous lemon dewdrop confections, and more wine. This was beginning to be a habit.

"Have to celebrate your first day," said Aunt T, cutting the cake while Hazel poured us a drink. We all gathered around and clinked.

"Thought I'd pick Squid up now. Figured the other dogs went home already and your day is over," said Red, once again walking in on drinking going on. "Oh, sorry to interfere."

"You're not interfering at all, Brian. Come on in for some cake and wine," said a jovial Hazel. She poured him a glass and handed it to him before he could protest.

But I noticed he drank it fast, almost in one gulp, refused the cake and left with Squid as soon as he could.

*Could he not even stand to be in my company for a few minutes*? Guess not, after I'd figuratively slapped him in the face when he'd helped me with Jim.

One of these days I'd get around to apologizing.

## *Fifteen*

"What would I ever do without you, Olive?" I crooned, feeling toasty and warm, curled up in my tree house while the rain poured down. I'd even managed to get Sadie up here and she was fast asleep at my feet, snuggled up in a blanket. Noticing a light go on in Red's window, being my usual nosy self, I leaned out and snuck a peek, watching him turn on his computer and sit down at his desk. I wondered what he was doing? I was hoping he'd turn on his T.V., as often I'd watch sitcoms with him. Since it was summer and his window was up with just a screen separating us, I could pick up the sound clearly. Not that he knew, of course.

Wait a sec. Is he getting up?

He walked over to the window, looked out and waved. Rats! He'd caught me. Ignoring him, I quickly ducked back inside.

Tired after a long week of work, I took a deep breath, let it out, sighing with contentment as I stretched out on the rug, and leaned back against a pillow I'd carried up for even more comfort. I was in one of those happy, peaceful kind of moods as I'd been busy calculating my finances and was thrilled to see that White's Waggles was in the black. Yep, we'd even made a small profit. Tiny but real. It warranted a party and if I'd had the energy, I would have gathered up Team White and headed out for a few drinks in celebration. But I guess it was for the best not to, in case I was tempted to spend what little I had.

Sure looked like the doggy daycare was going to work, or at least it had great potential to eventually provide a decent salary to Emma and me. Could there be law in my future again? Who knew, but certainly not for now. I was content taking care of furry clients who couldn't answer back, or bug me with annoying habits, and only brought smiles to my face.

Another good thing was that lately I found myself completely over Jim. That night at the restaurant sealed it, and ever since then his face was fading away, and I could barely even conjure up his smile. I thought back to all the errands I did for him. It was always, "Jessie, could you buy me this. Jessie, could you pick up my favorite beer?" It was "gimme, gimme" all the way. I rarely, if ever, got anything in return. In fact, it backfired on me. It was as if I were addicted to wanting approval from him but instead of respecting me more, he looked down on me. When would I ever learn the only approval I needed was from myself?

My life was finally taking on some normalcy, and tonight my mind was literally doing cartwheels while my body lolled about, hardly able to move. Man, I was bushed. Running after dogs was energy draining but another good thing about this job was that I was burning calories at a rapid rate. I'd already lost five of the eleven pounds I'd put on during my down in the dumps junk food fest. Another great feat.

I took a deep, reassuring breath as I allowed my happiness to flow over me like my old Raggedy Ann comforter on a cold night. Yep. That's how good I felt, even on a rainy day. Nothing like it.

The voice of Gloria Gaynor crooning out *I will survive* startled me. Not to mention Sadie's woof at the noise. I looked around until I realized it was my cell phone ring. I'd forgotten that Emma had set this tune up, guaranteed to urge me on to victory. It worked. But damn! For some reason, I didn't want to answer it. Intuition, I guess. You know how often in the middle of a good spell, when you find yourself enjoying life to the fullest, something always happens to ruin it? Like sad news would destroy everything or at least dampen your enthusiasm? Or something or someone would stir up trouble?

I had a gut feeling this call wouldn't be good and my contented little bubble would burst. But as it kept on ringing, I finally caved and grabbed my phone out of my back pocket. It could be another booking or something important. Wishful thinking on my part.

"Hello?"

"Hi, Jessie."

"Yes?" I had no clue who it was; just that it was a male voice.

"It's your father."

For the first time in sixteen years, I heard his voice again.

*Double crap.*

My intuition was spot on. I should never have answered.

Jerking straight up into a sitting position, I instantly felt sick to my stomach. Closing my eyes, I tried to summon up his face from long ago memories. But I couldn't. I'd blocked it out all these years until it was just a blur. A faraway image.

"Jessie? Are you there?"

Imagine asking if I was here when he was the one who was never anywhere for me. I felt like hanging up.

"Why are you calling?"

"Your mother asked me to," he said quietly.

Hazel? And she didn't mention this to me? And… he couldn't have called on his own? He had to be asked? And why after sixteen years?

Anyway, who cared! I didn't want to talk to him. Ever. What could I possibly have to say to someone who abandoned me? Zilch. A great big nothing.

"That surprises me," I answered, wanting to hang up but for some reason, not wanting to at the same time. As much as it killed to admit it, I was curious. "Didn't know you kept in touch."

"A recent thing." He paused.

I guess he was waiting for me to say something. Fat chance. He made the call; he could do the talking.

*But this felt awkward as hell.*

"Heard you were fired a while back," he finally said.

That did it. I was pissed.

He hadn't talked to me in years and that was what he had to say? That I was fired? To hell with him. Rage surfaced as I lashed back. "Great lead in, Dad. Instead of focusing on my failures, how about you tell me why you left and then never kept in touch? You're a real asshole."

I really didn't care if I sounded disrespectful or like a little kid who didn't get my way. I was all riled up. Did he really think he could waltz right back in my life with a phone call? Besides, I was sick and tired of always being nice. Especially with him. The man who said he'd be there forever. Lies. Nothing but lies.

"I know you're angry."

"You don't know the half of it," I answered.

"Can we meet and talk about it?"

"No."

A big pause, then, "So you opened up a daycare for dogs?"

"Yes." It was typical of him to change the subject. I remember when Hazel would get angry about something; he'd ignore her and try to move on to another topic. He hated confrontations and messy situations. Even as a kid, I picked that up.

"Great idea."

"Oh, I'm glad you approve," I said sarcastically. "Do you think I really care about what you have to say?" After all these years, he wanted to comment about my life? Dream on, buddy.

"Er… I'd love to see you." His hesitant voice had a touch of desperation as he sidestepped my comment. "And explain everything."

"Too late for that. Sorry but no. For one thing, I'm not traveling all the way to California."

"You won't have to. I'm in town."

"What? You're in Hamilton?" That was a surprise. I

looked down, making sure he wasn't watching me, like in one of those creepy movies where the person calls and they're actually just outside the door. Nope. No one around.

"Yes. I have a small condo in Stoney Creek."

No way. That was not too far from us. In fact, it was just down the road, another suburb of Hamilton.

He was that close?

But really, big deal. I wasn't visiting. Ever.

"Well, I'm kind of busy right now." But against my will, my heart pounded wildly and I had to admit, a wave of yearning set in. *My father was only about ten minutes away?*

Wait a sec. Who cared? I figuratively squashed that yearning part of me into smithereens.

"Sure, I understand. You're probably tied up with the new business and all. How about if I give you my phone number and you call when you have some time?"

"Okay." *Wouldn't be anytime soon.* I pretended to write down the number but in fact, tuned out his voice.

"Well, hope to see you," he said, and I was sure I detected a note of wistfulness. Too darn bad. He didn't deserve any contact with me after all the hell he'd put me through.

"Bye," I said quickly, as I hung up.

Shaken, I leaned back against the pillow, a host of memories swirling around. As if I needed this right now.

I never thought much about my father. Now and again, a flashback would surface, but I'd stuff it away as quickly as possible. Oh, sure it bothered me from time to time, especially when I was younger and my friends would be buying gifts for Father's Day, but as the years moved on, I pretty much banished him from my thoughts.

I closed my eyes and it was as if Pandora's Box flew open. Images of him were running rampant. Hearing his voice set off a series of snapshots of my younger days. Youthful, carefree times when I felt I had the best darn daddy in the world.

We used to do such fun, crazy things. Like the time he borrowed a truck and took me out in the middle of the night to watch the Perseid Meteor shower us with hundreds of shooting stars. We spread a blanket in the back of the truck where he had put together a picnic basket of sodas, cookies and chips, and we gazed up at the sky counting the number of stars we saw flying through the darkness. I sighed. That was such a great memory. A cherished one.

I could also recall laughter, pushes on swings and giant sandcastles built along the shores of Lake Ontario. We'd stay at the beach until darkness kicked in, creating a magnificent kingdom of turrets and moats. They were happy, glorious times and I thought they'd last forever. When Dad was around, it never bothered me that Hazel spent such long hours in her studio and that I rarely saw her, for I had my daddy. And... *I thought I'd have him forever.*

Then came the tears and tantrums when he left, alternating between hating my mother, for not seeming too upset, to hating my father for leaving me. For months, I kept expecting him to walk back in the door, and one night I snuck out in the middle of the night and rode my bike all the way to the exact same place where we used to watch the stars. I'd even brought along a bag of cookies and holding my flashlight close to me, I waited, hoping he'd show up. Of course, he didn't. Not sure why in the world I thought he might, nor why in the world I wanted him to be there. After all, he'd abandoned me without even talking to me in person. That damn piece of paper was all I had left.

I kept bugging Hazel about what happened, but she said little, just that he was off surfing in California. Surfing? I didn't even know he did such stuff. Couldn't believe he'd rather do that then spend time with me.

I even went after Aunt T, looking for answers or even how to contact him. She told me she had to stay out of it but said she didn't know much, although one night I overheard her telling Hazel off, and urging her to get on the phone and get him back home. As far as I knew, that didn't happen. The call, I mean because my father never returned.

One desperate night when she was out, I searched Hazel's bedroom, looking for an address or phone number for him, but came up with nothing. Google searches were also a disappointment. There were a couple of Rob Whites but when I contacted them, none of them were my dad. I figured he'd gotten an unlisted number to avoid my finding him.

Eventually, I'd tucked my pain and heartache away for I couldn't keep dragging up the hurt every single day. I survived, but mistrust of all men now entered into the equation. When it came to dating, I had lost all confidence in myself because if my father could leave me, being the one person who knew me the best, then I mustn't be worthy of love.

I had no idea Hazel was in contact with him. Why wouldn't she have mentioned that to me? Or at least prepared me for a possible phone call?

What was with all her secrecy anyway?

What was with the nights away from home, the late getting back from the studio, and all sorts of long winded phone calls she hid from me by speaking low and moving from the room, if I happened to enter. Did it have something to do with Dad?

I had to know. Now.

"Sorry, Sadie," I said, as I picked her up and made the climb back down the tree. I marched right into the kitchen where Hazel was cooking up one of her health food concoctions. I glanced at the glass pot. Did all her stuff really have to be lime green?

"Why didn't you tell me about Dad?" I asked, aware my voice sounded harsh, but too bad. I was frustrated and wanted information.

She looked at me vaguely. I knew that look. She was probably thinking about some detail of her latest painting, lost in her own private world. Too damn bad. This was important to me, so I asked again, louder, "Why didn't you tell me?"

"Tell you what?" She looked genuinely puzzled.

"That you're in touch with him."

Now she looked guilty and… a bit pleased as I saw her lips start to curl up into a brief smile. "So he actually called?"

"Yes."

"I'm surprised. Didn't think he would get the guts to do it. So I kept pushing."

"But why did he? And why does he want to see me now?"

"Come, sit for a second."

She gave the pot one last stir, turned the heat down on the stove, pulled out a wooden chair and beckoned me to it. She then joined me across the table, staring off into space, as if trying to choose her words carefully.

Finally, she spoke. "About eight months ago, I called your dad and suggested we get together and talk."

"You knew where he was?"

"Oh, yes. He always let me know in case we needed anything, as well as to get updates about you."

That was news to me. I never knew he was in touch. "Really? Why?"

"He cared about us."

"Funny way of showing it. I thought you hated him."

She looked at me strangely. "No, as a matter of fact, I love him. Always have, always will." She hung her head down. "Although it's taken years of therapy to admit that."

Therapy? She was in therapy?

"Why did you contact him?"

"In simple words, I missed him."

"Did he fall out of love with you? Is that why he left?"

A frightened look ran through her eyes.

*Had I hit a nerve? Was she afraid of my knowing the truth?*

"Well, things were rocky for a while but in hindsight it was all my fault. To make a long story short, I can sum it up in one word. Fear. *My* fear. I was afraid to love. After all, I'd lost my best friend when I was a teen. That completely destroyed me."

I'd forgotten all about that incident. Apparently, she and next-door neighbor Mary Jones had been out biking one Sunday and her friend joyfully raced ahead, was struck by a car and died on the spot. Hazel witnessed the whole thing. According to Aunt T, her hair turned white the very next day.

"After the accident, I suffered from survivor's guilt. Why Mary and not me? She was so sweet, kind, and good. Wanted to be a doctor. To save the world." She smiled. "She was actually a bit like you. So I poured my heart into my paintings, trying to forget her and not wanting to get too close to anyone again, in case I lost them. My artwork became my escape." She sighed. "I felt I was just half a person most of the time. The rest of me was buried with Mary. Then, your father came along. At first, it worked well because he was strong and supportive, but then he lost his job. That changed everything."

"He lost his job?" I didn't know that.

"Yes."

"Why?"

"He got fired."

Looked like we had a lot in common, but before she said anything more, there was one question I needed the answer to. I'd asked her before but she never responded. Just shrugged her shoulders and walked away. I thought I'd try again during this truth session, hoping to find out more. If she got up to leave, I was going to tackle her and even sit on her until she told me. I needed truth.

"When Dad left, why did he not make an effort to see me? That, I don't understand."

There was a long pause where Hazel just kept looking

at me. Finally she glanced away, then back at me. It was like she was trying to decide how much to say.

"I told him not to."

*What?*

Angry as hell, I slammed my fist down on the table. "How dare you? That was not your decision to make."

"I realize that now," she said, softly. "At the time he was a mess and I figured it was best for you. I thought he'd really upset you with his depression. I'm sorry. It was probably the worst decision I've ever made."

A tear rolled down her face, which shocked me. *I had never seen her cry before. Nor apologize.* My anger diminished a bit as I figured out how to handle all this emotion.

"So you're in touch a lot?" I asked, backing off as I got up, grabbed a tissue from the box on the counter and handed it to her, before sitting back down.

"Lately, yes."

"Are you getting back together?"

To my surprise, her few tears turned into a burst—like watching an explosion of sobs. Pretty scary stuff.

I waited a bit before asking again, "So are you? Getting back together? Is that who you've been with all those times you've gotten in late or stayed out all night?"

"Yes, we've been spending time together, talking a lot and getting to know each other again. And as for getting back together, I can only wish."

"What?" I'd always wanted that but grew used to them being apart. Had I heard her right? She'd like to get back together?

She looked over at me as she wiped her tears away.

"I let a good man go, Jessie. My lack of empathy destroyed what happiness I could have had."

"Is he married?"

"No."

"He's in Stoney Creek at the moment. But where does he live on a permanent basis?"

"Ah… here."

"Here?" I figured he was just on vacation.

"Yes. He moved back four months ago."

Once again, I was shocked. There was also probably no way I could avoid him now, especially if he and Hazel were hanging out together.

Abruptly, Hazel looked at her watch and stood up. "Sorry, sweetie, but I have to go. I have a meeting with a gallery owner in twenty minutes. Believe me if I could cancel I would."

She could go from one emotion to another in ten seconds? Were her tears fake? Did she really have a meeting or was she avoiding telling me something?

"But I'm not done here. I want to know more."

She sighed. "And you will. I should have told you ages ago. I promise I'll explain it all soon. But I really have to get to that meeting or I'll let down a lot of people."

*What about letting me down?*

To my surprise, she hugged me. A normal, sometimes everyday gesture among families, but if you knew Hazel, a big one. She was not much into physical contact.

"I'll hold you to it," I said, still feeling her abrupt departure was a fake job. She was hiding something.

"I know," she answered softly.

After she left, Sadie and I curled up on the couch trying

to watch some old reruns of *Happy Days*. Anything to get me in a better mood. But all I could think about was the fact my father was back in town. What in the world was his story and did I want to find out? Now that this whole matter was somewhat out in the open, I feared the truth.

*After all, what makes a father leave his daughter and never stay in touch?*

## *Sixteen*

*Was that the doorbell ringing?*

Roused out of sleep, I glanced at the clock—three in the morning. Couldn't be. I must be dreaming. No one would be at my door this late. That'd be insane.

I yawned so loudly Sadie looked up as if to say, "What's wrong?" What a great watchdog she was. *Not.*

I yawned again. No buzzing a second time so I must've imagined it.

It'd taken me quite a while to get little Gloria asleep and she had worn me right out. Exhausted, I snuggled down deep into my covers, prepared to drift back to la la land, or hoping to at least. I closed my eyes.

Hadn't planned to have dogs overnight, but Gladys begged me to keep her toy poodle. How could I turn her down, especially since she'd been called away to a family funeral? Death sure didn't happen on a convenient schedule for anyone.

I thought of taking the dog into the house but Gladys said she'd be fine out in the studio, after all she was used to it. She insisted she'd sleep right through the night, but every time I started to leave, she barked and whimpered. It broke my heart and I was ready to scoop her up and take her to my room, when she finally fell fast asleep. Almost keeled right over from exhaustion. I guess all that barking wore her out. So I'd tiptoed out, Sadie in my arms, in case I woke her and headed for my bed, where I hastily threw on my nightie and was out in about ten seconds flat.

Now I was awake. Wide-awake.

A new noise echoed from downstairs. My eyes popped open. Someone was hammering on my door. I wasn't imagining it this time, because Sadie started to growl, reacting to the sound. Finally, she was in watchdog mode, maybe because it sounded like the door was going to splinter and break. I sat straight up. Someone really was there. Hazel said she'd be out with a friend again, probably Dad, but maybe she forgot her keys.

Jumping out of bed, I threw on my housecoat and charged down to the door, holding a riled up Sadie who was now full out barking. Opening it up, I was surprised to find Red standing there with Squid, his hair rumpled as if he'd been sleeping, jeans on with a half buttoned up shirt, wrongly, I might add. He looked damn sexy. Once again my heart clipped along at a fast pace and my face colored. I wished I didn't find him so attractive for it would sure make my life a whole lot easier.

"Is something wrong?" I managed to squeeze out as I finally got control of myself and a few deep breaths steadied my heart rate.

"There's a dog yapping that won't shut up. Squid here can't sleep because of it and now I can't sleep because of him. What's going on? Is there some kind of problem?"

Oh no! Gloria. With the door open, I could hear her

barking in that shrill annoying way of hers. I must have been in a dead sleep not to have heard her before. Damn. As a way of keeping track, I should have gotten one of those baby monitors to hear how she was doing.

Instantly, I felt bad because Red really did look tired. He certainly didn't need barking keeping him up all night.

"I'm so sorry. I've taken in a dog for the night." I rolled my eyes in frustration. "She was asleep when I left her."

"Well, can you do something to stop the racket?"

Looked like he was trying hard to hang on to a temper on a short fuse. Fatigue and stress would do that to you. I knew from experience so I'd better get moving and quickly as well.

"I'll certainly try," I said, again feeling guilty as hell.

Grabbing my keys, Sadie and I headed over to the studio with Red and Squid right behind us. I could still hear Gloria's high-pitched yips, as well as frequent bangs as if things were falling over. I opened the door to a crazed poodle racing around the room in a circle. Not only was every dog toy strewn about, but two "accidents" of the poopy kind were by the door, as if she'd been trying to get out to the grass. So much for Gladys saying she was fully trained and slept through the night. It didn't seem as if she was frightened at all. Just looked like the tiny poodle was having her own private party and didn't even glance over to see who was joining her. If I hadn't a disgruntled Red on my hands, I'd think it was funny.

Feeling a thump against my leg, Squid pushed by and trotted up to the tiny dog. Gloria stopped dead in her tracks and stared up at the big canine with hero worship in her eyes. He leaned down for a sniff and the tiny poodle wagged her tail so hard, I thought it'd fly right off. I'd forgotten they'd become such good friends when Squid visited a while back. The Dane then laid down and much to my surprise, Gloria snuggled up to his face, rested her head on his snout, closed her eyes and was snoring away in a matter of minutes. Loyal Sadie stayed by my side for about five seconds before she too, joined them in their snuggle. Quiet at last and wishing I'd brought my camera, my heart oozed love at the adorable scene, until I remembered Red was here and turned to find him cleaning up the mess. I rushed to help him.

"So sorry," I said, again. "You don't have to do that."

"That's okay. I'm wide awake now," he grunted.

"Er… would you like some coffee or something?"

"No thanks."

I was wondering if he'd take off as usual, but after depositing the mess in a garbage pail, he plopped down on a chair, and I was sure his eyes softened at the sweet display of affection going on among the dogs. Not one hundred percent sure, but ninety-nine.

"I can wait to see if Gloria stays asleep. Anything to stop that darn yipping and yapping," he said.

I sat down as well, suddenly self-conscious to be out and about with my nightgown on. I pulled the housecoat even tighter when, all of a sudden, Red grinned.

"Can't afford a new one?"

I looked down and saw it from his eyes. The rose-colored fabric was faded almost to white with rips, some long, some small, sprouting up everywhere in the old, worn areas. It exposed my most unflattering purple flannelette nightgown, which at least had a high neck and revealed very little, especially my extra flab rolls. I was glad about that, but I was sure I looked horrible—like my old teddy bear I'd accidentally left out in the rain when I was a wee kid. When I finally found it, it was bedraggled and never looked the same, even after several washes. Guess I looked like that bear right now. Quite a mess.

But I grinned as well. Just couldn't help picturing myself through Red's eyes.

"It's like comfort food. Can't do without it," I explained.

It was then I noticed his expression change as his eyes raked over me and I wished I'd taken the time to at least comb my hair. I reached up to flatten down the tangles and saw his grin stretch even wider, as if he knew what I was doing, so I shook my head and stopped. Who cared anyway? I was off men for the time being. Who gave a hot damn if I looked presentable or not? And to hell with him anyway, for being so good looking but darn his hair looked amazing and he smelled good too. I took another whiff. It had to be Hugo boss cologne, my favorite. Jim used to wear it but for some reason I had a hard time conjuring up his face right now when Red was around.

"I understand," he said, breaking into my thoughts. "I have a few old sweatshirts I feel like that about."

Was this the kind side of Red peeking out? Trying to make me feel better? Hmmmmm… I actually liked this nicer side of him.

"I heard your father is sick. How's he doing?" I asked, concerned but also wanting the focus off me and my horrid clothes. Being in my nightgown made me feel kinda vulnerable.

A worried look shot across his face.

"Not so well."

"Is it serious?"

"Yes."

He paused and I waited to see if he'd say more. Finally, he said, "He's in the latter stages of prostate cancer."

"I'm sorry."

He ran his fingers through his hair. "Yeah, it's damn sad. Mom couldn't get him to go to the doctor all these years and when he finally went, he found out he had cancer."

"That's horrible. Is he in any pain?"

"Minimal. They keep him well drugged."

"Must be really hard to see him like that."

"Sure is."

I wanted to ask more but didn't want to upset him so kept quiet.

After a moment of uncomfortable silence when Red didn't offer more information about his father, I asked, "So how did you end up in a bank?" I figured this was a lighter subject plus I was dying to know the answer.

"My mother's the bank manager there and when the current loan officer suddenly took a sick leave, the new one couldn't get there for a few days. So she suggested or rather ordered that I fill in until then. I knew the job well as I'd done it before."

Odd how it happened to be just when I needed a loan. The fates were definitely working against me that day.

"Are you here for long?" I asked.

"A few months."

"Never realized you're an architect. A famous one, too."

He looked surprised. "Someone's been filling you in. I am an architect but not so famous, though."

"That's not what I heard. Did you take a leave of absence?"

"No. Fortunately, I can do quite a bit of work from home. Unless, of course, I get disturbed by people staring into my office when I'm trying to work, or dogs barking all night." But at least he tempered this with another smile. A cute one, by the way. To be even more honest, a heartstopping one.

I found myself staring until I realized he was looking at me oddly.

"Oops, sorry about that," I muttered. I was dying to ask him about his fiancée, but didn't have the nerve. That would be too much like prying into his business, as it would definitely be a sore spot for anyone.

"Do you enjoy your work?" I asked instead.

"Yes. I love the challenge of creating a home or building that fits in with exactly what the client wants."

"Must be rewarding." I was surprised by the look of excitement in his eyes as it, along with the smile, changed him into a totally different person. A less scowling one at least.

"Sure is. Do you enjoy running a daycare for dogs?"

A guy actually asking a question about what I was doing? At the risk of sounding sexist, this was new. At least for me.

"Sure do. So… you came home to be with your father?" Okay, I knew it was sounding like a game of twenty questions but I quickly changed the subject feeling unnerved having the spotlight on me. Couldn't help myself. Yes, it was great to have a guy care enough to ask, but it was uncharted territory for me. After all, usually I'd be trying to win their approval by asking the questions and being in control. Sad but true.

He gave me another odd look, probably at the quick jump in topics.

"Yes. He doesn't have long to live and I figured I'd never get this time back again. So work can go a bit on the back burner for a while. He's more important."

I wished my father felt that way about me and never left. We lost all sorts of moments together. Precious, precious moments. Now here he was in town and I didn't even want to see him whereas Red had come home to be with his dad. He was lucky to have such a close relationship. I envied him. I hadn't had that in sixteen years.

"Is something wrong?" asked Red.

I looked up to find him watching me closely.

"I've met your mother but not your father. Did he pass away?" he said quietly. "Is that why you look so sad? Did he have cancer too?"

"No, he left. They're divorced. Haven't seen him in years." I debated telling him about the phone call and the news that my father moved nearby, but couldn't bring myself to mention it. My reopened wounds were still too sore to share.

"Sorry. Didn't mean to pry." He looked genuinely concerned.

"That's okay. You had no way of knowing."

He looked as if he wanted to ask me a few more questions, but instead said, "By the way, I ran into James

Kite the other day. Your name came up."

Kite? Oh no!

"Really? How in the world do you know him?"

"Played football in high school together. He asked where I was living and when I told him, he recognized the street and the fact that you lived here as well." He looked at me and I swore I saw compassion in his eyes. "He's an idiot, you know. Always out for a buck. It's good you got out of there. No way would he be supportive of any act of kindness." He winked. "Said you were a hard worker, though. Just didn't have your priorities straight. I told him that he was the one with the wrong priorities."

What? Red was sticking up for me?

"Er… thank you." I had to admit, I felt kinda touched. It'd been a long time since any man had my back. As I said before, this was new ground for me and I was really enjoying talking with him, for he seemed to genuinely care about my answers.

"Do you miss law?" he asked.

"At times. After all, it's what I studied to do. But I'm enjoying running my own business."

"Seems to be doing well," he said.

"Getting better every day."

"You're doing a good job. I know a few of the people who bring their dogs here and they're very happy with you."

Wow! Red was complimenting me again. Surprised, I looked over. He was watching me and once again, I saw his eyes flicker down to my lips. He moved closer. *Was he going to kiss me?*

Nope. Instead, he glanced at his watch and jumped up,

looking embarrassed as he said, "Well, better get going. I have some work to finish. C'mon, Squid."

As his dog started to get up, Gloria immediately began barking her disapproval.

Puzzled, Red looked at me.

"This isn't going to work is it? My taking Squid."

"Would you mind if he stayed?" I asked. "Might be quieter for you as well as the whole neighborhood."

"Not a problem. Guess it'd be cruel to separate them."

"Thanks. I'll drop him by in the morning."

"If you don't mind, I have an early errand to do, so if you could tie Squid to the chain in the backyard, that'd be great. I'll leave his food and water out."

"Fine with me."

He hesitated for a second, then turned and went out the door saying, "See you."

"Bye," I answered.

Deciding to stay put in case Gloria went into one of her party moods and roared into the night again, I curled up in my chair, but just couldn't get my neighbor off my mind. Tonight he'd been downright delightful. Very different from his usual arrogant know-it-all stance.

Man, he was confusing. But then again, I guess I was too, blowing hot and cold, wanting to get to know him, but not really. It was just that it was okay if I did it but not him. Yeah, I know, self-centered as hell. But this was my time to reflect on life and figure out what I wanted. It was okay to be self-involved when trying to find oneself, wasn't it?

Strange indeed. If I hadn't sworn off men, I'd be tempted to get to know him better, just to see what made him tick, not to mention the fact that my heart thumped fast every time I was around him.

A huge red stop sign jumped out before me, warning to be careful. I hadn't shown good judgment with Jim and didn't want to get hurt all over again.

But still, I didn't remember any guy asking me much about myself. I must admit it felt good.

Tired as hell, I finally started to doze off, and all I could think about was one last thing.

*Was Red about to kiss me, and if so, would I have let him*?

## *Seventeen*

'Budda boom, budda bing.' The words from the T.V. commercial advertising the restaurant I sat in, flew through my mind. What a silly ditty to be thinking about, but I guess any distraction was welcomed as I tried not to get up and run right out of the building.

I was waiting for my father.

*Was I nuts*?

I wasn't even sure it was a good decision, but I just couldn't get Red's haunted eyes out of my mind when he talked about his dad. Here he was, wanting to be with his father more than anything, while I had a healthy one trying to make amends and I rejected him. What if he got ill or died suddenly? How would I feel after ignoring him? Especially, since he'd reached out. Sure, he'd left and I hadn't seen him in years, but we were still family. He was still my dad.

Maggie and Emma rang in with their votes. They thought I should meet him, deeming me too judgmental and felt I should at least spend time trying to find out the reasons for his actions. They pushed me to get an adult's perspective, not the teen's memory from sixteen years ago.

Urged on by their coaxing, witnessing Red's devotion plus a healthy dose of curiosity, I decided to give him a chance. At least once.

All for the visit, Hazel gave me his number, but it took two days before I got up the nerve to call and set up this luncheon date. I was terrified, angry, frustrated and every other horrible emotion that existed. I wanted to see him but also didn't, all at the same time. Yes, there was an eager, excited little girl deep inside who missed her daddy, but standing beside her was an adult woman who had been hurt and didn't know if she could ever forgive him for taking off the way he did. Just because he wanted to forge a relationship with me didn't mean it was going to happen. I wasn't planning to make this easy.

Looking around Eastside Mario's, I sniffed the delicious smells of garlic and onions. This place was known for its Italian food and had pizza and pasta to die for. Too bad I wasn't hungry. I was too nervous to eat anything. A rare moment for me.

I glanced at my watch. Ten minutes until he'd be here. I still had time to get up and leave. *No.* I was going to stick this out.

Would I even recognize him? Did he still have that big patch of dark brown hair with a cowlick that couldn't be tamed no matter how much he combed it or tried to slick it back? Once he used hairspray and it only made it stick straight up. He looked like a conehead and I couldn't stop laughing. He joined in and Hazel arrived home to find the two of us giggling away and we couldn't even find the words to tell her why. Needless to say, she was not amused.

I wondered if he still laughed readily with a zest for life that was infectious and caught me up in a spell of hope where I believed anything could happen?

Closing my eyes for a minute, I recalled the time he'd pushed me higher and higher on the swings at the playground around the corner from where we lived. I thought I was flying and laughed and laughed, never wanting it to end. When I was older, we'd go there to kick a soccer ball around or play some hoops. After he left, I couldn't set foot in that park ever again. Couldn't even stand to walk by. It was too darn painful.

I wondered what he was like now? Had he changed? What had sixteen years done to him? Did he hurt like I did? Had he suffered?

Getting more curious by the minute, questions that burned away at me inched their way up into conscious thought. Why'd he do it? Why'd he walk away? Why hadn't he talked to me about it? Maybe I could have helped make things better.

I sighed. Would I really find any truth today? Truth that might take away the pain in my heart or at least lessen it? Maybe I would finally understand a piece of my past that never made sense. Maybe if all my pieces clicked together, I could feel whole again. Less insecure.

"Jessie?"

Lost in my daydream, I jerked open my eyes and looked up to see a gray haired man peering down at me. He was tall and lanky, with a definite cowlick, but it was his eyes I remembered most. From way back in my mind, I was able to summon up those twinkling green eyes. While the rest of him had aged, they hadn't changed a bit.

"Dad?" Instinctively, almost against my will, I felt like jumping up and giving him a hug, but stayed put. That would be just too darn weird after all these years. He looked so familiar though, and even smelled the same. Old Spice and Irish soap. So much like the handsome prince I always thought he was when I was young and he was my hero. Just a bit grayer, that was all.

He handed over the paper bag he was carrying, and then sat down across from me. "Some dog toys for your business." He smiled. "I can sure recall from raising pups over the years how they chew through toys by the dozens."

"Thank you." I snuck a peak and saw about a zillion tug toys, then put it down on the seat. Was he trying to buy me with gifts? Wouldn't work. "Do you have a dog now?"

"Sure do. A yellow lab named Billy. Heard you have a Havanese."

"Yes. Sadie."

"Cute breed."

"Sure is."

Awkward silence followed, as both of us struggled for something to say. I felt like I was ten, walking into his bedroom and finding all his clothes gone. I wanted to scream, "Why did you leave me? Why?"

"Would you like to order now?" Our tense moment was interrupted by the arrival of our waitress. Thank goodness.

"Sorry. Haven't looked," Dad said.

"I'll give you a few minutes."

"That'd be great."

"I'll be back shortly. My name's Kate and I'll be your waitress tonight. Let me know if I can help you in any way," said the sweet girl.

*Could she help me talk to my dad?* Silly thought, but what in the world do you say to someone who abandoned you and then shows up out of the blue? Besides angry words, I hadn't a clue.

"Do you know what you're having?" he asked, interrupting my cluttered thoughts.

"Oh, just a burger, I guess." The rich spicy smell circling the restaurant was now making me feel sick, so I decided to stick with something plain.

"A burger in a pasta place?" he said, with a smile. "That brings back memories."

"Not sure what you mean, but they're really good here." Of course, I knew what he meant. Often when he took me out on jaunts we'd stop at restaurants where I'd always order a hamburger even though he tried to get me to eat other stuff. No way. It was a burger or nothing. But I didn't want to engage in any happy walk down memory lane with him. I was still pissed.

"Well, I'll get the same." He closed the menu. "So how are you doing?"

"You mean all those years since I last saw you?" I said harshly. A bit too harshly than I meant. Just couldn't help myself. I was damn bitter. "Do you really care how I've been? Don't you think it's a bit too late to try and pretend you do?"

I saw a flicker of pain cross his face. But I didn't care. Even though I'd decided to attempt to make amends, it'd hurt like hell not having a father all these years. I wanted him to hurt too.

"I know you must be angry."

"To say the least."

"Would you like to order now?" asked the waitress, approaching our table again, probably noticing our menus were closed. I wanted to kiss her, I was so happy for the interruption.

"Yes, I'll have a burger, plain, with fries," I answered, regaining some control.

"I'll have the same," said my father.

"It'll be ready in a moment." She flashed a smile and was gone.

My father reached over to take hold of my hand but I pulled it away.

We stared at each other. An impasse.

"I'm really sorry, Jessie. Sorry I wasn't around during your teen years or when you went off to university. I'm hoping you can forgive me."

"Sorry doesn't really cut it after all these years."

He hung his head as he said softly, "I know. But it's all I have to offer."

"Why did you do what Hazel ordered and not stay in touch?"

"I thought it was best."

My mind raced.

*Did I dare ask him my biggest worry?*

The one that kept me up at night? The one that bugged me all these years? The one I spoke of only in the quiet of my heart?

*Was it my fault he left?*

Aunt T always said it wasn't, but then again, how would she know. Maybe it really was all my doing. Maybe having a kid was too much for him. Hazel was always arguing with Dad about boundaries and restrictions. She felt he was way too lenient and complained that he let me do too much, or gave me too many treats. I noticed how often he'd agree with her but then do whatever he wanted, which worked out fine until she'd catch him.

I thought back to the day he left. We had a fight that morning about rollerblades. All my friends had them and I wanted a pair too. Hazel said no because she was afraid I'd hurt myself, but I kept bugging my dad, yelling at him, until he'd stormed off, angry with me. The next I knew, he was gone. Was I the real cause of his leaving?

Taking a deep breath for courage, I blurted out, "Did you leave because of me? Did I do something wrong?" *I had to know.*

I let out my breath with a loud whoosh. There, I did it. I'd finally shared the concern I'd held in all these years. I braced myself for his answer.

He looked up and put his hand over mine, and surprisingly I left it there, sucking in his warmth.

"No, of course not. Don't ever think that. You were and are the best part of my life."

"It wasn't because of the rollerblades?"

"What rollerblades?" He looked puzzled.

Okay, I'd leave that for now. He didn't remember so it mustn't have been important. At least that brought me a bit of peace.

"How can I be the best part of your life? You never phoned. Or came to visit."

He put his head down again. "It was the wrong decision."

"Why couldn't I have determined what was best?"

He sighed and looked up. "That's why I'm here now. I made a mistake." His eyes looked troubled and I sensed there was a lot more that he wasn't saying. Like Hazel, he was hiding stuff.

"But what have you been doing all those years? Having a great old time in California?" I was bitter but had to admit, curious.

"Yes, I did go there. Had a cousin who let me stay in his basement for free. Moped around, drank way too much. Used to sit on the beach, hiding my booze in a silver water bottle so you couldn't tell what it was." He looked away, obviously embarrassed.

"What made you get back in touch?"

"There was this man; I think he was the grandpa, who used to bring this little girl to the water to teach her to swim. They looked like they were having so much fun, laughing and splashing around. Every once in a while, the little girl would hug him and it reminded me of the two of us." He looked back at me. "The way we were. I found myself getting to the beach every day, just to watch, all the time thinking of you. I wanted you to be proud of me again and look at me the way that little girl looked at her grandpa. So one day, I walked off the beach to a phone booth, called AA, found the closest meeting and went immediately. I straightened up, worked at every odd job I could find, started sending money to your mother for you, then went back to school, upgraded courses and got a Master's in special education. I taught for a few years there, then in Toronto, until I secured a job at St. Jude's High." His eyes gleamed with excitement. "It took a while but I made it back."

"Really? You're working right here in Hamilton?"

"Yes. How apt. St. Jude is the patron saint of hopeless cases." His eyes still twinkled as he smiled. "But I'm not one anymore."

"So you're here for good?"

"Yes."

Fortunately, the hamburgers arrived, giving me time to absorb all this information. Nauseous or not I dug in quickly, once again using food as comfort. I wanted to know more, but a headache pounded away. Plus I was afraid to ask any more questions, worried I'd cry my eyes out, or puke at the answers. Or both. Either one would be embarrassing. Also… I was nervous of what I might hear. I shouldn't have done this in a restaurant, after all. Way too public. Why hadn't I considered that?

Thoughts of Red's dad hit me again. He was blessed with having a father he loved so much that he'd changed his whole lifestyle to be with him in the end. Was I lucky to have one around even though he'd really hurt me?

*The verdict was out on that.*

Realizing my dad was watching me, I quickly said, "Well, that's great. About the job." I was making an attempt to be upbeat even though it wasn't what I felt. My words sounded hollow even to me and judging by the upset look on my father's face, he knew I still had loads of mixed feelings.

"So tell me about this doggy daycare. It sounds interesting."

I guess he felt that talking about my business would relieve some of the tension. Maybe it would. So all through dinner, I explained what I was doing. I was reluctant to admit it but I enjoyed talking to him as he asked good questions and seemed to genuinely care. And, for however long it lasted, it felt kinda good having him here.

I still wanted to ask him more about what happened but didn't have the guts anymore and he wasn't forthcoming with information. For sure he was holding back, just like Hazel. My gut registered that it was something bad. Could I handle hearing it? Maybe another time when I felt I was ready. It seemed we'd at least called some kind of truce.

"More coffee?" asked the waitress.

"No thanks," I answered.

"Me neither," said Dad. After she left he asked, "Could we make this a regular thing?"

"What?" I knew what he meant, but I was stalling for time, thinking of an answer.

"Meeting for lunch."

He looked hopeful.

"Not sure, Dad. Not sure at all." I couldn't fake what I felt and I was still wary as hell.

Sorrow etched across his face.

"Will you at least consider it?"

"Yes."

That was all I could offer at the moment.

## *Eighteen*

Have you ever had one of those long, grueling nights of the soul? The kind where you can't sleep and you stay up thinking, problems taking hold of you and not letting go? You try to figure stuff out but it gets too much. Completely overwhelming. You feel you're sinking into quicksand and there is no way out. So you run to your latest addiction, chugging coffee or booze and shoving junk food down your throat. The goal being to anesthetize yourself so life doesn't hurt. So that your problems will all go away.

*Tonight was one of those nights for me.*

So far, I'd eaten myself through two sleeves of Oreos, a box of Laura Secord miniatures and a whole carton of chocolate milk. I was on my second. Not great since I was still trying to lose the extra weight I'd put on, but crucial in moments of extreme stress. I was even debating making a run to the nearest corner store to fill up on more goodies, that is, if any were open at four a.m. Anything to help me escape the confusion I felt about my father. Being with him was probably the worst thing I could have done. It probably would have been better staying in the dark where he was just a distant memory. It stirred up way too much inside me.

Damn. Why did he have to return now? Especially since my business was going well and I was happy for a change.

"Heard you had supper with your father last night?" asked Hazel, as she entered the kitchen, her bright cucumber green caftan swirling around her ankles.

Startled, I almost fell off my chair but caught myself in time. I hadn't even heard her approach.

Watching Hazel go straight to the coffee pot, I wondered again how I ended up with two screwed up parents. No wonder I was a mess. What could I expect with their genes floating around inside me?

Questions surfaced out of my muddled, food-infested mind. Since I didn't have the guts to push my father into more confrontations about the past, maybe Hazel could finally give me the answers. After all, she promised. Dad was holding back, sidestepping the truth. I just knew it. His eyes could never lie and I saw fear in them, the same fear reflected in Hazel's.

*What did they not want me to know?*

Somehow, I was stuck in this in-between world—wanting to know stuff but afraid to find out. In some ways, I felt as if I still had the emotional level of a ten year old and wondered if I'd stay that way forever. Like that movie *Groundhog Day* with Bill Murray. Every day I'd go through the same line of questions, never moving forward.

So just what was the real story behind it all? The real deal? Did I want to know or is ignorance truly bliss? A stupid question, indeed. *Grow up, White.* I knew the answer. I was still a lawyer at heart. I needed facts before I gave my ruling. I had to know. Everything. Only then could I get on with my life.

Forgive? Possibly. Forget? No way.

"Ahem."

I looked up to see my mother staring at me.

"Oh, what did you say?"

"I said, I heard you were with your father last night." She had a worried look on her face.

"Sure was."

"Are you all right?" asked Hazel, looking around at the empty wrappers.

"Yeah, yeah I'm fine."

I watched as she sat down and took a sip. It was time to take action. No more stalling. It was now or never.

"I still don't understand what happened between you and Dad. I think you owe it to me to tell the truth. You promised. After all, I'm not a child anymore, in case you haven't noticed. Haven't been for quite some time."

Looking thoughtful, Hazel set her mug on the table and popped some bread into the toaster. I was getting impatient but waited it out, knowing it wouldn't help to rush her. That never worked. Everything had to be done in her own time.

She smeared honey on the toast and took a bite. In between crunches, she finally said, "Do you really want to know?" Her forehead had those stress lines and she looked dead serious, like she meant business.

"I said I did, didn't I?"

She sighed. "Well, maybe it is time. I've kept you

sheltered long enough and after all, you're right, I did promise."

"Please." I clasped my hands tightly together, bracing for the worse.

She crunched on her toast again until I wanted to scream, "Just eat it." But I managed to keep quiet.

Finally, she took another sip of coffee and said, "I think you've been under the impression that your father left of his own accord."

"Well, yeah. That's what the two of you led me to believe."

"I know, but that wasn't the case. I just wanted you to think that, so you wouldn't be mad at me. Selfish, I know. But I was the one left to raise you. I wanted to be on your good side." She took a deep breath, expelled it slowly, then said, "The truth is, I asked him to leave. To be blunt, I kicked him out."

"You kicked him out?" I was stunned. I always felt he abandoned us. That he left without any warning, right out of the blue. My insecurities were based on mistruth?

"Why?" I knew my voice was harsh, but I just didn't care. I was pissed. Big-time. First I found out that she told him not to keep in touch with me, now I discovered she'd kicked him out. What else happened?

"As I mentioned before, he got fired." Her eyes took on a faraway look, as if reliving it all. "I tried to be patient at first. Tried to be all sympathetic and helpful, but he seemed to lose interest in everything, except you. He wouldn't even entertain the thought of looking for another job. His depression was growing as self-centeredness took over."

All I could think of was the childish retort—it takes one to know one. It seemed ridiculous that my mother would label someone else as self-involved when she was the queen of that. Hell, she could win awards for being selfish.

"So you kicked him out? When he needed help?"

"He didn't want help. He just wanted to hang around, watching T.V. until you came home from school."

She stopped talking and I felt she still wasn't telling me the truth. There had to be more to it.

"Did he have an affair?" Was that the missing link?

"No."

"So you kicked him out just for being depressed?"

"Er, yes."

"And he agreed? He didn't kick up a fuss? He didn't beg to stay?"

"Well, he voiced concern about leaving you but was in such a state of depression and on heavy duty medication, that he didn't fight me. Even agreed it'd be best for you." She reached out to put her hand over mine. I pulled away.

"But he was weak and vulnerable. You hit him at his lowest point."

"Yes," she said softly. "I was trying to protect you.

It was hard for me to even grasp the fact that my mother was trying to protect me, as it seemed so out of character. It was just as hard to imagine my father as that weak, sniveling person. He must have kept that side really hidden from me.

"Who gave you the right to play God?" I barked back. "You should have told me what was going on."

"I realize that now. Back then, I thought it was the right thing."

"It wasn't."

"I know. I'm sorry about that. It was all my fault."

Wow! It amazed me how people could think a simple sorry could resolve everything. Fat chance of that.

"Can you forgive me?" she asked, looking concerned.

"Don't think so," I said firmly. "It's pretty damn unforgivable to kick someone out when they're down."

"I agree."

"Well, at least we agree about something."

Could I forgive my mother for what she did? For depriving me of my dad all these years?

No way! As far as I was concerned, it really was all her fault.

Rage swept through me.

*I'd had enough.*

The walls of the kitchen seemed to be closing in. I needed to get out of here. Away from this selfish, selfish woman.

Standing up, I left without another word and headed to work. At least there, I could get my mind off everything for a while. This was all way too much to digest. I needed time to sift and sort. But right now, more than anything, I needed my furry friends.

They'd help me forget… for a while, at least.

# *Nineteen*

Work was just what I needed and Emma's chatter was therapeutic. Pushing my parental issues aside, I even started humming as I refilled the water jug, poured food into bowls, happily anticipating the arrival of the dogs. At seven a.m., Emma unlocked the door and I was surprised to see the golden retriever lumber in first.

"You sure we should be keeping Goldie so close to her due date?" I asked. She looked huge, as well as exhausted as she plopped down on the floor and rolled onto her side, panting like crazy.

"Oh, she's got a while yet," said Jill, shrugging her shoulders and looking like she couldn't care less.

"Really? She looks big enough to give birth now," said Emma. "Today, as a matter of fact."

"Trust me. Not yet. See you at five," she said, as she practically ran out the door, obviously not wanting to chat.

I didn't trust Jill, finding her immature as well as irresponsible, especially since she was always late picking up her dog. She worked in nearby Toronto and claimed traffic was horrific. I understood, as I'd driven in rush hour from time to time, but couldn't comprehend when she was sometimes as late as three hours. Especially since I smelled booze on her breath. My guess was she was going out after hours for drinks.

Jill always paid me for the extra time, but I warned that I wouldn't be able to accommodate her much longer if she kept this up. I was still trying to work on my "nice complex" and making an effort to toughen up. Lately, she tried harder to be here on time but I still didn't feel good about her and was concerned she was drinking and driving. I'd tried to approach the topic several times, but she claimed it was her mouthwash that smelled and she hadn't been drinking at all. I was pretty sure she was lying.

Worried about Goldie, I made sure there was a bowl of food and fresh water near her at all times. I asked Carl and Sam to keep an eye on her as well and then got busy with the other dogs. I had a full house today so I herded them all out to the back yard to play ball and threw until my arm was numb—back and forth, back and forth—while they managed varying degrees of fetching and retrieving. A few ran around, sniffing delightedly, and I was sure for some of them, this was the only time they got to stretch their legs. Most of their owners led busy lives and had little time for walks. Finally, they all tired out, so I brought them back inside and one by one they dropped for a nap.

Around two o'clock, when all the dogs were snoozing away, Emma searched me out in the farthest corner of the yard where I was gathering up wayward balls and toys that'd been tossed around.

"You have some visitors. Wait'll you see who," she said quietly.

I followed her in to find a tall man dressed in a gray suit, white shirt, black tie. Unfortunately, I knew him. Jack Kite. Looking as stiff and unyielding as always.

"What in hell is he doing here?" I whispered. He looked completely out of place and it sickened me to see Mrs. Whitmore off to the side, her beady eyes darting about, taking in everything. I was sure her critical, condescending mind was hard at work picking out all the faults with the business.

"Don't know," whispered Emma. "He said he'd only speak to you. Completely ignored me even though I used to work for the firm. But then again, unless I was important to him, and I wasn't, it wouldn't be worth his while to remember."

Deciding Kite wasn't going to make me feel bad in my very own business, I quickly used the sanitizer dispenser to clean my hands, gathered up courage and walked over, hand outstretched for a shake.

"Hello, Mr. Kite," I said, forcing a confidant tone of voice. He still had the ability to make my knees shake. So much for not letting him get to me.

"Jessica." He nodded his acknowledgement, but ignored my handshake as he looked around, clearly grossed out by the dogs. His lips were curled up in disdain and he reached down to wipe some dog hair off his trousers.

"Hello, Mrs. Whitmore," I said, in my most friendly voice.

She didn't even have the grace to acknowledge my greeting as she walked over to inspect a couple of pups who'd awoken and were playing with a tug toy.

"What brings you here? I take it you don't have a dog out in your car or something, do you?" I asked.

Ignoring my comment, an attempt for a bit of lightheartedness in the face of these sour people, Kite put his briefcase down on Emma's desk, opened it and pulled out a file. I caught a glimpse of several papers.

"I have a list of complaints from your neighbors about this er… " He turned his nose up. "Dog daycare. The constant barking throughout the day is disturbing their lives. Apparently, there was even one night a dog barked nonstop." He handed over the file with a smirk on his face.

I couldn't believe he would lower himself to deliver this personally. After all, he was a criminal lawyer, and as far as I knew I was no criminal. It was also clear he was enjoying this way too much, judging by the delighted look on his face. I opened up the file, glanced down and saw six signatures, recognizing three of them as neighbors that had lived here as far back as I could remember.

"This is just a warning. If things don't improve, the next time you see me you'll be handed a fine and a court date. Mark my words, I'll shut this place down." Kite snapped his briefcase closed, turned and left, slamming the door on his way out. Mrs. Whitmore looked around at the noise, saw he'd gone and scurried to follow him. I wondered again why he came himself instead of sending one of his servants. I was small potatoes to him. Maybe, they were both just being nosy and wanted to see what was going on.

"Wow! He brought a chill right into this room. Like a giant ice cube," said Emma. "Didn't even allow for discussion."

"Always was a jerk, always will be," I said, shoving the file in the desk drawer. "Mrs. Whitmore too. I'm just angry the neighbors didn't come and speak to me directly. We could have talked this out and come up with solutions."

Sam entered the room with two bichons he'd been out walking. Obviously, he'd caught part of the conversation. "Hate to tell you this, but we noticed a few folks 'round here aren't so friendly anymore. At first, they were all interested in the dogs, learning their names and stuff, even giving them treats. Now, they just ignore us."

"What are we going to do?" asked Emma. "Can he actually shut us down?"

"They can if things don't improve and they push it," I answered, frustrated at this new development. I didn't need any more hassles on my plate.

"Don't worry. I won't let that happen."

I turned to find John, my former legal assistant, holding a larger sheaf of papers than Kite had.

"Heard the big man was coming here today and I've been researching like hell. If you end up fined I'll make sure you have all the info to fight back."

Once again, I experienced that wonderful feeling when someone goes out of his or her way to help another. In this case, me. But John was always like that and I was grateful to have him as a friend.

I moved closer and reached out to hug him.

"Thanks," I whispered. "You're always there when I need you. But why in the world would Kite lower himself to get involved in something like this?"

"Maybe because one of the complainants is his sister. A Mrs. Foster."

"Mrs. Foster is his sister?" I was stunned. She was usually sweet, lived down the street for years, and was always asking me how I was every time I ran into her.

"Yes. She must have said something to him about the barking and he decided to get involved to retaliate. That man definitely needs a life," said John.

"Retaliate? Why?"

"He lost a big millionaire client after firing you," he said.

"Really? Who?" I didn't recall ever being near anyone with that kind of money.

"James Pape. Software expert."

"The CEO charged with insider trading?" I remembered the case as headlines splashed across the papers for months.

"Yes, that's the guy. He's a client Kite got off, free of charges. Of course, he made big bucks from Pape, as well as a string of referrals."

"What's that got to do with me?"

"Do you remember Christine Aylmer?"

"Of course. She was one of my pro bono cases." Her sullen face under a mop of ginger curls rose up before me.

"James Pape is her father. Aylmer is her mother's maiden name."

"Really? I never knew that. How's Christine doing, by the way?"

"No one knows. She ran away from home a few days ago. Word has it; she's living on the street somewhere. She missed her court date and there's a bench warrant out for her arrest. Her dad came looking for you to help and went crazy when he found out you were fired. Apparently, he tore a strip off of Kite and ended all business deals immediately. Kite's angry and has been maligning you every chance he gets."

"Figured. Thought it was just because I refused to obey him." Although I wasn't surprised. "So Christine missed her court date. Dammit."

"Sure did. By the way, your replacement won't touch pro bono cases so I don't go near her. Won't help her either. Watched her hunt for a file for two hours and just pretended I didn't know where it was when all the time it was on my desk."

"That's kinda mean." But it made me grin. Couldn't help but admire his loyalty.

"Not as cruel as she is to us. She makes it clear we're worse than the scum under her shoes."

He looked at his watch. "Gotta go. I'll leave these papers here for you to look at. With five kids I can't afford to be unemployed, and if I get going now, I'll make it back on time."

"Thank you."

"I'll be in touch. Kite won't know what he's up against." He stuck his fist up in the air. "Power to the little guys." Laughing, he took off.

I tucked the mound of files in a drawer for I had to focus now on getting the dogs ready to go home. Soon it'd be five o'clock and clients would be lining up to retrieve their pets. Kite and his crap could be dealt with later.

Finally, after every dog was reunited with his or her master, we were just left with Goldie. Emma tried to get hold of Jill, but her phone call went straight to her voice mail.

"You go home," I said. "I'll be fine by myself."

"You sure?" asked Emma.

"Positive."

"Well, okay. I've got a load of laundry calling my name."

I shook my head, still amazed that with all the money she had, she still did her own housekeeping, laundry and cooking. She was quite a woman.

After Emma left, I spent some time cleaning up and doing paperwork. Right in the middle of balancing out my expenditures, Goldie let out a loud groan. I looked over and realized she'd gotten up, was agitated as hell and panting loudly. Then she lay back down or fell down was more like it.

Oh no! Was this the onset of labor?

I panicked. Fearing something like this might happen here, I'd even read up about it, just in case. But my thoughts were so tumultuous I went blank.

What was I going to do?

*Get it together. The dog needs you.*

Goldie looked at me with trusting eyes. She was counting on me. I rushed to the cupboard where I had blankets stored. I then remembered a large kiddie swimming pool I had blown up and placed in the corner for the dogs to splash in when hot. Figuring this would make a good lair for a dog, I quickly put it down on the floor, spread a blanket over it and helped Goldie into it.

I next texted Aunt T, Maggie and Emma, hoping someone would see I needed help. I knew Hazel was at her studio but decided not to call her. Just didn't want to see her face at the moment.

I knew dogs usually took care of everything themselves, but I was afraid of complications. As Goldie panted more rapidly, I went into full-out panic mode, ran out of the house, and looked over to see if Red's car was in the laneway. Good, it was. What was that saying? Desperate times called for desperate measures? Desperate as hell, I raced over and rang the doorbell, several times I might add, praying he was there and willing to help.

Amidst Squid's barking, Red opened the door, struggling to put a T shirt on. I got a quick glance at his six-pack abs and, for a moment, forgot the reason I was there until he said, "What's wrong? Is there a fire or something? Did you fall out of the tree again?"

Breathless with fear or by the sight of his abs, I struggled to stammer out, "No. I have a dog in labor. Can you help?"

"Sure," he said, not hesitating a bit, as I turned to head back.

Red and Squid followed me to the studio. I was glad he didn't ask a whole lot of questions, as I was worried about leaving Goldie alone too long, and didn't want to go into long explanations. When we got back, much to my shock, one little puppy had already been born. Red dimmed the lights and we spoke in soothing voices in an attempt to comfort her and before long, there were eight tiny little golden retriever pups. I fired a prayer up to the heavens, as I was damn lucky. Goldie did it all herself, with no complications, at least that I could see. Whew! What a trooper.

"I can't get over how adorable they are," I said, looking up at Red. He seemed just as awed as I was. I mean, who could remain unmoved by these tiny miracles? But where in the world was Jill? I glanced at my watch. She was later than ever.

"Looks like things are never dull around here," said Red. "Is something wrong? You still look worried."

"I can't get hold of Jill, Goldie's owner. I wonder where she is?"

I'd left messages and even called her home phone. Much to my shock, it was now disconnected. I had a strange feeling she wasn't coming back for her dog.

"She's abandoned them, right?" he asked.

I looked up to see Red staring at me but I had to admit, his eyes were pretty darn compassionate.

"Seems so." Exhausted beyond belief, I felt like I was going to collapse.

To my surprise, almost intuitively, Red reached over to hug me and I held on tight, drawing from his strength. Warm and safe, I had that feeling of never wanting to let go.

But reality hit hard, as the door opened and in rushed Emma. "Tried to reach you on the cell phone but you didn't answer. Oops, sorry."

I pulled away quickly.

"Don't be." But I knew by her raised eyebrows, she noticed my face was flushed.

She looked back and forth between us, then continued, "Got your message about Goldie."

I pointed to the wading pool.

"Awwww..." She noticed the puppies and went right over and knelt down. "Such beauties. Wait until Jill gets here. She'll be so surprised."

"I think she's skipped out on us," I said.

Emma stood up, looking concerned. "What do you mean?"

"I can't get hold of her."

"Really?" She picked up her phone and texted someone.

"Are you trying to reach her?"

"Nope. Sending a message to a friend of mine who's a vet. She owes me big time since I babysit her kids from time to time. I asked her to drop over and her answer came back immediately. Said she'll be here in about an hour."

"Thanks. The pups look okay and so does Goldie but at least we'll know for sure."

"By the way, did you figure out what to do about the complaints?" asked Emma.

"That really bothers me," said Hazel, entering the room and continuing on with what Emma was saying. "What in the world's got into these neighbors? Those dogs are so happy they rarely bark and besides they're happy barks."

"Bugs me too," said Aunt T, trailing behind along with Maggie.

Guess they all finally got my text messages and someone called Hazel, but how did they know about the petition?

"Sorry," said Emma, obviously noticing my surprised look. "Told them about Kite."

"That's okay." But I snuck a glance at Red, hoping he hadn't heard. After all, I'd kept him up all night with Gloria's barks and he might want to sign that petition himself. Looked like he hadn't heard though, as he was busy tidying up the room. I went over to help him, anything to get away from my mother, as well as stop the conversation about the neighbors.

"You can go home now, if you want. I think everything is under control."

"No problem. I don't mind staying for a while," he said. "Hear you have a problem?"

Rats! He knew.

"I've lived with these neighbors for thirty-five years and never had issues before. To think they went behind my back to a lawyer," raged Hazel, who had walked over to join us. I still couldn't look her in the eyes.

"A disgrace," said Aunt T.

At that moment, Goldie let out a soft woof and both of them stopped as they spied the puppies and went over to ooh and ahh over them. I quickly ran over as well, worried something was wrong, but it seemed she just wanted to show off her gorgeous brood. I didn't blame the proud mother one bit.

"So the neighbors are complaining?" asked Red, coming up behind me.

"Unfortunately, yes." I sighed. "Guess this wasn't such a good idea after all."

"Don't think that," he said firmly. "I'll have it soundproofed by Monday."

"What?" I turned to look at him.

Had I heard him right? He was going to help? Again?

"I'll call my buddies and fix this room up so no one will ever hear a bark again. I'll go and arrange it now."

In total shock, I watched him walk away.

He kept surprising me. One minute he was ignoring me, the next he was helping. The dichotomy again. Hopefully, one day I would figure him out. But for now, I was grateful for the help.

I needed it.

## *Twenty*

Huddled up in the tree house, I just couldn't get Christine Aylmer's freckled face out of my mind. Her eyes haunted me. Not even the Seinfeld re-run Red was watching could pull me out of my funk. Tonight I was a big ball of worry.

*Christine! Where are you?*

I pictured her scared and lonely, living somewhere out on the streets, which could be dangerous to a kid not schooled in street smarts. No telling what she could get into or be lured into doing.

Closing my eyes, I summoned up her image that first day I met her. Joey McAdams had practically dragged her into my office where she refused to sit, just stood by the door as if prepared to bolt at any moment. Sullen looking, with a definite pout going on, she wouldn't meet my eyes and I had a hard time getting information out of her. With Joey's coaxing, I managed to uncover she had been caught shoplifting. Angry, desperately seeking some attention, it was a game to her to see how much she could sneak out of stores without clerks knowing. Just one problem. She was lousy at it, got caught several times, had plenty of warnings until one shop owner had enough and charged her. She'd stolen from that particular store five times. Bail wasn't required as the police released her into the custody of her father and Christine seemed to enjoy the attention, saying it "shook my dad up" with a huge grin. She wanted revenge. To make him suffer the way his long absences from home on business made her suffer.

Apparently, her father always paid for the stolen merchandise and even got her expensive legal help to take care of the charges, but when the lawyer started spouting off a list of rules she had to obey, she told him to go to hell. "Forget it. I'll handle it myself", she then told her dad.

Hence, my appearance on the scene via Joey.

It took quite a bit of time and several meetings, but with a lot of tenacity, I discovered she was a sweet kid; well, not actually a kid as she was eighteen, an adult in court. But she always seemed young for her age, having been sheltered and protected by an apparently overbearing father. Who knew it was Pape? All I knew was her mother had died a few years ago and her father was a really busy guy. Christine felt abandoned. I could relate.

In time we bonded. Who would have guessed we were both fans of the Hardy Boy mystery books? Guess her dad had the series from when he was a kid and she'd plowed her way through reading every single one. So had I, and with mutual crushes on Joe Hardy, we'd connected. I was supposed to be there for her assigned court date. I'd had it all planned out, hoping to get her into a Diversion Program where she'd do charity work and attend lectures on the evils of shoplifting in return for the Crown withdrawing the charge. Dammit! I'd let her down. And now she might end up in jail.

A hard truth smacked me in the face. Much to my disgust I realized I hadn't thought about any of my pro bono cases since getting fired. On a personal quest to help others, I'd stood up for my clients with Kite, and then dropped every one of them, caught up in my own battles. I knew they'd be wiped out of the firm the minute I left, yet I just ignored them. Forgot about them. Left them on their own.

*Why didn't I check on how they were doing? Call them? Help them? Finish what I'd started?*

Hell! I was no better than Hazel and my father, walking away from people in need. What had I been thinking? That I only help people when it's convenient to me and drop them the minute life gets too hard?

I sat straight up. That was it. Enough of this moping around.

*I had to go find her and right my wrong. Now!*

Glancing at my watch, I realized I had time before I relieved Emma from puppy duty. We were all taking turns watching the new puppies around the clock, making sure they were okay. I had about five hours to do some sleuthing. I needed to get moving.

"Gotta go, Olive." I eased out of the tree house opening, prepared to climb down.

"Hey, what's up? Not watching the show tonight?"

I looked over to see Red hanging out his window, with a large bowl of popcorn dangling from his hand. "Want some? It has extra butter," he taunted.

"No thanks," I answered, mortified that he obviously

knew my little secret of watching T.V. with him.

I quickly climbed back down to the ground trying to put thoughts of Red behind me. I had no time to think about him right now. I had to find Christine.

Not having a clue as to where she could be, I jumped in my car, headed downtown and cruised up and down the streets, searching for any sign of her. A couple of times I thought I saw her but nope, it turned out to be someone else. I headed to Mac's Milk, hoping Joey would be there and have information as to where she was. Pulling in, I hurried into the store.

"Howdy, Ms. White."

Thank goodness, he was working.

"Hi Joey. Hey, I'm looking for Christine Aylmer. Any idea where she is?"

His eyebrows pushed together in a squint. "Sorry. Don't know where she is."

*Was he lying?*

"You sure?"

"Positive. Used to be she'd tell me everything but this time she took off and didn't let anyone know. Least of all me, because she knew I'd be worried and tell her dad."

"Does she work anywhere?"

"No. Did once at McDonald's, but quit after a month."

"Do you know where her hangouts are?"

"Sure. Parks. She loves hanging at Gore by the fountain and Confederation by the waterworks. Those were the two places I'd usually find her but not lately. I've been worried as well. Rumor has it she's been getting high quite a bit."

Guilt washed over me. Dammit. This was all my fault.

"Thanks, Joey. Could you let me know if you hear from her?" I handed him a card, writing my cell phone number on the back.

"Sure will."

I headed to Confederation first, driving slowly down the road beside the park, searching for any sign of her. Nothing. Next, I parked my car and headed down to the Wild Waterworks section of the park, which attracted hundreds of teens looking for aquatic thrills. It was a warm night and maybe she was cooling off by going for a swim. Walking up and down the fenced in area, I couldn't see her and left before I got pegged as some kind of freak, watching young people in pools. I then set off through the camping section, filled with trailers and tents, but came up empty. Almost ready to give up, I noticed a group of teens hanging around a picnic table and headed over, hoping they might at least know her or point me in the right direction.

"Hi there," I said, watching them all eye me suspiciously. No one answered.

"Was wondering if any of you know a girl by the name of Christine Aylmer?"

"Wouldn't tell you if I did," said one of the girls, blonde hair tucked up under a baseball cap, but I was sure I detected a glint of acknowledgment in her eyes. I'd bet money on her knowing where Christine was.

I sighed, but didn't blame her for not saying anything. I was once like that and knew a teenager's code was to mistrust adults until they earned your respect. Handing out my card anyway, I figured I might luck out or at least I hoped so, when she had time to think about it.

Next, I drove back down King Street to Gore Park, situated in the center of town. Managing to find a parking spot a few blocks over, I hurried to the Park, perusing side streets, looking for her as I walked. Finally arriving, I circled all around the main landmark—a gigantic black fountain—scouting out every person there, even handing my card to several people, but there was no sign of her. It hit me how ridiculous I was, expecting to locate her in a city which was the eighth largest in Canada with a population over five hundred thousand. Hardly likely, I'd find her.

Not wanting to give up, once again I drove up and down streets, and when I found myself back on King Street heading downtown again, on impulse I turned right onto Mary Street. Driving slowly beside a skateboarding park, searching for her with no luck, I pulled over across from the Good Shepherd Centre, a large brown brick building. It was run by the Brothers of the Good Shepherd who provided free food to those in need.

Would she be here? Glancing at my watch, I realized supper hour was over but I was wondering if she was at the food bank they held in their warehouse. She'd get hungry sometimes and with no money, this would be an ideal place for her to go. I knew she'd heard about it, as I'd once given her a list of shelters and organizations that would help, when she talked about taking off from home. Fortunately, she'd stayed put that time, where at least she had the basic comforts of food and shelter.

I hurried across the street and entered the building, went up a small flight of stairs, which lead me to a room filled to the brim with canned goods. Standing just inside the doorway, I scanned the scattering of people picking up food or sitting, chatting. No sign of her. I was just about to go over to talk to some of them when a loud voice spoke up behind me.

"Excuse me. May I help you with something?"

I turned around to find a young man wearing a black shirt with a white collar, indicating he was one of the brothers. I checked his nametag—Brother John.

"Do you work here?" I asked.

"Sure do." He smiled, making me feel a bit hopeful after my search had turned up nothing so far.

"Maybe you can help. I'm looking for a girl by the name of Christine Aylmer. Do you know her?"

"A runaway?"

"Yes."

"Sorry. We don't always know everyone's name. As a matter of fact, sometimes they give fake ones. What does she look like?"

"Long red curls to her waist. Blue eyes, about five feet six."

I watched him closely as a hint of recognition lit up his eyes.

"The red curls are a giveaway. I think I have seen her here a few times. Has a penchant for peanut butter, if I'm not mistaken."

"That's her, for sure. She loves peanut butter." Found that out when she sat through a whole meeting one time, scooping it out of a jar with her finger and sucking it down. Totally grossed me out.

"Any idea where she's staying?"

"Couldn't tell you if I did, for confidential reasons. Is she in some kind of trouble?"

"Can't go into detail either, but yes, she is."

I pulled out my card and handed it to him. "Could you give her this if you see her again?"

Eyebrows squeezed together, he said, "Sure will."

Walking back to my car, a thought struck me. Brother John looked genuinely worried about the girl, more so than if she was just one of a group of random people who ate there occasionally. Appeared to me like he knew her a bit better than he let on, but I could understand why he couldn't say. Sixteen and up, a young person could legitimately take off without police getting involved. At eighteen, she could do whatever she wanted.

*But this got me thinking of another place where she might be hiding.*

I headed back down Main Street, turning right on Pearl and parked in front of a large red brick building called Martha House, also run by the Good Shepherd. I knew I'd circled this on the list I'd given Christine and had explained the intense privacy this house afforded you. It was a haven for battered and hurt women who needed to hide out. Whether I knocked or phoned, they would never give away the identities of who lived there. They would simply say, "If that person is here, I'll let them know."

Standing on the porch, I rang the bell and a pleasant looking young woman answered. Given the pat answer, I waited, holding my breath, crossing my fingers.

*Was Christine here? If so, would she see me?*

Minutes passed but it seemed like hours before the door opened. Out walked Christine, and I could have cried right there, right then. Tears of joy, not sadness. At least she was safe.

"What do you want?" she snarled. Her scowl said it all. She was really pissed and I didn't blame her one bit.

Do I give excuses? Tell her what happened? No. I figured that wouldn't work with her. Best to accept the blame and ask for forgiveness. Several times, if I had to.

"I want to apologize for leaving you in the lurch. I'm so sorry."

"Too late now."

"Yeah, I know. But figured too late was better than never."

She looked down at her feet. At least she was still here, not taking off back inside the house.

"How are you doing?" I asked.

"What's it to you?" She stared me in the eyes. The anger there clear to see.

"I care," I said softly.

Silence.

"Glad you're here and off the streets."

"Was there for a while."

"Heard about that. Also heard you missed your court date."

"Checking up on me, are you?" But she seemed a bit pleased by that.

"You know there's a warrant out for your arrest?"

"Yep."

I sighed, feeling pretty broken-hearted about what I'd done to this girl. Here I was the brilliant lawyer out to save her by my skills, and hell, I might have if I hadn't walked away.

"Hey, Christine," I said hesitantly, deciding to try one more time. "I let you down and there's no excuse for that.

I'm hoping you could find it in your heart to forgive me and we can try again."

"You mean you'd be my lawyer?"

"If you'd take me on."

"That's what you said the last time."

"I know."

"Don't know about you anymore."

I handed her one of my cards. "At least think about it. Give me a call or drop over and I'll help."

"Will they put me in jail?"

"I'll see what I can do."

"Well… I'll think about it. Maybe."

She turned, went in the door and slammed it in my face, obviously making it clear how upset she still was with me.

Once again, I didn't blame her.

## *Twenty-one*

"But I did no such thing, dear," said the obviously startled woman, standing in the doorway staring at me.

"But Mrs. Foster. Your name is right here." I held out the petition pointing to her signature.

She was last on my list of neighbors to make peace with, after Red finished soundproofing the studio and the dog's barking could no longer be heard. I'd left her to the end because she was Kite's sister and figured she might give me a hard time. Hopefully, she was nothing like him but… *this was odd.* She was saying she didn't sign the petition?

"Let me get my glasses, hon. Come on in. Why don't you wait for me in the living room." She pointed to a room just off the hallway.

"Sure," I said, plopping down on a comfy beige sofa.

The room was lovely with wall-to-wall pictures of children and obviously happy times, marred only by a few of Kite. I went over to take a look at one of them, which showed him with a blonde woman and two children sitting in a canoe. They were all smiling and I sure hoped his wife was strong and kept the children from knowing what a horrible man their father was. But then again, I was biased. He probably was a wonderful husband and dad. Yeah, right.

Bifocals on, Mrs. Foster came back into the room, so I scuttled over to where I'd been sitting.

"Here, let me take a good look at that."

Staring at the petition for quite some time, she finally said, "That's not my signature." She put the file down and went over to open up a drawer in a desk on the other side of the room, bringing back a notepad and pen. Sitting down, she wrote her name and held the paper up. "See? The whole way it's written is completely different."

She was right. Not even close. It was my turn to be confused.

"Where did you get this?" she asked. "It's a forgery. Someone else signed my name. And by the way, I would never protest your doggy daycare, dear. I'm an animal lover and I think it's great what you're doing."

Weird as hell. All the other neighbors were annoyed and glad to know the room was soundproofed. Their complaints were legitimate. But this was Kite's sister. *Wasn't she the one who started it all?*

Before I even got a chance to respond, she said, "Oh, don't tell me." She slapped the paper down hard on the coffee table. "This is all my brother's doing, isn't it."

Guess she noticed his name at the top.

"Yes, by the way, it did come from him."

"Well, wouldn't you just know it? Jane down the street, a big dog hater by the way, probably complained to him. He's her lawyer you see, and her name's first on the list. He probably put this together to get back at you and figured the more signatures he had the better, so he signed my name." She looked at me sympathetically. "Heard he fired you. A bloody shame." She shook her head. "But don't worry about this, dear. I'll set him straight. Someone's got to rein him in." She winked. "I'll tell him I'll press charges if he ever does this again. He'll lose a lot because I babysit his children quite frequently."

"Well, thank you." For once, the fates were with me. Kite's sister was on my side; however I was surprised she knew about my being let go. Probably Hazel told her.

"As a matter of fact, I'm going to pay him a little visit right now and put an end to this. Forging someone's name is a criminal act and he's not going to get away with it."

*I'd sure love to be a fly on that wall,* I thought, as I left her getting ready to confront her brother and headed back to the studio, glad this petition was behind me. Hopefully, Mrs. Foster would make sure there wasn't another.

As soon as I walked in the door, the rustling of a bag caught my attention.

"Sunny, get out of there," I chastised, barely able to get the words out through my laughter, as I watched the tiny pup's wiggling tail hanging out of a bag of dog food sitting on the floor. While Emma was busy filling the water bowl, he must have tipped it over and was having a great old time snacking away. Watching his little legs trip over each other as he backed out of the bag was hilarious but he finally made it and scooted over to see me. I squatted down to give him a quick snuggle and was rewarded with a few licks. In a dog's world, I believed they were called kisses and to be the recipient of such an endearment made all the hard work of raising them worthwhile or helping to raise them, I might add. Goldie proved to be a wonderful, capable and loving mother. I was just her human nanny from time to time.

"I'm a bit worried about little Sunny there," said Emma, finished with her chores and coming over to join me.

"Why?"

"Check out his left hind leg. He seems to be limping off and on."

I watched him for a bit and noticed the same thing. "I'll keep an eye on him and take him over to the vet if he keeps it up." I looked at my watch. "Thanks for staying late and holding down the fort while I met with the neighbors."

"No problem. Sam and Carl were a big help."

"Sure are." The two guys were working out amazingly well.

"Did everything go okay?" she asked. "Is everyone all happy now?"

"So far."

After I explained the whole Kite/sister thing, Emma grinned.

"We're definitely toilet-papering his house one night. For sure," she said.

"What's with you wanting to vandalize people's homes? First Joseph's, now Kite's."

"Revenge is fun. As a kid, Halloween Eve, I never missed a Devil's Night of mischief. Or got caught."

"And you're proud of that?"

"Sure am. I was the queen of pranks in high school."

Her pleased expression set me off on a round of

laughter. The good thing about Emma was her fun side, which balanced my more serious view of things.

"Now scoot. You've been here too long as it is," I ordered, after getting myself back in control.

"Okay, I can take the hint and besides, I have some stuff to do. See you tomorrow."

Like a whirlwind, she headed out the door.

After Emma left, I got busy cleaning up, reflecting on how quickly time flies when raising puppies.

We had blocked off a section of the room where the pups could have some privacy, but Goldie never seemed to mind her new friends and family checking up on them. She always seemed quite proud to be showing off her babies. Weeks had passed in an instant and before I knew it their eyes were wide open and they were able to walk a bit, or wobble was more like it.

I was completely enthralled with watching them every spare moment I had, caught up in all the ways they could get into trouble as they explored their worlds for the first time. Curiosity was rampant as they sniffed everything and everyone, often getting tired all at once and ending up in a pile, snoozing away. Watching them helped me get my mind off problems I had with Hazel, Dad and now Christine.

Dammit. I still hadn't heard from the girl. I'd made a few calls and even figured out another course of action but couldn't implement it without her okay.

The other thing that really bugged me was that after Red's hug the night the pups were born, he went back to being cool towards me. Barely even spoke to me the day he and his friends soundproofed the room. Why, I hadn't a clue and decided to just forget about him. I thought we had the beginnings of a good friendship but that was certainly nipped in the bud as it looked like we'd regressed. Oh well, I was better off without him anyway.

Still concerned about Sunny's leg, and about another pup that had started puking up water, I decided I'd stay the night in the studio, keeping an eye on things. I always worried about them eating something they shouldn't for I'd heard horror stories about dogs being operated on to extract various things from their bellies. I'd puppy proofed their area, but was always on the lookout for something they could get into or find and swallow.

Feeling a bit hungry, I made myself a peanut butter sandwich from the stock we kept in a back cupboard and snuggled up in a chair, prepared to get some snoozing done between checking up on the dogs. First, I took inventory making sure the pups were all okay by doing a quick head count. Yep. Everyone was here.

Watching Goldie, I still felt frustrated that we never did locate Jill. I'd driven by her house several times and knocked on the door but no one answered. Her cell phone went to an answering machine and one day a For Sale sign appeared on the front lawn. I'd even called the real estate agent asking how to get hold of her but he was tight-lipped about her whereabouts and said he'd give her the message. Of course she never called back. Ringing her work number and pushing for answers revealed she'd quit her job.

So it looked like I was the owner of eight golden retriever puppies. How someone could give up these beautiful creatures was certainly a mystery. But at least all of them had a home. Sadie and I had fallen in love with the littlest one who was actually the lightest in color. I called him Sunny as he reminded me of a ray of sunshine when he swished around, trying out the strength of his legs. So I decided to keep him. Maggie, Emma and Joey each wanted one, Gladys, after she saw how much her dog loved Squid, laid claim to two of them to keep her little poodle company, and the other two were going to Sam and Carl. And... much to my shock, Hazel adopted Goldie. Distant from people, she was not, I discovered, that way with animals. Sure, she loved Sadie but she adored Goldie. They were quite a pair.

Speaking of Sadie, she was having the time of her life, already best friends with all the dogs and strutting around as if she were their boss or at least their big sister. Fortunately, Goldie seemed to love her little assistant and welcomed her as a co-parent to her brood.

Hearing Sadie bark a warning to one of the pups, I looked over to see what was going on. Sunny, obviously the most curious of them all, had now fallen headfirst into the water bowl. It was unbelievable the mischief these dogs could get into.

A car started up nearby and nosy, I glanced out the window and saw it was Red. I looked at my watch. One in the morning. Pretty late for him to be going out. I hoped that didn't mean his father had taken a turn for the worse.

Much to my surprise, his car pulled out and stopped in front of the studio. He jumped out and headed to the door while I tried to flatten down my hair and tuck in my shirt. I guess he noticed the lights were on. I opened it up to a tense-looking Red, while Squid pushed by to run over and see Goldie, Sadie and the pups.

"Saw your light on. Everything okay?" he asked.

"Everything's fine."

"In that case, I was wondering if I could leave Squid here?"

His words sounded hurried as well as strained.

"Sure can. Is it your father?"

"Yes," he said, rubbing his eyes as if trying to wake up. "Squid seems to have picked up that something is going on and won't stop barking. I figure if he was here he'd settle down."

"No problem. He can stay all night if you want."

He looked so harried that I wanted to wrap my arms around him and purely on instinct, much to my surprise, I did. He hugged me back hard, then just as abruptly pushed away muttering, "Sorry." He then turned and ran down to his car and took off.

I sat down or almost fell down, to be exact.

*What the hell just happened?*

Why did I hug him when he'd been aloof for days? It was way too intimate a gesture, and it wasn't as if he needed that right now, especially since he was rushing off to the hospital. And another thing, *why did it feel so good?* Reaching out to touch him seemed completely natural but I'd been unprepared for my reaction. Hell, I could have held on all day long. *Get a hold of yourself.* I pushed my thoughts away. They were too disturbing to think about so I got up to see how Squid was doing.

I smiled as I saw him join in with Sadie, watching over the group, even nudging the puppies back to their mother when they got too far way. I glanced at my watch and decided I couldn't sleep now and desperately needed coffee. Figuring the pups would be okay for a few minutes with Goldie, Squid and Sadie on duty, I headed over to the house to grab some caffeine and something more substantial to eat. I needed some good food to keep me going.

Much to my surprise, I found my father sitting at the table sharing one of Hazel's health food shakes. How they could down anything lime green so early in the morning was beyond me. A dog, probably his dog, was barking at me.

"Hi there," he said, looking sheepish. "Don't worry, he won't bite. He's just very protective." He looked down at the dog. "Billy, meet Jessie."

I bent down to give him a pet, while I tried to gather my wits about me. This was the first time I'd seen him since our lunch and it felt awkward. Damn awkward. Billy, maybe sensing how distracted I was and wanting my full attention, stopped barking and raised his paw, nudging me until I looked down. He obviously wanted a shake.

"Good boy," I said, humoring him, delighted he'd settled down so quickly.

"He sure likes you," said my dad.

I couldn't think of anything to say, so stayed quiet.

"I have to go out of town today. Would you mind if I left Billy with you? I'll pay, of course," said my father.

I just nodded.

"I'll bring him over later. I'd love to see your place."

More silence.

For some reason, I was struck dumb by seeing the two of them together for the first time in sixteen years. It was much like it was years ago, yet so different. My tired mind just couldn't wrap around it.

"Here, have some coffee," said Hazel.

Hunger and a need for a caffeine fix prevented me from turning and dashing out the door.

I pulled over a tray and put the coffee on it, adding a bowl of cereal. After pouring milk over it and sprinkling on some sugar, I quickly headed towards the door.

"Won't you join us?" asked Hazel, looking alarmed.

Finally finding my voice, I said, "No, I need to get to work."

Ignoring the sad look on my father's face and the disappointed one on Hazel's, I just kept right on going. I didn't feel like dealing with either one of them right now. Okay, I knew I was acting selfish, but I just didn't care. I was damn tired of all the secrets surrounding them.

Not having an appetite any longer, I pushed the food away and somehow managed to snooze for a bit, awakening when the door opened and in walked Emma, who handed me an extra-large cup of black coffee from Tim Hortons.

"Thank you," I said, as I took a sip and sighed. "Just what I needed."

"You look like you've been here all night."

I glanced down at my wrinkled pants and sweatshirt. "That's because I have."

"Is everything okay with Sunny?"

"Looks like it. He finally stopped limping. He must have just banged it or something. All the pups seem okay now."

"What's up with Red?" She pointed towards Squid.

"He got called to the hospital to see his dad." To my surprise, a tear drifted down but I quickly wiped it away, hoping Emma didn't notice.

"Nice outfit," I said, changing the subject, pointing to her shiny electric blue pantsuit.

"Thanks. Fifty percent off at Zellers," she preened. "Love it when I get a good deal."

"Well, it looks terrific on you." I stood up and headed to the washroom where I always kept a fresh set of clothes. "Guess I better change before a client arrives and I scare them away."

"That would be my advice. You look like you rolled outta bed."

"More like rolled out of my chair."

I quickly threw on a clean pair of jeans and a T-shirt and came back, clutching my coffee, hoping the caffeine rush would keep me awake.

"Much better," said Emma, nodding her approval.

I had no time to answer as a flurry of owners arrived. Ten minutes later, my father showed up. He looked around, saying, "You've done a good job here."

"Thanks. I tried." I smiled, relenting a bit.

"Hope Billy behaves for you."

I glanced down at his dog, who was licking my hand and wagging his tail. "He will."

"Thanks," was all he said as he walked out the door.

I felt bad, because he obviously felt unwelcome. Usually, being curious by nature, he'd want to know and see everything that was going on. Or at least that was what he was like in the past. I guess he felt he'd better get out of here fast since I wasn't that friendly with him. Oh well, no time to think about that now. I had work to do.

The day was hectic with a lot of poopy messes going on in the studio. It was sometimes hard for the new dogs to understand that they would be let out on the grass and it was difficult to keep track of them when they went to the door wanting to take a bathroom break. Unless they barked their urgency, I often missed them. Emma and I spent a lot of time with mops and cleaning solutions.

It was about two o'clock before Red showed up. One look at his tired face said it all.

"I'm here to pick up Squid."

"How are you doing?" I asked, concerned at how tired he looked.

He paused for a second, then said, "My father passed away."

*Oh, no!*

"I'm sorry to hear that." I waited to see if he'd say more, but when he didn't I added, "Hey, why don't you leave Squid with me. I can drop him over later. It would be no trouble at all."

He hesitated, then said, "You sure?"

"I'm sure."

"Well, that would be a big help. I just came home to make phone calls and stuff but I didn't want Squid to overstay his welcome." He looked relieved.

"Let me know if there's anything else I can do."

"You're doing enough by watching my dog."

As he turned and left, I noticed his shoulders were hunched over. Once again, it hit me that he would give anything to have his father alive, while I didn't want to give the time of day to mine.

## *Twenty-two*

"You have company," said Emma, yelling to the back of the room where I was tending to a couple of terriers, hell-bent on getting into trouble by knocking over a water dish. Mopping up the floor, I tossed a tug toy, hoping that would keep them busy.

"Really? Who?" I asked, turning around.

Oh my goodness. The jean-jacketed girl waiting by the front door was Christine, flanked by two women.

Never had I been so glad to see someone. She'd been on my mind constantly and I was so worried about her I was tempted to go back to Martha House and force the issue. I knew that wouldn't work so I just kept hoping she'd show up or call.

"Glad you made it here," I said, as I rushed over to greet her.

She stared down at the floor, refusing to meet my eyes. "Wouldn't have come if it wasn't for Sylvia and Melanie."

I looked at the two women, recognizing both of them.

"My goodness. Sylvia Hawk? Is that really you?"

She smiled. "It's me all right."

She sure looked different. Her dark hair was bleached blonde and she'd lost about thirty pounds. Her slim figure was encased in skinny blue jeans and a black T-shirt. She'd been one of my pro bono clients as well, coping with a violent husband who looked at beating her up as a recreational sport.

"How've you been?" I asked, guilt surfacing. I'd let her down too.

"Turns out Christine and I are both at Martha House," she said. "I snuck a peek out the window when you were talking to her and recognized you. I knew you got fired so I told her all about it. That it wasn't your fault you'd left the firm."

"But I should have called and let you know. How did you find out?"

"A guy named John told me, when I came looking for you. He let me know where you were and I was actually going to pay you a visit."

Good for John. Always on the lookout for me.

I turned to the other girl. "You're the girl from the park."

This time she grinned. "Yeah, Melanie's my name. Figured if you went to all that trouble searching through Confederation Park for Christine, it must be important. Pushed her to come here as well. She needs to get her act together."

Christine rolled her eyes, to which Melanie said, "Sorry, but you do."

"Well, I'm thrilled all of you are here. Come on. Let's go talk." I led them to a side area where a few chairs were set up.

"Do I have to go to jail?" asked Christine, swinging her feet back and forth, finally looking at me with eyes of terror. "For missing that court date?"

"Are you willing to turn yourself in?" I asked.

A long pause ensued until Sylvia nudged her. Finally she said, "Might as well."

"Good. It's the right thing to do. Now excuse me for a moment, I just have to make a quick phone call to check a few facts."

Not wanting anyone to hear, I took my cell phone outside and quickly dialed a number.

"Officer Jason Locke, please."

He was a grandfatherly type cop down at the central Police Station on King William, seasoned at the job, who took me under his wing when I started at Kite's. He'd been on duty the first time I'd paid a visit to the courthouse, getting my bearings. Showing me around, he gave me his cell phone number and told me to call if I needed any help. Today, I did.

Fortunately he answered and after explaining the situation, he proved to be a worthy ally by helping me plan out a strategy. Thanking him profusely, I hurried back to Christine.

"I can pick you up first thing tomorrow morning and take you to the police station. An Officer Locke will meet us there, do the paperwork and escort you over for a bail hearing. I'll be there on your behalf."

"Will I make bail? I don't think I could take a night behind bars." Her lip quivered and a tear rolled down her cheek, making her look way younger than her eighteen years. I'd put her at ten, at the moment.

"I'll do my damndest to keep you out of jail."

"Okay. Guess I'll show up, since I have no choice." She wiped her tears away with a Kleenex Melanie gave her. "But hey, you don't have to pick me up. Sylvia here will take me."

"It's a deal," I said. "Promise you'll be there?"

"Promise. But the bigger question is—will you be there?" Her eyes held mine and the depth of vulnerability there, shook me. Once again, I didn't blame her for not trusting me.

"Promise." I reached out my hand for a shake, and after a moment's hesitation, she reached out as well.

A wave of relief washed through me. Now, I just had to make sure I didn't let her down, ever again.

After they left, Emma and I said goodbye to the last dog heading off with his owner and she took off for the evening. Noticing Red's light still on in his computer room, I decided to wait until later before bringing Squid back home. I figured he was still busy doing stuff and decided to give him lots of time, especially since Squid was no trouble at all. Sadie loved having his company and the two of them romped around the back yard until they were exhausted. Right now, they were dozing in the living room.

I felt so bad for Red and not knowing what else to do I strapped on an apron and baked some oatmeal muffins and chocolate chip cookies. I had to take action somehow. I mean, what do you say to someone who just lost his father? Words seemed trite but goodies might at least assure that he ate something and anyway it was the thought that counted. I sure hoped he'd recognize my thoughts as kind ones.

After my baking cooled, I bundled it all up in a Tupperware container, roused the dogs and headed next door. Ringing the bell, I waited a second and could hear him running down the stairs to answer.

"Sorry," he said, as Squid came barreling in the door, wagging his tail, obviously thrilled to be home with his master. "The time just raced by. I meant to come over earlier to pick him up." He leaned down to pet his dog, just as Squid jumped up and covered his face with dog kisses. It was actually quite sweet as I noticed a smile appear on his tired, haggard face. Nothing like a dog's devotion to get you in a happier frame of mind.

"No problem. Squid's fun to be around," I said, holding out the goodies I'd brought. "I made you some snacks."

"Thank you," he said, his eyes lighting up as he took the container, pulled up the lid and peeked inside, leaning closer to suck in a long whiff. "Are those chocolate chip cookies?"

"Sure are. Hope you like them."

He sighed happily. "I'm sure I will. Haven't eaten much lately."

"Figured you hadn't."

There was an awkward silence until he said, "Er… would you like to come in for a bit?"

"Well, I don't want to bother you."

Crap! I didn't want to go in at all. I didn't want to cope with the feelings he drummed up in me. I'd planned on dropping off the dog and baked goods, then taking right off, but I'd hesitated a bit so as not to appear rude. I should have just turned and made a quick getaway.

"No bother at all." He stepped aside to let me by. "I was just making some phone calls, letting everyone know, as well as making arrangements. I'm trying to reduce the stress on my mother."

"Oh, how is she doing?" I cared, but I was also stalling, not sure of what to do.

"Not so good." He ran his hands through his hair just as Sadie raced by to join Squid. "So, are you coming in as well?"

Damn traitor dog. "Well, okay. Just for a few minutes." Maybe he didn't want to be alone. I sure wouldn't, at a time like this.

"Follow me," he said, walking briskly down the hall.

I shut the door behind me and as he led me through the living room, I snuck a look around. It was quite simple with just a brown leather couch and love seat on a plain beige rug. With no pictures on the wall, it came across sterile looking and in actual fact, seemed like he barely used this area at all. Guess the Petersons had taken all their furniture with them and Red just added the basics.

The room he led me into was the kitchen. It looked a bit more inhabited with boxes of cereal on the counter and newspapers lying on the large oak table surrounded by matching chairs. He pushed them aside to put my treats down and leaned over to fold up what looked like a blueprint. He pointed to a chair and said, "Make yourself at home. I'm having a beer. Would you like one?"

"Sure would," I answered, as I sat down. Once again, there were no pictures or even a calendar on the wall but he definitely used the toaster, as I noted the bag of bread sitting beside it. It was obvious that this was just a temporary place for him for he certainly hadn't settled in with any little homey touches.

"Oh, a bottle's fine," I said, as I saw him about to pour it into a glass.

"You sure?" he asked.

"Positive."

As he handed it over, he said, "A girl after my own heart."

I was startled to hear him say something so personal and I guess he was too, as redness covered his face and he busied himself pouring food into Squid's bowl. The hug we'd shared, not to mention that kiss at the restaurant, loomed before me, and I could feel a blush covering my own face as well. Damn. We both looked like sunburned fools.

"Is it okay if Sadie has some as well?" he asked, as she ran over to the bowl and Squid, always the gentleman, moved to allow her access.

"Sure, no problem."

However, Sadie, ever the picky eater, sniffed a bit, then went off to play with a ball that was lying by the cupboard.

Squid, on the other hand, amazed me by devouring the whole bowl in about twenty-three seconds, while Red dropped on a chair across from me, took the lid off the Tupperware and tasted a cookie.

"Delicious," he said.

I settled back in the chair and relaxed. Figured I was here so might as well get comfortable.

"Hey, I'm really sorry about your father." I wasn't sure

if it was too painful to talk about his dad or not. I was just throwing it out there, just in case he wanted to get some stuff off his chest.

"Me too. I'll miss him." He looked thoughtful as if reliving past memories. "Wasn't that way in the beginning, though."

"Really?" That surprised me. "I assumed you were always close, to actually move here while he was er, sick." I didn't want to be too blunt and say, while he was dying.

He leaned back in his chair and closed his eyes. After a few minutes, he finally opened them and said, "Nope. He was a workaholic. Good old Edward. First one to arrive at his office. Last one to leave. Hardly saw him at all as a kid."

"Really?" That was a shocker. And here I thought they'd had a perfect relationship right from the start.

"Yes," he picked up a muffin and took a bite. "He had quite the temper and at one point, my mother gathered us up and left. He begged her to come home, saying he'd changed. She did and the same thing happened all over again. So at that point she took us to a shelter and was planning on filing for divorce."

"How did you end up getting close after all that?"

"Dad had a heart attack. Changed him completely."

"How so?" I urged him on, intrigued as well as surprised he was actually sharing this much.

"Faced his mortality, I guess. Got his priorities straight and figured out what was important in life. He wanted his family back, but we'd moved to an apartment and my mom wasn't keen on trusting him again, so they took it slow, dating again and seeing a counselor. When things were stable we moved back home for the last time. Dad started paying more attention to me, taking me fishing and stuff. I found myself forgiving him for all the beatings, but my sister had a harder time."

"Beatings? You mean your dad hit you?"

"Sure did. He had an old, black leather belt that he frequently used."

"How horrible."

"Yes, it was. His father beat him and he was just carrying on the tradition."

I was at least lucky in that respect. My parents never laid a hand on me. Poor Red!

Staring into his beer, he remained quiet and I wasn't sure if I should pursue this line of questioning, fearing it might upset him, so I changed the subject saying, "So you have a sister?"

He smiled. "Yep. Izzy, short for Isabelle. She's flying in tonight from Halifax."

"Did he try to spend more time with her, too?" Just couldn't help myself. I was curious to hear more about his family. Hopefully, he wouldn't think I was prying.

"Yes, but she didn't buy it. She had a hard time accepting his realization that he'd been cruel and wasn't going to be like that anymore. She kept waiting for it to start all over again." He sighed. "Just got off the phone from her. She was really upset, as she never really made peace with him. I guess she felt she'd have more time. Guess we always feel we have time."

"You didn't find it hard to forgive him?"

"I did. Especially at first. But the more I became aware

of my own failings, it was easier to accept his. Actually, I admired the fact that he got it together. He really did change."

"Amazing." Was it possible that my parents could change? And to the good? *Could I, as well?*

"But enough about me. I take it you and your mother have a strange relationship?"

"What makes you say that?"

"It's obvious by the way you look at her. Or don't look at her, to be more honest."

"Oh." Was I that transparent or was he just really insightful? "Well, yeah, it's kinda weird."

"Notice you also call her Hazel."

I shook my head. "She doesn't deserve the title Mom."

His eyebrows rose at that, but I didn't add anything more, not wanting to talk about her.

"It must have been hard losing your father so young," he said.

I guess he got the hint, but talking about my father wasn't much easier.

"It was."

"And you never heard from him?" He got up to grab us both another beer.

"Well. Shocker of shocks. He just recently moved back to Hamilton. Stoney Creek, to be exact."

"And he wants to see you?"

"Yep." I took a big swig as if fortifying myself with ammunition to get up the guts to talk about him. After all, Red had been honest with me and I felt I owed him the same. "I don't know if I should let him back into my life or not. I have mixed feelings about the whole thing."

He was quiet for a second, then said softly, "Let him back."

"Yeah? Why?"

"Everyone deserves a second chance."

Christine's eyes flashed before me. That was what she'd given me—a second chance.

"And that's what you did?" I asked.

"Yes."

"And you really thought it was worth it?"

"Certainly."

I shook my head. "Just not sure if I can."

"Promise you'll at least consider it?"

I smiled. "Promise."

Deep in thought, my eyes flicked around the table and I noticed a photo of Red sticking out of the newspaper. I picked it up and stared at it, checking out the blonde in his arms. Was that his fiancée?

"You look nice here," I said, fishing for information or maybe just a distraction from talking about my dad.

He took the picture and laid it face down. "I was going through some old files and found this one of my ex-fiancée. I was just going to throw it away."

"I'm sorry." So she definitely was an ex-fiancée, not a current one. A wave of joy hit me, as well as confused me. I'd have to figure out why later.

"Don't be. She cheated on me with one of my partners. Ex-partner. They married and are already headed for a divorce."

"Wow. That's pretty bad."

"Not really. I realize now it was the best thing that ever happened to me."

"Honestly?"

"Yes."

"Er, have you found someone else?"

I couldn't believe I just asked that. It was really crossing the line. Hell, it was none of my business.

*Would he answer*?

There was a period of silence and then he said, "Yes."

*So he was off the market.*

I felt like I'd been sucker punched and all of a sudden, I wanted to get out of there. Too many emotions were surfacing.

I jumped up.

"I'd better get going."

He looked startled, as he got up as well.

"Thanks for the beer," I muttered, as I raced down the hall yelling, "C'mon, Sadie."

At the door I turned to look at Red, aware he'd followed behind, remembering why I was here in the first place.

"So sorry about your dad. Let me know if I can do anything to help."

He just stared at me and I swear he looked at my lips again. Feeling a strong wave of attraction, I was tempted to just grab his face and plant one on him, but figured it was inappropriate as hell on the evening of his father's death, not to mention he had a girlfriend, or thoughts of getting one. So I quickly looked down at my feet and willed my hands to stay put.

"Good night," I said, as I turned and walked out, Sadie following.

"Good night," he said, sounding confused.

*Did I really have feelings for him?*

Was that why I was upset to hear he was interested in someone?

*Was I falling in love with him*?

No way! It could only lead to heartache. That was what I thought I felt for Jim and look where that got me. And besides, love was too strong a word to describe how I felt. Hell, I barely knew the guy.

Maybe the word "like" was more apt. Or "big like", as it was more than just plain like. That was it. Big like.

*C'mon, White. Don't fall in "big like" with Red. It will only lead to more sadness.*

But I suspected my warning to myself fell on deaf ears.

## *Twenty-three*

I didn't want to be here one bit.

Grimacing, I looked around the cemetery and it struck me again how everything was gray and bleak and the thousands of tombstones lined up in rows were depressing as hell. Even the sun refused to shine and raindrops added to the gloomy scenario. Everyone was huddled under umbrellas trying to stay dry as well as warm, for of course a cold wind just had to pick up at this particular moment.

Sadness emanated from Red's family, as we all stood around the opened ground where they were going to place his father. I stamped my foot in frustration.

Where was the priest? I wished he'd get here and put an end to this. Let's get it over with.

Okay, maybe I sounded selfish, but I found this whole mourning process just too hard to take, especially because it made me think of death. I mean, who wants to focus on that, if they could help it?

I knew I sounded immature, like a little kid not wanting to do anything I didn't want to, but it was hard to be at a funeral for someone's dad, when I was so mixed up about my own father. This whole service had me thinking about him, which upset the hell out of me. Not everyone could be like Red, forgive their dad, and be there for him after years of abuse. I didn't think I could. But Hazel and Dad were going to the funeral, as well as Emma and Maggie, so I figured I should too, to pay my respects. Besides, I was his neighbor. As Maggie said, sensing my reluctance, coming here was "the neighborly thing to do", especially after all he'd done for me. Carl and Sam were holding the fort until we got back, so I couldn't even use work as an excuse.

Another thought niggled away at me. One that'd been bothering me for days, driving me absolutely crazy. Was I really falling in "big like" with Red?

That was another reason I didn't want to be here. Probably the main one. I thought I was starting to care for him a little too much for my sense of wellbeing and decided avoiding him would benefit me enormously. So much was going on, I really couldn't deal with a love interest, especially since he liked someone else. Hell, I even wanted to kiss him the other night! I could have made a complete fool of myself. *Stop! Forget about that. Put it out of your mind.*

Hard to do when he was standing two feet away.

I stared at his mother. Anyone but Red.

It'd been interesting meeting her at the funeral home, a few nights ago. She had a capful of auburn hair, a slightly duller shade than her son's and appeared sad but still warm and pleasant. She also knew all about the roof, and I was actually surprised Red had mentioned it to her, as he seemed so tight-lipped about his life. Or maybe, that was just with me, although he sure opened up the other night, much to my great surprise.

Red's sister was delightful and chatty, sporting the same vibrant color of hair as her brother's. They could almost be twins. I didn't talk much to Red while I was there. He was busy with a line-up of friends and relatives eager to pass on condolences, but he seemed grateful to see me, even giving me a hug, albeit letting me go as quickly as possible. Don't think I didn't notice that he held on to Emma and Maggie much longer.

I sighed. I'd gotten through the funeral today holding back my tears, but being at the cemetery was hard, really hard. It was so damn final and I was just barely holding it together for against my bidding, happy, fun memories of my dad broke free from their buried storage unit deep in the back of my mind. Sadly, they floated up, reminding me of the times when my father was my best pal.

*Sheesh! Don't think about that, either.*

Was my self-searching and trying to emerge from being too nice making me narcissistic? Was I going from one extreme to another? I should only be thinking of Red's loss, not about myself and all my problems. What was wrong with me?

Much to my embarrassment, tears drifted down my cheeks drawing surprised looks from Maggie and Emma.

"Allergies," I said, suspecting my friends wouldn't be fooled by that.

Probably hearing my voice, Red looked over, raising his eyebrows. Embarrassed, I quickly wiped them away as the priest finally arrived and the small service was about to begin.

After leading with an opening prayer, Father O'Malley

said to the family, "I pray that you will leave here in peace but before I say the final blessing, I invite any of you to say a few words, if you wish." He handed them each a rose. "You may place your flower on the casket, after you've spoken.

Oh no! I couldn't bear any more tear jerking stories. But once again, I had to remind myself that this was not about me.

Silence reigned.

Finally managing to shake myself out of my self-absorbed feelings, I snuck a look at Red. He looked solemn, with one arm wrapped around his mother's shoulders and another around his sister's. My heart went out to him. I was sure he was trying to be strong for them as both were weeping openly. It really upset me to see this usually confident, in control guy look so grief stricken and I wished I could run over and give him a hug, but I stilled my thoughts when Red's mother began to speak. With tears running down her cheeks, she shared her love for her husband. Then, his sister talked about how she never really forgave him for the way he was when she was young and regretted that. I guess she was still trying to make amends. I then noticed his mother dig an elbow into Red's side, obviously wanting him to speak as well. I was curious to see if he'd comply or keep to his usual silence, but when he cleared his throat, I knew he was about to say something.

"I struggled a lot to get along with my father. At times, I completely wrote him off." He paused for a second, as if for effect. "But I persisted and ended up forging a strong bond with him, learning a lot in the process."

Hell, all I'd learned from my father was to run when the going got tough. Wait a sec! Had Red's eyes really flitted over to mine? Or had I imagined it? Did he have more to say? I tuned back in.

"The last words Dad said to me were a thank you for giving him another chance. I am grateful I did because I finally got to really know him—the good and the bad. I was proud of him and it sure goes to show you that people really do change and forgiveness is one of the greatest gifts we can give to one another. It's a lesson I'll never forget." He placed his rose on the casket. "May he rest in eternal peace. He deserves it."

Crap! Was he saying those words just for me? Continuing his thoughts from the other night? Was he making a point? To give my father a second chance? To forgive him? Or at least that was the message I was getting. I looked over at my dad. He was looking right at me and I felt his eyes begging me to let him into my life. I quickly looked away as I was not sure of what I wanted to do yet, being still thoroughly messed up about both my parents. It seemed as if all they thought about was themselves or disguised their selfish thinking by saying it was best for me. Where did I fit into the equation? Were my wishes ever important? But hey, who was being self-centered now? Especially at this funeral?

I then remembered Red saying something about being aware of his own mistakes, which helped him forgive his father's. Okay, yeah I made and make lots of mistakes, especially abandoning my pro bono cases, but it was still hard to think of my parents as less than infallible. Especially my father. He'd been way up there on a pedestal. At twenty-six, I should already know that moms and dads don't always do the right thing, after all, I listened to Maggie joke about her mother and her constant forgetfulness, but I hadn't had a normal upbringing. My family life had been screwed up and I hadn't learned lessons others did.

Another horrid thought hit me.

Red talked about giving second chances. Was that what he was doing with his ex-fiancée? Was that why he had her picture out that night? He was getting back with her? Was she the one for him?

The priest spoke again, thankfully interrupting my muddled thoughts. As he prayed the final prayer all I could think about was thank goodness it was over before I made myself into a slobbering fool. Wiping more tears away, I finally got it together as I quickly walked toward my car to head back to work. I needed a good dose of furry friends to get me back on track. The rain had stopped, so I leaned up against the car, waiting for Maggie and Emma to join me.

Much to my surprise, I saw Red say something to his mother and head over.

"Hi there," he said, a brief attempt at a smile on his face.

"Hi, yourself," I answered. "You okay?"

"I will be. At least my father won't suffer anymore."

"That's some comfort, but I'm sure you wish he was still here."

"Yes, but life doesn't often work that way. Nice of you to come, though. I'm sure it wasn't easy."

*Could he see into my mind? Did he really know how*

*hard it was to be here?*

"Just wanted to support you." Man, if he only knew I'd come close to not coming and was actually pissed I did. Not only that, I had thought of my own troubles most of the time instead of what he was going through. In short, I was a selfish wench.

"Well, I'm leaving for Dubai in a few hours. Didn't want to go without saying goodbye and thanking you for taking care of Squid all those times."

*He was going away?*

"For good?" I managed to croak out, controlling myself, trying to sound calm.

"Yes, but I'll be back and forth, helping my mother."

"Er, where exactly is your office?" Okay, I was being nosy now, but I felt the need to know.

"Toronto."

Good. Not too far.

"Well, take care."

That was lame but I didn't know what else to say. He looked like he was going to say more, but instead turned and walked towards his car. I wanted to run after him and beg him to stay a while longer but couldn't bring myself to do so. After all, his only intention was to thank me. He didn't mention getting together or anything.

As I watched him leave, knowing I might never see him again, I knew at that instant I was going to miss him. Badly. I also realized something else. C'mon Jessie. Admit it.

*Double damn. I think I really was in "big like" with him*

I guess what sealed it was the fact he seemed like the

kind of person who would always be there for you, no matter what. Look how much he helped me already and I was practically a stranger. As I mentioned before, it was new to be on the receiving end of kindness, especially from a guy. I liked it. A lot. Not to mention the fact my heart still pounded away, my face went red, and I always had this urge to wrap my arms around him whenever I was in his general vicinity. I'd never felt like this towards anyone else, and I knew with Red, a relationship would be a two way street. A fifty-fifty deal. Oh, crap. I was getting all mushy again not to mention teary eyed.

*Leave it to me to acknowledge my feelings while at a cemetery.* Certainly wasn't romantic circumstances by any means, but it was a solemn moment, which I guess forced me to be serious. Yep, I really think I "big liked" this guy. Horrible that it was too late, but then again, it wasn't too late to do something I should have done ages ago.

"Hey, Red." I was shocked to hear his name come out of my mouth but I needed to say a few things and now was my only chance.

As he turned my way, I ran over.

"Just wanted to thank you for helping me with the tree house, the roof, the sound proofing and for replenishing the lumber pile." I'd never acknowledged that before and a thank you was long overdue. I felt I had to say it, before he walked out of my life.

He grinned. "So you like Seinfeld as much as I do?"

I grinned back. "Yes."

Awkward silence.

"Gotta go," I said, before I threw my arms around him and asked him to stay or begged to go with him. I made it back to my car in two seconds flat, feeling like an idiot but glad I did it. I'd made peace with him, at least a little bit.

Feeling like I was on a roll, I had one more person I had to see.

Spurred on by Red's words about his father and my promise to think about it, I had to get this over with before I chickened out. It was now or never. I walked over and knocked on the window of Hazel's car. The passenger side.

"Hey, Dad."

Looking shocked, he rolled down the window, surprised to see me there as I basically ignored him at the funeral. Even refused to sit with him.

"Would you like to go for a walk sometime?" I asked, before losing all courage.

"Sure would."

"How about tomorrow?"

His eyes lit up. "Name the place and time and I'll be there."

"Port Dover?"

"Know it well."

Of course he did. It was one of our hangout spots.

"Around 1:00?"

"Fine with me."

"See you there."

I noticed Hazel was beaming.

# *Twenty-four*

"C'mon, c'mon. Dammit, where are you?"

A cop stopped in his tracks, turned and looked at me, before I even realized I'd spoken out loud.

I waved at him saying, "Just anxious."

He stared, then fortunately left me alone as he hurried into the building. Probably to get away from me.

*Pull it together or they'll be arresting you. For being crazy.*

Pacing back and forth in front of the Central Police Station, I sucked back some coffee, hoping like hell Christine would arrive. Crap. I couldn't help but notice that my hands were shaking. I'd been up all night worrying about whether I could really help this girl. Sure she got herself into this mess, but I didn't help matters by letting her down. Being a rookie lawyer, I just prayed I could handle things right today. Our bond was tenuous to begin with, and if I screwed up, it'd be severed. For good. I wish I could have picked her up. That way I'd make sure she got here. What if she took off again? I told Officer Locke I'd bring her in at 9:00 sharp.

I glanced at my watch for about the one-hundredth

time. Ten minutes to nine. Christine was cutting it tight.

Dropping my coffee cup in a garbage can, I looked down the road again, squinting into the sun to see if I could see her.

*Were there really three women walking briskly towards me?*

Was one of them Christine?

Moving a few steps closer, I made out what looked like a redhead among them. One of them waved. Sylvia. Oh, thank goodness. Christine was here and looking sharp in a smart looking black suit, hair pinned back into a ponytail. Neat and clean.

Racing to meet them, Christine smiled. "Bet you thought I wouldn't show up?"

"Well, to be honest, I was a bit worried."

"We wouldn't let that happen. Just had trouble finding parking," said Sylvia.

"Loaned her my suit," announced Melanie, looking proud. "She's all official-like now."

"It's perfect. You look great, Christine." Nervous, I glanced at my watch. "Well, come on. Let's get this over with."

We marched into the massive red brick building where I promptly went up to the counter and asked for Officer Locke. The policeman on duty immediately buzzed him down and told us to wait at a side cubicle. Glancing around, I couldn't get over how busy this place was. Cops were everywhere, people milled around and lineups were forming, especially in the area where fines were to be paid.

"Get me out of here," said Christine.

I looked at her pale face and encouraged her to sit down.

"Won't be long. I promise."

I searched the crowd looking for Locke and was relieved to see him coming down the hall, a big smile on his face.

"Hello, Miss White. And this must be Christine." He reached out and shook her hand.

Impressive. I guess he could tell who was in trouble by how scared and white she looked.

"I'll take over for now, you go on over to Sopinka and meet us there."

"Thank you so much for helping out," I said, grateful the first part of my strategy was going smoothly. Let's hope the rest did too.

"No problem. You remind me of my daughter. Glad to help." He winked. "Don't worry, we won't be too long. I've got everything arranged."

"See you soon," I said, to a worried looking Christine. "Keep smiling. We'll get through this."

"What's a Sopinka?" asked Melanie, looking a little white herself, as I led them by foot over to Main Street.

"The courthouse. It's named after the late Judge John Sopinka of the Supreme Court of Canada. Here it is." I watched as she gazed with awe at the steps leading up to the tall brown building. Lots of glass and official looking people scurrying in and out.

"Looks scary," she added.

"Just make sure you never end up here," said Sylvia, as we hurried in.

"Not me. No way," said a solemn looking Melanie. "I

can't believe we have to be checked out." She pointed toward the guards on duty.

"Well, they can't take any chances," I said, as I was directed to drop my cell phone and loose change in the bowl and enter through the turnstile.

The two of them followed behind.

"Which courtroom is it in? I count eighteen of them," said Sylvia, staring at the huge sign depicting names and the floors they were on.

"It's on this one. Follow me." I led the troops to the left of the elevator where the signs stated that this courtroom was used for bail purposes.

"Let's check for her name and make sure she's scheduled today," I said, going up to the wall where clients' names were printed on sheets of paper.

"There she is," said Sylvia. "Ten thirty."

As I leaned in to check it as well, a booming male voice bellowed out, "Well, well, well. Look who's here."

*I recognized those guttural tones.*

I turned to see Kite standing right behind me.

"Guess they let all sorts of riff raff in here," he said, with a smirk. He turned to the guy beside him. "This here's Jessica White. The lawyer who got your daughter into this situation in the first place."

"What are you doing here?" The man beside Kite came towards me like an angry bull. "Haven't you hurt Christine enough?"

This was obviously Mr. Pape, Christine's Dad. John said he was mad as hell with Kite for firing me. Guess Kite smoothed that over and now he was focused on me.

How had they known she might be here? Did Kite have

a hotline to the police station?

Holding my head up high, I said, "I'm still her lawyer."

"No, you're not. She has one." He pointed at Kite. "Lowered myself to hire him, but at least he'll get her off."

"I'll take over," said a pompous Kite, looking smug, thoroughly enjoying this.

"You will not."

All of us turned to see Christine, escorted by Officer Locke, come up behind, hands on her hips, looking dead serious.

"Jessie is my lawyer.

"Honey, I've bought the best," said her dad, trying to hug her, but Christine stepped out of his reach.

"I already have the best." She moved to stand beside me.

I was blown away by her faith in me, especially since she still looked terrified and Kite really was the more experienced choice.

"C'mon, Jessie. Let's go," she added.

As she marched by, Kite stood in front of me. "You're done here."

I sucked in a deep breath, then said, "No, you are. Now move your butt or I'll have you up on charges of forging your sister's signature."

He stared. I stared.

Then he turned and walked away. Guess it wouldn't look good for a criminal lawyer to be charged. A small victory but it felt good nonetheless.

Willing myself to put it behind me so I could concentrate, I directed Christine to an interview room just outside the courtroom. Not sure where her father was but I hoped he left too. Man, that guy was intimidating just by size alone. Bet he weighed at least three hundred, give or take a few ounces.

Directing her to sit down, I said, "Now remember. No talking to the judge. Keep quiet at all times. I'll be sitting up at the table with the other lawyers and when you see me approach the microphone, come up and stand beside me."

"Okay." But she still looked like she was going to pass out.

"It'll be fine," I said reassuringly, as I glanced at my watch. "Time to head in. Oh, and Christine…"

"Yes?"

"Thank you."

"No problem." She grinned. "We're a team."

"Yes, we are."

I crossed my fingers. Somehow I had to do my best for this girl but I was the one who looked terrified when we stepped into the courtroom and I got a glimpse at who the judge was.

*Oh no!*

I just stood there blinking several times, hoping I was wrong. I wasn't. Corrina Stevens. The worst-case scenario possible. She was known as a tough cookie especially when it came to young people. She came down hard on them, hoping to stop their criminal activity—nip it in the bud. For sure, she would take the toughest stance possible against my client, especially after she skipped the court date and ran away from home.

Christine grabbed my arm. "What? Are you okay?"

Guess she noticed my reaction.

"I'm great." I summoned up a fake smile, as I led her over to sit down, my mind churning.

"Looks like church," she murmured.

"You're right. It does." The room was full of wooden benches that mimicked pews. At least they had cushions on them, making them comfortable.

Just as I was about to head up to sit with the other lawyers, she grabbed my hand and leaned over, whispering, "I can't go to jail. I just can't."

"I'll do all I can to make sure that doesn't happen."

But a sense of doom followed me down the aisle to my seat. Miracles happened, right? Because I certainly needed one today. Nervous as hell, I concentrated on deep breathing to calm down, but when I stood up for my turn, I could feel my legs shake. Damn it.

"Your Worship, my name is Jessica White and I'm here to speak on behalf of Christine Alymer."

I looked back to beckon her to come up and stand beside me, noticing her father sitting at the back of one of the rows. He was glaring at me. Guess he hadn't left after all, but I ignored him, concentrating on his daughter coming down the aisle. Seeing how scared she was reined me in. *Get it together.* This girl needed me.

"Is this the young lady who missed her court date?" asked the judge. Loudly, I might add.

One of the Crown attorneys answered, "Yes." Was that a smug expression on his face? He looked like a Kite clone. Asshole.

The judge glared at Christine for at least two minutes. I wasn't kidding. Two friggin minutes! Do you know how long that can be? With total silence in the court? Finally, she opened her mouth to speak.

"Young lady, I have very little to say to you. You are a menace to society. A disgrace. Repeatedly stealing merchandise. Running away from home. Skipping your court date. You have shown no remorse for your actions, proving you are irresponsible and not taking this seriously. Bail denied. That should teach you a lesson." She hit her gavel hard, driving home her point.

I hadn't even gotten to say a word in her defense.

Christine grabbed my arm gasping, "Please. Make this stop."

*I had to do something.*

Ignoring the fact that the room was full of clients and lawyers and that I was about to commit career suicide, I said loudly, "Your Worship, it's not Christine's fault that she missed her court date. It was mine. I ask that you change your ruling."

A gasp went through the court as Judge Stevens lifted her head up from the papers she was reading and stared at me—another full two minutes. I stared back, not wavering.

"You're out of line," she barked. "Another outburst like that and I'll hold you in contempt of court."

"But Your Worship, I was fired and let this girl down. Don't take it out on her. Please put me in jail not her," I said firmly hoping to come across confident, in control, and not like some wild freak making a scene. Inside I was a quivering mess knowing darn well that you never question a Judge's ruling.

More silence. More staring. Then a quizzical

expression crossed Steven's face.

"Please, step up here." The judge beckoned me closer.

I approached the bench, walking tall, shoulders back just like Aunt T taught me. She'd be proud.

"What's this all about?" hissed the judge.

Not holding back, I said, "Your Worship, it's not fair that this girl should suffer because of my actions. It's a travesty of justice."

The judge paused and I could almost hear her mind tick away.

"What's your name again?" she asked.

"Jessica White, Your Worship."

"White. Hmmmm… you the girl Kite fired?"

*She knew?*

"Er, yes."

"For representing pro bono cases?"

"Yes."

Oh crap! Did I just doom Christine? Did I make it worse?

"I see." She paused again, looking deep in thought, then finally said, "Come and see me before the end of the month."

"Er, yes, Your Worship." *That was a weird invite.*

"Now, go on back to your client." To my surprise, she winked.

A pale Christine, clutching onto the podium so she wouldn't keel over, greeted me with eyes that were full of tears. Her father had moved to the first pew right behind her. He personified the expression "if looks could kill…" as he stared at me.

"Am I in more trouble?" she whispered.

"I don't know," I answered honestly. *What was that wink all about?*

A loud bang of the gavel startled everyone.

"In light of new evidence. I will place bail at $5000.00."

*Had I heard right? She changed her ruling?*

Christine clutched my arm and let out a huge breath. "Thank you," she whispered.

"I have one condition," continued the Judge.

Oh, oh!

"You must return home to your father."

I looked at Christine, not sure what she'd do. Would she prefer being behind bars to this?

"That's okay. Anything but jail." She smiled.

A huge sense of relief swept through me. At least I'd gotten my client out of a jail stay. For now. Next I'd try hard to get her into the Diversion Program like I'd planned. Hopefully this would be her last court appearance.

*But what in the world did the judge want to see me about?*

## *Twenty-five*

The drive out to Port Dover was a trip down memory lane. About forty minutes away, the small tourist town was situated on Lake Erie, where my father took me for picnics almost every weekend in the summer. Hazel rarely came, too busy painting of course, and it became a special time for just the two of us. I loved every minute of it. A magical place full of fun adventures where I felt carefree and happy. Swimming and frolicking at the beach for hours at a time, my dad had to practically drag me out of the water to go home. I figured it might be therapeutic to meet at a place that was a genuinely happy bond between my father and me.

As I pulled into the huge parking lot on Walker Street, just down from the lake, I realized how much I'd lucked out, for I couldn't have asked for a more beautiful day. The sun was shining, it was warm out and lots of people were enjoying the nice weather, walking, biking and jogging.

I got out of the car and stood for a moment watching the sailboats flit among the waves. What was it like out there without a care in the world? I'd love to be skimming the water right now but instead, here I was about to meet my dad. I wasn't sure I was up for this but figured I might as well get it over with.

I turned and headed to Willie's Ice Cream Place, where I knew he'd be waiting for me. A cone was usually the first thing we got when we arrived and sure enough, there he was, anxiously pacing back and forth. He stopped when he saw me approach.

"Hi there," he said, a shy grin on his face. He looked pretty hip in his blue Nike shirt and shorts, sandals on his feet. Young and sporty, despite the gray hair.

"Hi yourself, Dad." Butterflies kicked up big-time in my gut.

"Would you like some ice cream?" he asked.

"Of course. Don't I always?"

Would his version be the same as Hazel's? Was he really that depressed? Was there more to it? Dammit! I really needed to get the facts straight once and for all. I was tired of dreaming up all sorts of horrid situations that may or may not be the truth.

"Here's your cone, lady."

I snapped out of my reverie to take the ice cream. Chocolate for me, maple walnut for my dad. Old traditions died hard as these were the exact same flavors we both had sixteen long years ago.

We ate in silence as we took our ritual walk down Harbor Street to the pier that led to the lighthouse. No matter how cold or windy, and sometimes it got really windy along Lake Erie, I always insisted that we walk down and back. I loved the blue and white lighthouse, a tower of strength, a beacon of hope to sailors, and today to me as well.

Finally, as per tradition, we headed along the beach where I took my shoes off and waded in. The water was warm and soothing. So far, we'd both remained quiet but after a bit, Dad pointed to a bench back among the grass, which offered us some privacy.

"Why don't we sit there and talk?" he asked.

"Okay." I guess it was time, since I couldn't procrastinate much longer.

After settling ourselves, I waited for about ten seconds, before asking, "So is it true, Dad? Hazel kicked you out?"

"It's true."

"Why didn't you tell me that? I thought all along you left on your own. That you got tired of the whole family scene and wanted out." I paused for a second before adding, "That you were tired of me."

"Never even once was I tired of you." He sighed. "I didn't tell you because it would put your mother in a bad light. She thought she was doing the right thing."

*He was sticking up for her?*

"Couldn't you have taken me with you? I was closer to you than to Hazel. You knew that."

He sighed. "Well… there's one more thing you need to know. Your mother didn't want to tell you, figuring it was my story. She also didn't want to mar your image of me."

Finally the truth. The last piece of the puzzle was about to be offered. Was I ready? Could I handle it? I wrapped my arms around my waist and held on tight, gearing up for what was coming next.

Dad paused so long, I thought he chickened out of

telling me, or had fallen asleep. Finally, he said, "To be blunt, I tried to kill myself way back then." He hung his head down, obviously not proud of what he was revealing.

*He tried to commit suicide? Had I heard him right?*

"You did what?"

"Your mother found me in the garage, car running. Just in time, I might add."

No way! My father, my superman, my hero tried to end his life? It was too horrid to even think about, but now I knew what everyone was trying to keep secret from me. My dad tried to check out of life. To leave us for good.

"And if she hadn't?"

"I'd be long gone." He looked up and his face was pale. "She called 911 and I was rushed to the hospital."

"Where was I?"

"At your newspaper meeting. I made sure you weren't home."

I remembered. I was editor that year and he'd been so proud of me. I thought hard, vaguely remembering him being in the hospital.

"Why, Dad? Why would you want to leave me?"

I looked over at him, and found him staring out at the lake, the saddest expression ever on his face. I wondered if it was worth dragging everything up as it was obviously a painful time for him, but I really did need to know in order to let it drop. I needed to give it a proper burial.

"I was trying to leave myself, not you. Sounds lame, but it's true. A selfish, selfish reason. I know that now." As if gathering up courage, he took a deep breath and let it out. "When I graduated from high school and decided to go to university, my father insisted I take accounting, which I hated. I was bad with math and anything to do with business stuff. I begged him to let me study what I wanted but all he said was, "Too bad. I'm paying." He sighed again, even louder than the last time. "So I picked courses that he chose and got a job in a field he wanted. But my heart wasn't in it. Day after day I slogged away at something I hated. Inevitably, it wears you down. Meanwhile, Hazel was ecstatic about her painting. She had found her heart's desire." He looked over at me. "I envied that about her."

"Couldn't you have found something you liked? Teaching, for instance?"

"It would require me getting into teacher's college and I didn't have the marks. As I said, I hated accounting, so barely scraped by. I would have needed to upgrade my courses."

"Why didn't you?"

He smiled. "Because you came along."

"You're blaming me?"

"Of course not." He put his arm around me and gave me a brief hug. I allowed it, which surprised me.

"Well… where did I fit in?"

"When I found out your mother was pregnant, I was thrilled."

"But… ?"

"We were poor back then. Just scraping by before your mother's artwork took off. I couldn't afford to go back to school and since I increasingly hated my job, it soured my whole outlook on life. You were the only bright spot in it. Then I got fired. Your mother was angry and I didn't blame her. I got let go because I couldn't concentrate and made silly mistakes. I kept telling myself that I had to work hard to provide for you, but as I said, being in a job you hate gets to you and every day became a hell. I was a lousy employee and deserved to be kicked out."

I thought back, but couldn't remember a time when he was depressed. But then again, I was busy at school and he was probably good at hiding his feelings around me. I also couldn't reconcile the man I remembered with the one who worked in a job he disliked. He was always telling me to "shoot for the stars" and that "anything is possible." But then again, maybe he was trying to make sure I didn't do the same thing he did.

"Looks like getting fired runs in the family. But keep going," I said, urging him to say more. "I need to know everything."

"You at least did the job. I didn't." He groaned. "I was out of work at the same time Hazel's paintings found a market. She was thrilled and so enthused about everything that I felt like I was bringing her down and eventually you. I decided the two of you would be better off if I was out of the picture. I was nothing but a failure. A complete and utter failure."

"How could you think that?"

"Easy when you're in a depressed state of mind." He gazed off towards the lake again. "I convinced myself leaving was for the best, since I couldn't maintain being the happy, positive father I tried to be for you. My sad side was taking over so I decided to end it all. I couldn't take it anymore. I wanted to die. I even researched ways to do it and decided carbon monoxide was the way to go. Luckily your mother got home in time although I was plenty mad at the time. She wrecked my plans and she was so angry she asked me to leave and to stay away from you as well. Sadly I went along with that, thinking it was the right thing to do, since I was in such a pathetic state. A huge mistake on my part. I realize now it was wrong but I didn't want to make a reappearance until I'd gotten myself back together. So over time, I worked hard to turn my life around."

"Did you really go to California?"

"Yes, I did. All that was true."

He paused for a second.

"Please don't be too angry with your mother, honey. Don't forget about how her friend Mary's death impacted her. Mary would have done anything to live and here I was choosing to take my life. It was her worst nightmare. Your mother couldn't bear to be around me after that, and by the way, she really was trying to protect you."

I still found that hard to believe.

He squeezed my shoulder.

"I love you, Jessie. Always have, always will. I wonder if you can find it in your heart to forgive me? A poor excuse of a father who finally saw the wrong he did and tried to fix it. Could we start again?"

Crap! It sure was tough when your bubble burst when it came to your parents. Everyone wanted to think their dad was their knight in shining armor who'd protect them from harm and always be there for support. It was hard to think of my dad as depressed, a basket case who tried to kill himself, then skulked away. But… I guess I could understand depression. Look how I'd been when I first moved into Hazel's. So depressed I'd even stolen lumber from my neighbor when I was actually the type who'd return an extra nickel to a store employee who'd given me too much.

But could I forgive him and move on? Did he deserve that after all the pain he instigated in my life? Had he really changed?

Thoughts of Red sliced through my mind. Second chances worked for him and I was grateful to Christine for giving me one. I knew firsthand how someone could get so caught up in their own issues that they forget everyone else's.

I looked over at my father. He'd been through a lot and seemed to be really trying to pull it all together. I saw him reach for my hand and I moved to touch his. He hung on tight and it hit me how vulnerable he must feel right now after opening up to me.

I knew what my answer would be.

"I think so, Dad," I said softly.

He looked hopeful.

"That's more than I can ever ask for."

## *Twenty-six*

"So here's the deal," I said, laying out several papers I'd prepared. "It would be almost impossible for Drew Fitzgerald to contest your grandfather's will. He'd have a greater chance of winning the lottery. But just in case, I prepared all sorts of information for you, as well as a few case studies."

"Really?" asked Emma, still looking worried.

I'd been looking forward to our Wednesday night get together and, as per tradition, we were all at Jake's. It was an important time for Emma as it was the night she was meeting Drew. That was why she made the meeting on this particular date; we'd all be here for support.

I'd promised to check up on the legal grounds to contest a will, and to be honest, the research unsettled me. I hadn't done anything law related in a long time and here I was involved not only with Christine but also Emma. I had to admit, it was pretty darn exciting being back in the game.-I really did miss practicing law at times.

"Ahem," said Emma.

"Really." I pushed away my law reminiscences. "It would be a waste of time, effort and money for Fitzgerald to even attempt it. According to what you said, your grandfather was lucid to the end and a reputable law firm drew up his will. No chance this Drew character would win and he'd spend big bucks trying to do so."

"Will you represent me? If he does?" she asked.

"But you have a lawyer."

"I want you. You care for me and I know you'll go to the ends of the earth to help me."

"Well... okay." I was grateful for her faith in me and I was glad I said yes when I saw the relieved look on her face. Hopefully, this Drew guy wouldn't do such a thing.

"Do you miss him?" interrupted Maggie.

I turned and watched her take a long swig of her scotch.

"Ahhhhhhhhhh… ," she moaned in bliss. "Just what I needed. It's been a hell of a day."

She looked so satisfied after the drink, I thought she'd start purring and forget about her question, but instead she looked over.

"So… do you?" she asked again.

"Who?" I knew who she meant but played dumb. I didn't want to talk about anything that could possibly make me sad, frustrated, angry or all of the above. I was trying to escape.

"Red, of course."

"Yes, do you?" chimed in Emma. "I still remember the sight of you two clutched together when the pups were born. Figured you were headed for romance, for sure."

I sipped my beer, thinking about their question. I'd been really enjoying the evening. Did they have to go and ruin it by mentioning my neighbor? And… honestly, did I miss him?

Oh, who was I trying to kid. *Of course I did.* But no way was I letting them know.

"Nope. Barely even knew him so how could I miss him?" I wondered what they'd say if I just burst out that I was in "big like" with him. Or at least thought I was. Should I tell them that just thinking of him got my heart beating fast and my face reddened and all I wanted to hear was his voice again and again? That I almost kissed him one night? But I wasn't ready for anyone to know and couldn't stand to see their sympathetic looks. Unlucky in love was my mantra at the moment.

"But he helped you. Fixed your roof and soundproofed the room. You owe him a lot," said Maggie.

"I know and I've thanked him. But it doesn't mean I have to miss him," I said.

"A gorgeous hunk like that living next door? I'd miss just staring at that beautiful face," crooned Emma. "Not to mention, his butt."

"You must be talking about Squid. Him, I miss. Sadie does, as well."

That got them laughing.

"Leave it to you, to miss the dog, not the owner," said Maggie.

"Dogs are easier to get along with," I said.

"Ain't it the truth?" agreed Emma.

"More drinks, ladies?" asked Jake.

"The rest of you can. Remember, I'm the designated driver," said Emma. "I need to be alert tonight."

"Okay. I'll have one more," I said. "Make it a light one."

"Oh, why not," said Maggie. "Throw me another."

Noticing Emma's repeated looks toward the door, I waited until the bartender left before asking, "Are you worried?"

"A bit. Just concerned about what that guy wants."

"I noticed that you've dropped some weight," said Maggie, checking me out, giving me the once over and obviously not wanting the conversation off of me.

What was this? Pick on Jessie night?

"Sure have. Running around after dogs is great exercise."

"Do you ever hear from Red?" asked Emma.

Man, they just wouldn't let up but I wished they hadn't brought it up right now. Today a For Sale sign had gone up on the front lawn, which made his moving away all the more final. I guess the Petersons decided to sell. In my fantasies, I hoped Red would come back one day and stay there, but fat chance of that when his office was in Toronto.

"No. No reason to," I answered.

"Too bad about his ex-fiancée," said Maggie.

"Whose?"

"Red's of course."

*She knew about his ex-fiancée?*

"Why? Do you know anything?" I asked.

"A bit. Dave was talking about him last night at dinner."

"Oooooo… so you're seeing Dave?" asked Emma.

Maggie blushed. "Not at all. We just met to chat about his daughter."

"So what's Dave's story, anyway?" I asked, deciding I really shouldn't be talking about Red anyway. It upset me too much. I wasn't sure she was going to answer but after hesitating a bit she said, "He's divorced with a horrid ex-wife."

"Oh, they all say that," said Emma.

Sheesh! Cool it Emma. Was she so nervous she was picking a fight?

"Just so happens, I know the ex. Do you remember Josie Fife, Jesse?"

"You mean Junkie Josie?"

"Yep. The one and only."

"How'd she get that name?" asked Emma.

"She was a gossip junkie. Loved to spread junk about everyone. Didn't even care if it was true or not," I explained. "But get out! That's his ex-wife?"

"Sure is. How he married her in the first place is a shocker."

"I can see why. She was good at pretending to be nice while she searched for juicy tidbits. Then used it against you to get what she wanted."

"Well, she got what she wanted. Full custody. Dave's fighting her all the way."

"How old is the boy?" asked Emma.

"Five and a real cutie," said Maggie.

"You've met him?" I was surprised at that.

"Went with Dave to the park once."

"Is this serious?" I asked.

"Just friends."

"Sure," said Emma.

"We are," she argued. "Now let's talk about something else."

"Well c'mon, then. Don't leave us hanging. So what

did Dave say about Red's fiancée? You never did finish that story," asked Emma.

"Just that the day Red found out about his dad's cancer he walked into his colleague's office to tell him he was going home for a while and found the two of them sprawled out on a couch. Total nudity was involved."

"How awful," exclaimed Emma. "That man should be castrated and she should be hung up by the ankles in the lobby for everyone to spit at."

"Ouch! Such visual imagery," said Maggie.

I kept quiet, shocked at what I'd heard. Poor Red. Imagine having to go through that.

Maggie was looking at me, so I quickly said, "That's horrible."

"How long ago?" asked Emma.

"About two years. But Dave said Red's never been the same since."

"How so?" I asked.

"Well, you know that old saying "once bitten twice shy"? Well in his case it's one hundred times shy. He's only been on one date since."

"What happened to the ex and the colleague?" asked Emma.

It was great that Emma was asking the questions, as I was getting all my information, without appearing too nosy or interested.

"The colleague left for another firm. It was either that or get fired and I guess he married Red's ex but they've broken up already. Dave said she's trying hard to get back with Red."

"Really? Are they dating?" I asked. Couldn't help

myself. Was she the one he had 'found' again?

"Dave wasn't sure." Maggie stared. "Interested, are you?"

"Not at all," I lied, shaking my head. "Just curious."

"Hey, speak of the devil. There's Dave now," said Maggie.

"Well, he can't join us. You know the rules," said Emma, impatiently. "Tonight is only an exception because I need you here when I meet Drew."

I also knew she had no use for men at the moment after the Joseph fiasco and valued these girls nights out even more.

"Yeah, I know," said Maggie. "Don't worry. He knows as well."

"How are you ladies doing?" asked Dave, but I noticed he only had eyes for Maggie.

"Fine," she said.

As I watched her stare at Dave, I swear I saw sparks fly.

He finally dragged his eyes away from her to ask, "How's the new roof holding up, Jessie? Red wanted me to call to see if anything else needs to be done, so I'm glad I found you here. Jeb, Mike and I assured him we'd take care of things if you need help."

"Don't worry, everything's going fine."

"Well, I'll leave you guys alone." He looked at Maggie. "Sorry about intruding on your night but it's my cousin's birthday and he wanted to come here. Had no say in the matter whatsoever." With a tip of his baseball cap, he went off to join his friends by the pool table.

"Sure it's not more than friends?" I asked Maggie,

curious, as I hadn't seen her show any interest in the opposite sex in years. She'd been too busy with her practice.

"No, that's all."

But her cheeks were flushed and her eyes sparkled.

"Well, your red face says it's way more than that," added Emma, much blunter than I could ever be.

"Not at all. How about you guys. Any men on the horizon?"

"No, for me," I said.

"None for me, neither," added Emma.

"Sure you don't have a thing for Red?" asked a persistent Maggie.

*Could she just not give it up?*

"Nope. Sorry to disappoint you." I glanced at my watch. It was almost time. I looked towards the door.

"Hey, don't want to alarm you, but is that him?" I whispered.

We all turned to take a look at a tall, fair-headed man, carrying a briefcase, standing at the door looking around.

"That's him all right," said Emma.

"What makes you so sure?" I whispered.

"He said he'd be wearing a blue sweater over a yellow T-shirt."

I looked again. "Well, he has all that going on."

When he looked our way, Emma stood up and waved him over.

"Emma Blake?" he asked, with a sweet lopsided smile.

"That's me," she answered, as she stuck out her hand for a shake. "And these are my friends, Maggie and Jessie."

"How do you do?" He reached out to shake our hands

as well while we both murmured that we were doing fine, then he pulled out Emma's chair and after she sat down, he did as well, putting the briefcase beside him.

"What would you like to drink?" asked Emma. "I'll let Jake know."

"Oh, just a coffee. It's been a long drive and I'm struggling to stay awake."

"I'll get it," said Maggie, as she pushed her chair back and headed to the bar.

"Where did you come from?" I asked.

"Well, I work in Ottawa, but was up visiting friends in Sudbury. We don't see each other much, so we stayed up all night shooting the bull and then I drove straight here."

Was it my imagination or did he seem a bit put out we were with Emma? He even looked like he was pouting. Too bad. We weren't moving until we were sure everything was okay.

"Here's your coffee," said Maggie as she put it down in front of him, and sat back down.

"Thank you." He immediately took a sip and sighed with pure pleasure. "Caffeine, this'll keep me awake."

"Well, please don't keep me in suspense. What did you need to see me about?" asked an impatient Emma, drumming her fingers on the table.

He smiled. "Just wanted to meet you. I adored your grandpa and he adored you."

"Really? But I never knew him."

"Well, he kept track of you." He reached down, opened up his briefcase and pulled out a scrapbook. He placed it in front of Emma. "This is the reason I'm here. I figured you'd like to have this."

Emma opened up the book. As she glanced at each page, she looked up, a confused expression on her face. "He had pictures of me?"

"Yes. While he was alive, he had you followed from time to time."

"He did what?" Emma looked stunned and I didn't blame her. It was certainly odd and kinda freaky, to be stalked by your estranged grandfather.

"He wanted to get to know his only grandchild, but was too proud to contact you. Instead, he treasured pictures of you."

"Excuse me, Maggie. Just wanted to see if everything is okay here?"

We all looked up to see Dave standing there. He kept staring at Drew and I realized Maggie must have told him. His visit here tonight was probably planned, to make sure we weren't in any kind of trouble. The story about the cousin was probably a hoax.

"Everything's going well," said Maggie.

"Are we still on for Saturday night?" asked Dave.

"Yes," answered Maggie.

Hmmmm… sure looked like dating to me.

"So this is what you wanted to see me about?" asked Emma.

"Yes. My mother and I thought you'd like to know how much you meant to your grandpa."

"You don't want my money?" she blurted out.

*Real subtle, Emma.*

He looked shocked. "Of course not. I make more than I'll ever use. What gave you that idea?"

"Ah, no one. Just used to it, I guess."

"Well, you have no worries from me in that regard."

"Just in case, keep in mind that Jessie here's a lawyer as well and she'll take your ass to court if you ever try anything."

I attempted to look fierce, displaying my best lawyer look, firm and determined with a don't mess with me attitude. I used to practice before a mirror to get it just right.

"Wouldn't think of it," he said.

And somehow, I believed him.

Maggie turned and asked me to play a game of pool with her.

"Thought we should leave them alone," she whispered.

"Good idea."

He seemed like an okay guy.

## *Twenty-seven*

"So how did it go last night?" I asked a tired looking, yet radiant Emma, as she strolled in the door dressed in a mini lime green dress under a bright purple jacket. She'd switched to tights and long sweaters lately, more in keeping with dog duties, so I was unprepared for the whole bright, outrageous ensemble she used to sport at the law firm. I had to blink a few times to adjust my eyes.

"Great," she smiled. "Drew and I stayed up all night swapping stories and today we're meeting for supper."

"Really? So he's definitely not out for your money?"

"Not at all. The best thing is I'm getting to know my grandpa through him."

"Did your mother ever talk about why they were estranged?"

"Rarely," she answered with a sigh. "She did mention one day after Daddy disappointed her that her father was right and her husband really was a low life. But I was young and didn't ask her to explain. I wish someone could tell me what really happened. Must have been pretty bad to keep them apart all those years."

"Maybe the housekeeper knows."

"That's what I'm thinking. Drew invited me for a visit."

"Are you going to go?"

"Maybe."

Hearing the door open with the first pet owner to arrive, I quickly said, "We'll have to talk later but I'm dying to hear everything. Every juicy little detail."

"Trust me. You will," Emma said, with a smile.

I had to admit, she sure looked happy.

It was a busy day but I was able to carve out a few quiet moments to scour our business records. I had a surprise for Emma and wanted to make sure everything was in order first.

During a lull, when the dogs were napping, I strolled to her desk and handed over an envelope.

"What's this?" she asked.

"Your very first White's Waggles pay check."

"Really? But I don't need one."

"Yes, you do. You're not working for free and I'm proud to be able to finally pay you something. It's not much but better than nothing."

"But…".

"No buts. You're taking it. That's an order."

"Yes, ma'am," she said, as she slid it in her purse. "Thank you. This is good news, right?"

"The best." I was so thrilled to be finally making a bigger profit that I felt like doing cartwheels but was too damn tired. Wasn't like I could do them, anyhow. "Now skedaddle and go get ready for your date. I can take over."

"Hey, thanks, Jessie," she said. "This is what I'm wearing, but I'd love to get to the restaurant first to freshen up my makeup."

"Well, get going."

She hurried out the door, while I got to work tidying up the room and getting the dogs ready for pick up. Envying Sadie who was snoozing by the window, I decided I was going to crash as soon as I was done. Man, I was tired. I'd stayed up too late at Jake's the night before.

But about ten minutes after the last dog had gone home, the door opened and in walked Hazel. A serious-looking Hazel. She even had on much more subdued looking clothing, I observed, taking in her black caftan, quite a switch from her usual bright colors. Something was up. My gut radar was flaring out of control. I hoped it wasn't to ask for my forgiveness again. I still wasn't ready for that.

"Hi there," I said.

"We'd like to talk to you," said Hazel, her eyes flicking everywhere but at me. She looked really nervous. Crap! I hoped nothing bad had happened.

Wait a sec... "We?" I looked to see if anyone was behind her.

"Your father is waiting in the house."

"Really? Is something wrong?"

"No. Just want to share some news."

"Good or bad?" I was hoping nothing would wreck this day as I was still flying high from cutting a pay check for the first time.

"We think it's good."

Good news? Well at least no tragedy had happened if it was supposedly good.

"Okay. I'll be there in a few minutes. Just have a bit more tidying up to do."

"We'll be in the kitchen."

She said this so seriously that I almost laughed. Like I wouldn't be able to find her or something. Usually when she was home, she was in the kitchen experimenting with her new concoctions. That'd be the first place I'd look.

As I pushed the dog beds back against the wall and swept the floor, all I could think about was *what in the world did they have to tell me?* Was it really good news or was she softening the blow? Was one of them sick? Was it terminal? Was Dad leaving town again? No. He wouldn't do that to me again. Would he? Not after we patched things up. Unless… Hazel asked him to. He seemed to obey her.

Stalling long enough, I finally joined them before I worked myself up into a frenzy of worry. Hazel handed me a cup of coffee as soon as I walked in the door and pointed to a chair across from them at the kitchen table.

"Please, sit down."

She sounded nervous. Like she had done something wrong and needed to confess or something.

I sat down, taking a quick sip, struggling to remain calm.

"What's up?" I asked.

After a long pause where no one said anything, I finally looked at Dad and noted he, too, seemed nervous. This whole thing seemed kind of spooky. Real eerie like. *What was going on?*

Finally, Hazel said, "Well, I won't beat around the bush any longer." She took hold of Dad's hand. "We're getting married again."

"What?"

As a kid, it was what I longed for when Dad first left. I'd stayed up nights thinking about ways to get them back together. Now that I couldn't care less, it was actually happening? I peered at Hazel. Yep, she looked ecstatic. I looked over at my father. He seemed thrilled as well as he reached over and put his arm around Hazel's shoulder.

"I popped the question and she said yes," he said, with a big grin.

"When's the wedding?" It was all I could gasp out.

"In about two weeks. That's just enough time to get everything organized," said Hazel.

"So soon?"

"I'm not letting her get away this time."

Hazel reached over and put her hand over mine. "I'd like you to be my maid of honor."

Pulling my hand away, I sat in silence, trying to fathom all of this. As Hazel started fidgeting, I realized I hadn't answered her.

"I'll think about it." I hated wiping that smile off of her face but just couldn't stop myself. I seemed to be able to forgive my father, but still had trouble with Hazel. Kicking my dad out and telling him not to contact me was still pretty horrific, in my eyes.

I knew it was none of my business and at the risk of pissing them off, I just had to ask, "What makes you think it will work this time?" I was curious about how they got to this again—their second marriage—to each other.

"I think I've grown up," said her dad, looking not the least bit upset at my question.

Hazel leaned over and gave him a hug. "We've both grown up."

Seeing the look of tenderness between them unsettled me. I needed to get out of here. Now. This was way too much information to process.

I jumped up. "I think I'll take Sadie out for a walk."

Fastening her leash, we took off. I didn't even care I had acted rude.

Aimlessly, I walked up and down the streets, my mind a muddle. I felt lost. Confused. I'd spent ten years with an adoring father who walked out of my life and left me with self-absorbed Hazel. Then I found out that the events were different than I thought which reshaped my whole history. Now I had a much nicer mother, a returning father and they were remarrying. I could hardly even grasp these turns of events and how I felt about it all.

Sadie let out a small woof. Looking down, I saw that she was staring up at me wagging her tail, and then she tugged on the leash, raring to go. I looked over and realized I was at the park my father used to take me to and Sadie was itching for a run.

Ahhhh… what the hell. I unclipped her leash. "Okay, buddy. Go stretch your legs."

I enjoyed watching her run free, but had to admit I felt uncomfortable. I hadn't been here in sixteen years and it brought back those glorious memories of playing with my father. I looked over at the soccer field. Thanks to him, I made the school team but quit the day after he left. It just didn't feel the same, not having him cheering me on from the stands.

I went over and sat down on the swings. I closed my eyes and recalled all the times he'd pushed me on this very swing. I sighed. So much had happened. My dad said we could begin again but was it just all talk?

A loud bark broke through my thoughts. My eyes popped open as Sadie raced across the field. Much to my surprise a familiar dog was running towards her and the two of them barked their excitement. Wait a sec! I knew that big brown dog. Oh my goodness, it was Squid.

It couldn't be. I peered into the dark. *Was that really Red walking towards me*? I rubbed my eyes and looked again. Nope. I wasn't hallucinating. It really was him. I was so stunned, I couldn't move. Just sat and stared.

"Hello there," he said, when he was a few feet away.

I took a deep breath and managed to say, "Hi, yourself."

"Mind if I join you?"

"Not at all."

Did my hair look okay? Was my face clean? I glanced down at my dirty jeans and grubby T-shirt, wishing I'd changed after work.

"Wasn't sure if you wanted to be alone," he said, sitting on the swing next to me.

"No, it's okay. How's Dubai?" I tried to make my voice sound cool and in control. No way would I let him know I was dying to see him.

"Hot. Exhausting. Busy. With little time to sightsee."

"Are you home for long?"

"Just for the day. I'm helping my mother take care of a few things. Then, it's back to Toronto."

"How's work going?" My heart raced and a familiar red flush crept over my face. I hoped he wouldn't notice.

"Okay. How about you?"

"Good."

"Really? You look upset about something."

I was taken aback by his directness as well as his insightfulness. I didn't know what to say so just kept quiet.

"Actually," he said. "To be honest, I saw you leaving and followed you here."

"You did?"

"Yes. I was next door and was going to pop over but as I came out of the house, you were already down the street. Is something bothering you?"

"Well... Hazel and my father just told me they're remarrying." I was surprised I was so honest. I guess it was because he sounded so concerned. But somehow saying it made it more real and upset me even more.

"Really?" he said, his voice gentle. He reached over and brushed a tear away. "Obviously, you're not too happy about that."

*Why did he have to touch me like that? It set off a wave of longing.*

"Oh, I don't know," I answered, trying to cover up my reaction to his nearness with words. "It was what I always wanted but now everything is happening so fast. I feel caught on a merry-go-round. Going round and round and never stopping. There's been so many lies."

His sympathetic eyes warmed me. Man, it felt so good to be with him. He radiated a strength I felt I didn't have at the moment.

"So they found themselves again," he mused. "I guess true love never dies."

"You getting all sentimental on me?"

He smiled. "Not really. I just believe in love that lasts."

He leaned closer, watching me carefully. "Have you forgiven them yet?"

"Pretty much my dad. Not Hazel."

"You'll get there. It's tough to do and important to do it in your own time. It's hard seeing a parent's weaknesses, mostly a product of their pasts."

He was right about that. Each of them had a ton of baggage, and along with mine, we'd fill up a huge storage rental.

"I guess I should try. I haven't, really. At least with Hazel."

"It's worth it. The results can be amazing."

There was a comfortable pause. A peaceful one where I felt in tune with him, although it didn't last long when all of a sudden our dogs ran over, as if finally remembering we were here.

"Guess I'd better go" said Red. "Have to drop some more stuff off at my mother's house."

"I think I'll head on back, as well."

"C'mon," said Red, as he stood up and reached out his arm to pull me up as well. "I'll walk you home."

His touch felt good, and I looked up and saw something warm in his eyes. Something I liked. A lot.

*Was he going to kiss me? What should I do? Back away?*

But no, he let go and reached down to strap a leash on Squid.

I did the same with Sadie.

We walked in comfortable silence all the way back and when we got to my door, he said, "I wish you all the best."

It sounded like a goodbye forever line and although I felt sad, I said cheerily, "Me, too. I hope things go great for you."

To my surprise he hugged me and to my shame I held on tight, but all I could think about was that other woman, whoever she might be. Lucky girl.

I pushed away. "Let me go," I finally muttered, knowing this was all wrong especially when his heart belonged to another.

He dropped his arms immediately.

"Jessie, there's something I'd like to tell you."

Oh, no. Was he going to tell me about his girlfriend? I couldn't bear that.

I placed my finger over his mouth to stop him. "Don't," I said, as I quickly turned and ran down the lane into the house, slamming the door in his face.

Hazel and Dad were still sitting drinking coffee.

"I'll do it," I said.

Although my father looked puzzled, Hazel understood immediately.

"You'll be my maid of honor?"

"Yes."

She teared up. "Oh, sweetie that's wonderful news."

Feeling fragile from seeing Red and not wanting to deal with her emotions, I took off quickly and headed to my room to watch T.V., a sure escape from everything.

To think of Red with someone else ripped me apart. But hey, I'd survived getting fired, evicted, and losing Jim all on the same day. I could damn well get over "big like" with my neighbor.

*At least, I thought I could.*

# *Twenty-eight*

"Just one more lap," I yelled over to Sadie, who had given up ages ago and was just sitting off to the side watching me, under the cool shade of a maple tree. She nodded as if she understood, but I think she figured I was crazy. Too bad. I had to do this.

I'd dragged myself to the track at a local school and was trying to jog five miles before I gave up. Today was the day Hazel was taking me shopping for a bridesmaid dress and I wanted to be in tip-top shape. My weight had been on a roller coaster for quite some time now—lose, gain, lose again, gain again. At the moment, I'd just finished shedding the extra weight I'd put on a while back and was trying to pare off a few more. I was determined. Running after dogs required me to be in good physical condition to combat their four legs against my two. It was sometimes hard keeping up with them. Not to mention, I wanted to look fairly decent at the wedding. After all, I was the maid of honor.

When I finally limped to the finish line, Sadie greeted me with her usual licks and we headed to the car to get back home. I hated shopping with a passion but since

Hazel decided to wear her original wedding gown she focused her whole being on buying me the perfect dress. I was really doing it for my father, glad he was back in my life again but man, she was obsessed with the gown, even buying fashion magazines to scout out latest trends and styles. I guess I could understand why. Knowing me, I'd probably leave it to the last minute, panic and purchase the first one I saw on the rack regardless whether it suited me or not. Dressing up was not my favorite thing to do and witnessing disdainful looks from sales clerks because I wasn't a size two, or even a size ten, left me avoiding shops altogether. The only time you saw me in stores was if my clothes were so threadbare I could no longer wear them. However, Hazel wanted to spend some bonding time with me—her word not mine—so I was going along with it. I didn't want to ruin this happy time for her and was calling a truce, for the time being.

The wedding was originally to be small, but my parents were so ecstatic at finding themselves again, as Red put it, they wanted to share it with everyone they were close to, so the list grew. Apparently there were over a hundred people invited. It was taking place at Incarnation Parish on Nash Road, the reception at Carmen's Banquet Hall. Even I had to admit I was getting excited, especially seeing how thrilled they were to be back together. Sometimes I felt like screaming, "Get a room," after walking in on them kissing away like a couple of teenagers, but basically it was kinda cool having the family unit as one again.

"'Bout time you got home," Hazel said with a smile, as I walked in the door. "I've made you some oatmeal. So hurry and eat. I can't wait to get started."

"All right, all right!"

She was like a little kid, all eager to get going. Not wanting to cause any arguments, I gulped down my food, changed into jeans and a buttoned up shirt, easy to strip off when trying on dresses and bid Sadie goodbye. We headed out, an excited Hazel behind the wheel, unusually chatting away.

"I thought I'd try out that new wedding place, Sara's Sizzling Bridal Gowns at Limeridge Mall. I looked at their website and they have the most gorgeous bridesmaid dresses."

"Sure. That's fine." I decided to be totally agreeable as we headed down the Lincoln Parkway to the shopping plaza.

Turning into the parking lot, she quickly found a spot and took off into the plaza, with me trailing behind. Not one to waste time, Hazel went right to the customer service kiosk and located Sara's, up the elevator and down five stores.

"Shall we take the stairs?" asked Hazel.

"Good idea." I knew she'd been trying to lose weight as well but was impressed at how she bolted up to the second floor leaving me in the dust.

At the top, I could spot our destination right away. A beautiful mannequin stood in the window dressed in a gorgeous white confection with her bridesmaids lined up beside her in fire engine red. It was definitely not the kind of store I'd go into as it was way too trendy for my taste. I always felt so out of place in these glamour locales.

"You sure this is where you want to go, Hazel?"

"I'm sure," she said, as she took hold of my arm and

marched me in the store.

"My name's Linda. May I help you?" said a sweet young girl with a huge, friendly smile.

"Yes. We need a sharp-looking dress for my daughter here."

She smiled. "And you'll make a beautiful bride," she said, eyeing me up and down, probably calculating my size.

"No, I'm the bride," said Hazel. "She's my maid of honor."

"Oh."

I almost smiled at how confused the girl looked. After all, Hazel was no spring chicken and with her white hair, looked older than she was.

"A certain color?" she asked, attempting to regroup.

I looked at Hazel. After all it was the bride's prerogative.

"A sexy black number," she said.

"What?" I gasped.

Do you know what it's like to be overweight a long portion of your life? Even when you lose the pounds it was hard to believe you could ever wear something sexy. I was thinner on the outside but still felt fat on the inside. No way would I look good in a "sexy black number". Besides, why in the world would any mother want their daughter to dress like that? Something suspicious was going on here as she never bared flesh and wasn't a fan of women who did so. This was unusual.

"Trust me, honey," said Hazel, with a twinkle in her eye. "You'll thank me for it."

I shrugged my shoulders, still trying not to make

waves, while Linda took a moment to take my measurements. "I have just the dress," she said, as she went over to a rack and carefully selected one, holding it up for me to see.

I was aghast at how skimpy it was.

"Try it on," whispered Hazel.

"Do you have a few others?" I asked. "Just in case?"

"Sure do." She came back with five of them.

I left the skimpy one until last and whirled and twirled my way through all five, hoping Hazel would pick one a bit more conservative. None of them even produced an inkling of a smile from her.

Frustrated, I just stood there, a green sheath hanging on me. "Can't we just go with this one?"

"No way. Try the first one on," she urged.

Not being able to stall any longer, I did.

The black material was soft and silky and actually felt good against my skin. It was quite modest in length, coming to just above my knees but the cleavage was way too low for my liking and the back was non-existent. I felt naked.

"Come on out," said Hazel.

I slowly came out of the room, feeling like an ass. A naked ass. I just hoped my ass wasn't naked.

"Turn around," said Hazel.

Reluctantly, I did as she said.

"That's the one."

"Really? I can't imagine wearing this."

"I can," she said, with a smile. "Trust me, it looks good on you."

Not about to make a scene—after all it was just one

day I'd have to wear it—I pulled out my credit card but Hazel waved me away.

"It's on me."

"I can't let you do that. It's a lot of money."

"Please. I want to."

Reluctantly I let her, knowing the cost would wipe out my bank account.

The salesgirl fussed about, tucking material in here and there saying, "It needs to be altered. I'll have it ready in two days."

"We'll need shoes," said Hazel, as she stared down at my runners.

"Sure. How about I meet you down at Lisa's Footwear in a few minutes?"

"Okay," she said, as she happily headed out the store, looking eager to do more shopping.

After squeezing out of the dress and putting my shopping clothes back on, I sought out the salesgirl again to retrieve Hazel's credit card.

"Excuse me."

She looked up.

"Any chance you could raise the dress higher? I can't stand how low it is and how much cleavage it shows."

She looked shocked.

"But Miss White. The dress barely shows anything."

"Just raise it if you can, please."

"I'll try." But she looked doubtful.

Okay. Maybe it wasn't that low because anything not up to my neck was too low for me, but I wanted to be comfortable. At least I'd tried.

I joined Hazel in the shoe store as she searched for the

perfect ones to match the dress. She inspected every pair in the shop and centered on a black strappy pair she liked. Looking at the price tag, I gasped. They cost a small fortune.

"Try them on," she urged. "Don't worry, I'm paying. After all it's my wedding and I'm saving a fortune by wearing my old dress."

"Er, okay." And… of course they definitely were the perfect ones to match the dress. Even I could see that.

After Hazel paid for them, I asked, "Could you do something for me now?"

She looked surprised. "Of course."

"Then follow me."

I led her to the Old Navy Store and took her right to a display of jeans. Gathering up a few that might be her size I directed her to the change room.

"What in the world?" she asked.

"Try these on, Hazel. I've been dying to get you out of those shapeless shifts."

"Oh, all right."

At least she was a good sport about it. I suspected she was just humoring me but I ignored that thought and set off to find a few nice Tees. After searching out one that was multi-colored with all her favorite paint hues, I stuck my arm over the door of the change room saying, "Try this on too."

Minutes went by before a shy looking Hazel came out. I was stunned. She actually had a gorgeous figure, hidden under those billowing gowns.

"Wow," was all I could get out.

As she preened in front of the mirror, I even thought I saw a smile on her face.

"Looking good," said a sales clerk, as she passed by.

"Oh my goodness," was all Hazel could get out.

As she headed back to change I stopped her saying, "No. Keep it on. It's my wedding gift to you."

"Really?" She seemed nervous in her new attire.

"Don't worry. You look good."

"Well then, thank you." She pulled out her wallet.

"No way. This is my gift." I quickly handed the salesclerk my card and couldn't help but notice Hazel was beaming and I suddenly realized I was having fun. A lot of fun. I'd even found myself laughing out loud a few times at her witty remarks and observances. She was actually quite delightful as a shopping partner.

Heading past a Tim Hortons in the Food Court, Hazel pointed saying, "How about a coffee?

*Was she as reluctant to end this shopping spree as I was?*

"Sure."

After settling in with coffees and low-fat blueberry muffins, Hazel asked, "So do you like Brian?"

I almost spit my coffee out.

"Who?"

"Our ex-neighbor, Brian."

"Oh, Red. He's okay, I guess."

"Not more than okay?"

What was she getting at? I was starting to feel uncomfortable. Never have I discussed any romantic interest with her. Never.

"No. Just okay."

"Well. In case you don't know, your eyes light up when he's around."

Sheesh! Could she see inside my heart? Did she know I was in “big like”?

“They light up with anger. That’s what you’re seeing. He’s too arrogant for my taste.”

Hazel smiled again, almost knowingly, then reached into her purse and pulled out an envelope.

“It’s tradition for the bride to give her bridesmaids a gift. Here’s yours.”

“But you already gave me something. The dress and shoes.”

“Open it up.” She smiled.

Puzzled, I lifted up the flap and pulled out what looked like official documents.

“What’s this?” I looked up at her.

“The deed to the house. It’s yours. We’re planning on moving to a condo in Stoney Creek.”

Oh, right. I’d forgotten they’d have to live somewhere.

“Would you like me to move out instead?” I asked.

“No, honey,” said Hazel. “A condo suits us fine. Your dad will be working all day and I’ll be painting. This way there’s no yard work to do and the both of us can concentrate on our own stuff.”

“How about I buy it from you? Or rent it until I have more money saved?”

“Your father and I would like to give it to you. Consider it your inheritance.”

“You don’t have to do this, Hazel."

“I know. But I want to.”

Shaking my head, I said, “I just can’t accept this. It’s way too generous.” I was also too independent to take charity from her since I liked to work hard for what I wanted. I handed the papers back.

She reached over and put her hand over mine. This time I left it there.

"I've never been a good mother to you."

I started to protest, feeling bad that I was making her look so sad on what was supposed to be our special time together. She cut me off.

"No, it's true. I know that's why you call me by my first name. Like your father, I'm asking for a second chance. This house is my gift to you. I know you're independent and want to make it on your own, but it's all I have to give. It's my way of making up for all the things I never gave when you were growing up. This will help you financially, give you the chance to pay off those loans and make your life easier. Please take it. It's the least I can do. My apology is wrapped up in this deed. I'm not expecting you to forgive me now. But maybe one day."

I was so stunned I just sat and stared at her. I rarely saw this honest, vulnerable side of Hazel and couldn't even get any words out, mainly because I couldn't figure out how I was feeling. Fortunately, she seemed to understand, as she folded up the papers and stuffed them back in her purse.

"At least think about it," she said softly, looking disappointed.

## *Twenty-nine*

"Be ready in a second, honey," yelled out Aunt T from her bedroom.

"No problem, I'm early. Take your time," I shouted back as I carefully sat down on her couch, not used to wearing skintight clothing and boy, was this new dress snug. Form fitting was how the salesclerk described it and my biggest hope was that I didn't rip it before I even got to the church. I sure didn't want any more of my so-called form showing.

I reached up to make sure my French braid was intact after my drive over with the air conditioning on full blast. It was hot outside and I didn't think sweat stains were particularly attractive when you're the maid of honor. Of course, the black would hide them well so that was at least one good thing about this dress.

Hazel insisted I get my hair done, along with a professional makeup job and I barely recognized myself when I looked in the mirror. I still felt naked. Like hell, the saleslady raised the cleavage level. It still seemed way too low for me but at least Hazel allowed me to wrap a shawl around my shoulders, so I'd look decent in church.

But I'd wear it proudly in Hazel's honor, not wanting to insult her. After all, it was her wedding. Her special day. I was going to do my part to make it a good one.

Trying to distract myself from how uncomfortable I felt, I looked around Aunt T's living room. I loved it here. It was cozy and warm and it'd been my place of refuge all my life, not to mention, she lived on top of the escarpment and had the best view possible of the city. At night, it looked like an imposing kingdom presiding over the thousands of twinkling houses below. Everything was so familiar and brought instant comfort. The white lace curtains hanging alongside the big bay window, the comfy chairs, including the one I was sitting on, the shelves of angel knick-knacks, the treasure chest she kept by the far wall that was always locked, filled with her "secrets". She always said that one day I could take a look. That day never came.

*Wait a sec!*

I wiggled my way to a standing position and moved closer. The chest wasn't locked and the lid was up about three inches from the base. That was odd. I looked toward the hall leading to Aunt T's bedroom. No sign of her.

Dare I take a look?

Years of curiosity overpowered me and almost without thinking, urged on by sheer nosiness, I reached down and slowly pulled up the lid, staring in shock. I didn't know what to expect, but it sure wasn't this.

*A picture of Mr. T stared up at me.*

*Mr. T?*

*What the...?*

You remember Mr. T, don't you? You know, the guy

from the television show—The A Team? The one with the Mohawk and dozens of gold chains? He was part of a group of soldiers who were set up for a crime they didn't commit. They were on the run but used their talents to help the less fortunate. It was an action packed drama and hilarious, all at the same time and I used to watch old reruns with my aunt. We'd pop up some corn and chow down while enjoying the escapades of Hannibal, Faceman, Howling Mad and of course Mr. T.

Noticing writing on the photo, I picked it up to take a closer look. *To Martha from Mr. T* was written across the bottom. Martha? I knew that was my aunt's first name. I looked back in the chest. With the picture gone, I saw tons of Mr. T memorabilia—mugs, T-shirts, bobble heads, pens, pencils and more photos of the actor.

Once again, all I could think of was—*what the...?*

*Clarity hit me hard.*

Aunt T? Mr. T? My aunt named herself after Mr. T? No way. That was just plain crazy.

"So you found my dirty little secret?"

I jumped, caught in the act, holding the picture but all I could do was just stare at her in shock.

"I was going to tell you one day."

"So you really are a big fan of Mr. T? You're the Martha he mentions?"

"A fan? Hell, I run his fan club. I'm the head honcho. Mr. T himself gave me the name and I decided I liked it."

I started to laugh and couldn't stop. After all the years of trying to figure out her name, I never dreamed of this. I also surmised that Aunt T didn't leave the chest open accidentally. She was too precise to do that. For whatever reason, she wanted me to know.

Finally, back in control, I asked, "But why didn't you tell me when we were watching all his shows?"

"Because I knew your mother was too preoccupied to mother you, your dad was gone, so I was all you really had left. I thought you'd think I was nuts if you knew and wouldn't respect me."

"But why? I could have handled it and I'll always respect you."

"Well, even though Mr. T was innocent, he was on the run from the law. I didn't think he was appropriate role modeling for a young girl but now I figure it's time you know." She glanced at her watch. "Sorry, honey. We have to go. Let's talk on the way to the church or Hazel will kill us for being late."

Now that it was out in the open, Aunt T gabbed nonstop about her Mr. T fan club on the ride over. It was obviously one of her favorite topics. Who would have guessed?

"Have you ever met him?" I asked.

"Sure have. That was how it all started. Went to one of his appearances and we were all trying to get his autograph. Someone banged into me and knocked me down. Mr. T stopped everything to assist me, made sure I was okay, and gave me not one but three autographed pictures of himself. He reminded me a lot of your grandpa."

"Really?" I'd never met my grandpa, as he'd passed away the year before I was born although I'd heard lots of wonderful stories about him.

"He was a real gentleman."

I snuck a look at her and her eyes shone. It was kinda sweet seeing her so enthused about something but to be the head of Mr. T's fan club and to name herself after him still blew me away. Another secret in our family uncovered. Weird as hell. Surely, there couldn't be any more?

As we pulled into the parking lot at Incarnation Church, I tabled my questions as we went to find Hazel in a room off to the side of the altar. She had her back to us, fiddling with her veil in a mirror and as she turned around, I gasped. I had seen the dress in pictures as a kid, but she'd gotten rid of the photos when Dad left. This was the first time I saw it up close and it was stunning. A form fitting creamy white gown that fit her like a glove. With her hair flowing down in soft curls, she looked absolutely beautiful and once again, I was stunned at how svelte she was.

"You look amazing," I gasped out.

She smiled. "Thank you. I'm just glad I can still fit into it. I thought I'd wear it, reminding me of how much we were in love when we first got married. You look gorgeous, by the way. That dress really does suit you."

"Er, thank you."

"Well, are you ready?" asked Aunt T, who'd been given the task of walking her sister down the aisle.

"Sure am," said Hazel, but she looked nervous.

*Time to act upon a decision I made just last night.*

I moved closer. "Good luck, Mom," I whispered in her ear.

Shock, surprise then sheer joy lit up her eyes. She stood back and stared at me.

"I didn't imagine it, did I? You really called me Mom?"

"Yes." I smiled.

She reached out to hug me and when I responded, she held on for dear life, whispering, "Does that mean all is forgiven?"

"Sure does."

I finally did it! I took the plunge and told her I forgave her. It felt damn good. A long time coming.

"Oh, lordy," said Aunt T. "You'll make her mascara run." But she looked pleased as punch. "Now skedaddle, Jessie. Time to get this show on the road."

As I pulled away my mother whispered, "Love you," and I whispered back, "Love you, too."

I'd finally figured out my parents deserved to be happy, as well as have my forgiveness and I wanted to make sure that they knew I was on board, at last. It took a long time but I made it!

"Now get going," said Aunt T. "The music's starting."

I could hear the vocalist singing the Ave Maria, as I walked out to the aisle. Nervous, legs shaking, I headed down, feeling reassured when I saw a smiling Maggie and Emma and… oh, no!

Was that Red sitting in front of them? Couldn't be. But it had to be. Very few people had that exact shade of hair. I glanced over as I passed and he smiled. Oh my goodness. He was here. It was really him.

*Hazel invited Red? And he came?*

What in the world, for?

But I finally got it. Now I knew why she wanted me looking good in a sexy dress. She was doing a little matchmaking, trying to dress me differently than in my usual dog hair-covered jeans and T-shirts. That was why she asked about my feelings toward our neighbor. She was hoping we'd get together. I was sure of it.

My knees wobbling even more, I decided to at least not be rude and nodded at him. When he smiled even wider, I sort of smiled back, and he looked so good in his black suit that my heart started beating erratically and I had to look away quickly or I'd pass out. That'd be just great. Fainting in the church. I took a deep breath and slowly let it out. This was my parent's big day and I didn't want to ruin it. I needed to block Red's face out of my mind. *Look over at your father. Concentrate on him.*

Dad winked at me, I winked back and we both turned to watch my mother arrive. She literally floated down the aisle and the two of them looked so happy when they acknowledged each other with a hug, I could only wish all sorts of happiness for them.

All through the ceremony, I tried hard to concentrate on what the priest was saying but all I could think about was the fact Red was here. I even snuck a few peeks at him and found him watching me. Sheesh. Nothing like making me more nervous.

When the priest finally said, "You may now kiss the bride," I stared in wonder as my father leaned down for a smooch. If I was unsure what to make of it all, I wasn't now. Judging by the look of pure joy on their faces, it was definitely the right thing. They were in love and that was obvious. At twenty-six, I had both my parents back together. A mom and a dad. Go figure.

I had to admit, I'd been feeling better about them as the days rolled on, understanding their weaknesses and factoring in the human element. To tell you the truth, I admired them for working through their own battles and emerging victorious. It was a lot like what I was trying to do. After all, when we make mistakes, all we can really do is ask for forgiveness. Many long hours spent with Olive made me realize I really needed to put the past behind and push forward into more adult relationships with my parents. I did already with my father. Today I made the first step with my mother. Another brand new beginning.

"Get going, daydreamer," whispered Aunt T.

I looked over and noticed my parents starting to move down the aisle, so I got in gear and followed. My smile was real, finally glad to be part of this celebration.

After a flurry of photos on the front steps, I gathered Aunt T and we headed off to the reception at Carmen's, which was back up the mountain.

After chatting about how beautiful the ceremony was all the way there, as we pulled into the parking lot, Aunt T said, "I'm proud of you."

She didn't have to explain. I knew why.

"Thanks," I said.

"You've come a long way."

She was right. I had. But there was no time for introspection for I just saw Red pull in and I needed to get out of there. I couldn't bear to greet him and have all sorts of feelings stirred up. I needed to be focused on my parents and their big day.

Carefully jumping out of the car without ripping my dress, I said, "I'll meet you in there," and hurried into the building. I knew Aunt T understood.

I quickly found my place at the head table and sat down, waiting for the arrival of the bridal party. Looking around the room, I was moved at the display of paintings mounted on the walls. All Hazel Hul originals and mostly of my father and me. Noticing one of the three of us, I went over to take a look. We were all smiling, happy and looked like the perfect family. I noticed it was entitled *Hope* on the card pinned below.

"I painted this a year ago."

Startled, I turned to find my mother right behind me.

"It's beautiful."

"Yes, it is. This picture holds all my dreams and today you made another one come true. Thank you." She reached out to hold my hand. We hung on hard.

My father came up behind, wrapping his arms around the both of us, joining us as we all stared at the picture.

I hadn't felt this contented in years. *Hope* had been the perfect title for our new beginning. The three of us—together at last.

Finally, he said, "C'mon. We'd better get seated. Dinner's about to start."

He led us back to the head table and I saw Red sitting with Maggie and Emma. Good. At least he wasn't among strangers.

After a feast of chicken for the meat eaters and veggie lasagna for the non-carnivores and a ton of toasts to the wedding couple, the first dance began. To the song *At last* crooned by Etta James, my parents danced, and to my surprise it brought tears to my eyes. I'd just finished wiping them, when my dad came over to claim me.

"Drop your shawl, honey," whispered my mother. "Give everyone a look at how breathtaking you are."

Yeah, right. But what the hell. If it made her happy, I

would. So I did and my father led me off into a waltz.

"Congratulations, Dad," I whispered.

"Thank you," he whispered back. "You made me proud today by forgiving your mother. I finally have my family back together."

"Yes, you do."

"At last," he said happily.

And now I knew why they chose that song for their first dance.

I snuggled closer, feeling his warmth and glad he was once again back in my life. Enjoying how good I felt for a change, I was sad when the song ended. But just as we were about to go back to the table, someone tapped me on the shoulder.

"Excuse me."

Looking around, I inhaled sharply when I saw a smiling Red standing behind me.

"May I have this dance?" he said.

"No, thanks. I really should stay with my parents," I said, feeling bad as his smile disappeared but I still didn't want to be that close to him and be all confused again. Especially when I was in a good mood and just wanted to enjoy the rest of the evening.

"Go ahead," urged my Dad. "Go have fun."

"Yes," added my mother, coming over to claim her husband. "We can spare you for a while."

"Well, okay," I said, not knowing how to get out of this gracefully. But when the band started playing Elvis Presley's *Can't help falling in love* I felt doomed. Wouldn't you know one of the most romantic songs ever would have to be sung at this particular moment?

As Red wrapped his arms around me, I had to admit, I liked it. A lot.

*Too bad it was forbidden territory.*

"How have you been?" he asked.

"Fine," I answered, looking up at him. "I didn't know you were coming."

"I wasn't sure I could make it." He smiled. "But I'm glad I did."

*Me, too,* I grudgingly thought.

He held me tighter and finally I laid my head on his shoulder, knowing I may not have any tomorrows with him, but at least I had right now. Might as well enjoy it. After a bit, I felt his arms tighten, and confused I looked up again. Was his face really moving closer? Oh crap! Was he going to kiss me? Should I allow it? What about the other girl?

"You look beautiful," he whispered.

"Oh! Please don't make me gag," said a loud shrill voice behind us.

We both stopped in our tracks and I looked around to see a tall, beautiful blonde, hands on her hips, glaring at the both of us. She was absolutely stunning looking in a long red gown. I backed away.

"Get away from my man. I think Brian's fiancée should be the only one to dance with him to this song."

She stepped in front of me and put her arms around Red.

Fiancée? I looked over at him. His face was completely white.

Furious, I turned and stomped away, just as I heard him say, "Jessie. Wait."

But I didn't. I kept on going, running to the washroom and shutting the door with a loud bang. Hiding in a stall, tears flowing, all I could think about was *why in hell did I dance with him in the first place?* I knew it would only lead to heartache.

"Is everything okay?" yelled Aunt T, from outside the stall.

"No," I said back. "But I'm not going to let it ruin my parents' night. I'll be out in a minute." I wiped my tears, blew my nose and walked out into Aunt T's arms. She wrapped them around me.

"Saw the whole thing," she whispered.

"Horrible, huh?"

"Not so sure. Wait until you hear from Red. He probably has a good explanation."

"Yeah, right. I never want to see him again."

"We'll see," she said as she led me back to the head table.

Maggie and Emma had me out on the dance floor in the space of two seconds and dancing up a storm helped me get through the night. Neither mentioned the Red situation, knowing I would talk about it when I was ready, although I could tell they felt bad by how attentive they were. I hoped I hadn't ruined their evening.

I was just glad Red and his woman left. I'd seen that girl before. She was the one in that picture I'd found at his house. His ex. They must have gotten back together.

I should have stayed away from him.

*When would I ever learn?*

## *Thirty*

"Please, take a seat," said the secretary, a warm smile on her face. "Judge Stevens will be here shortly. She's on her way to court, but said she'd squeeze you in."

"Thank you," I said, sitting down, nervous to be in her chambers and wondering for the thousandth time, why the Judge wanted to meet with me. Must be serious if she was "squeezing me in". I couldn't even begin to imagine the reason why and I'd chewed my fingernails to the quick this past week waiting for this appointment. It had to be something bad. I just knew it.

*Was she going to discipline me for speaking up in the courtroom? For questioning her judgment?*

Nervous as hell and trying to distract myself, I gazed around the room, noticing three watercolors hanging on the beige wall. They depicted several realistic shots of the Devil's Punchbowl Falls in Stoney Creek and were truly magnificent. Very eye-catching. Next, I peered at the large oak wall-to-wall bookcase and got up to take a look. It was a researcher's dream for I swear she had every law book on the market. John would have gone crazy seeing all of this. A million sources of valuable information at your fingertips. Speaking of fingertips, mine itched to hold a law book in my hand. It'd been a while. Too long, I might add.

Picking one up, I cradled it in my arms as I took a look at her university degrees displayed behind the desk. York University. I didn't realize we shared the same alma mater. As I moved in to take a closer look, I bumped into a brown leather chair that looked comfortable and regal, fit for a judge. I looked toward the door. No one in sight. I plopped down on the chair, sank into its softness, closed my eyes, and still hugging the law book, pretended I was a practicing lawyer again. Man, it felt good.

"Enjoying yourself?"

Opening my eyes, I jumped up to find the judge standing in front of me. At least she was smiling.

"Er. Excuse me." I hastily returned the book and sat back down on the chair in front of the desk.

"Sorry about that," I said, feeling a blush coming on strong.

"No problem. My father was a judge and I used to do the same thing when I visited," she said, as she sat down as well.

*Yeah, but I was no kid.*

Thank goodness, she wasn't upset. Kite would have had a fit if anyone trespassed in his domain.

"Your paintings are beautiful." Gesturing towards them, I was hoping to divert her from my escapade.

"My daughter did those."

"Really? She's quite talented."

"I think so and so do many art galleries. She's not as famous as your mother but does quite well."

So she knew who my mother was. Would that work for me or against me?

"Would you like some coffee?" she asked, getting up and walking over to a pot brewing on a silver trolley off to the side. "It must be ready by now."

"Love some." I got up as well, but she waved me away.

"I'll get it. How do you take it?"

"Black's fine."

She handed over the mug and as I held on to it, I saw that my hand was shaking. I quickly clasped it with my other hand as well so as not to spill anything. I looked up, hoping she hadn't noticed. She had, but said nothing as she sat back down behind her desk, the picture of composed authority.

I waited, taking a sip. Actually, I really should have skipped the coffee. I certainly didn't need a dose of caffeine getting me all riled up, for I was tense enough as it was. I just wished she'd get on with the reason behind this meeting. I couldn't stand the suspense.

"That was quite a performance you put on the other day," said the judge.

Oh! Oh! Here it comes.

"That was no performance. I meant every word I said."

"Even though you could have gone to jail?"

"It was what I deserved. I failed that girl."

"Good answer."

"It's the truth."

The judge took a sip of coffee as she watched me, a thoughtful expression on her face.

"You know, I've been meaning to get in touch with you before you turned up so dramatically in my courtroom."

"Really?"

"Heard about how you stood up to Kite for your pro bono clients."

*What?*

I was prepared for a blast, not a discussion about my previous job.

"May I ask who told you?" *Does everyone know?*

"A research assistant by the name of John. He speaks very highly of you."

John strikes again.

"I think highly of him. He'll make an excellent lawyer when he's called to the bar." Figured I'd put in a good word for him. After all, this judge was pretty influential.

"So are you."

"Pardon?"

*Had I heard her right?*

The judge smiled.

"You're a good lawyer, too. I've done some checking up on you. Top student, hard worker, compassionate as well. Not afraid to take chances. Qualities we need more of in the law field."

"Thank you."

"I want you to know that I admire your stand with Kite, just as I admire your stand in my courtroom the other day."

"You do?" Shocked, I put my coffee down on the desk before I spilt it all over me.

"Yes." She smiled. "It was very effective. You got me to change my ruling."

"For which I'll be eternally grateful."

"You know, you remind me of myself. I'm a firm

believer in striving for high ideals with no compromises, willing to risk getting fired or jail time. That's why I wanted to talk to you. Years ago, I was fortunate to work for Legal Aid and I knew all about Kite and his strong-armed tactics. He'd pretend to care about victims of poverty or abuse but do everything in his power to slaughter them."

She was dead on, but I was surprised she was so honest.

As if reading my mind, she added, "I'm not speaking behind his back. I've said all this to his face and I stand by it. He was one of the reasons I became a judge. To administer justice. Fair and honestly." She leaned forward. "If you don't mind me asking, have you been blacklisted here in Hamilton? I've heard rumblings about this. Am I correct?"

"Yes. No one will hire me." I wasn't going to beat around the bush. It was the truth.

"Thought so, but wanted to hear your take on it." She sighed and shook her head. "So Kite strikes again."

She picked up a piece of paper, got up and moved to stand in front of me, leaning back against the desk.

"We need good lawyers like you in this city. Lawyers who really care about their clients. I want you to know that I'll make sure my words counteract Kite's here in Hamilton. You'll be able to find a job in no time. I even have the names of several firms looking for good lawyers. I'll recommend you." She handed me the piece of paper. "Have them call me for a reference."

*Judge Stevens was backing me?*

Overwhelmed, I didn't even know what to say or do.

Paralysed, I just sat there, staring at her.

She smiled. "I hope to see you practicing again."

A wave of longing hit me hard. Being in such an intense law environment with a judge who believed in me made me realize how much I missed it all. I missed clients who challenged me to seek justice for them. I missed using my skills, honed after years of intense study, to do my part in making this world a better place. Yes, I was still an optimist and always felt I could make a difference fighting for people's rights. My dreams had been shot down by Kite but today Judge Stevens was giving me a second chance. I couldn't believe this was happening.

"I appreciate this," I said softly, struggling through my emotions to get out my words of gratitude. "More than you'll ever know. Thank you so much."

"You're welcome. Now, you'll have to excuse me," said the Judge, pulling me out of my shocked state. "I have to prepare for court. Maria will see you out."

"Um, sure," I mumbled, managing to get up and head to the door. Just as I was about to exit my mind kicked in.

"Your Honor."

"Yes?" She looked up from a file she was flipping through.

"It's about that matter of diversion for my client, Christine."

"A well prepared document."

"And?"

"I'll okay it." She smiled.

I didn't think my own grin could get any wider. Christine was going to be okay. I'd managed to help her despite my abandonment.

I almost skipped back to my car and settling behind the wheel, glanced at the paper the judge handed me. There were four big law firms written there. Powerful ones.

Excitement got a hold of me, as thoughts of practicing law filled my mind.

*Should I call them? Or should I keep working at the dog daycare, which I also loved?*

I wasn't sure what to do or what I wanted anymore. Judge Stevens had certainly rocked my world.

Olive, here I come.

Time for some heavy-duty truth sessions.

## *Thirty-one*

"What's wrong?" asked Maggie. "Is it to do with what happened at the wedding?"

"Why do you ask?" I was puzzled, as I thought I was putting on a pretty good show of smiling, laughing and being all happy, fake though it was, these last couple of days.

"Please. This is your best friend talking. Don't think I can't see that sad, preoccupied look in your eyes when you think we're not looking."

"I'd rather not talk about it." I picked up my beer and took a swig. "I've been looking forward to this night at Jake's and don't want to ruin it by discussing my ex-neighbor."

"I think you have to," said a persistent Maggie. "I haven't bugged you about it but I think it's time you got it off your chest."

"I agree," added Emma, sliding onto the stool beside me. "Sorry I'm late, guys. Heard the phone ringing as I was dashing out the door and thought that maybe it was one of you calling. Instead it was Drew." She looked at me for a second before saying, "Wish I could fix whatever's bugging you. Those dark circles under your eyes don't become you. They've gotten worse since that horrid girl interrupted your dance with Red."

Unwillingly, that scene at the wedding shot through my mind. Instantly, I felt Red's arms around me, warm and strong, and I remembered gazing up at him. Somehow, the look in his eyes made me feel that something was going to happen. Like a kiss perhaps. Or maybe I was just hoping. Dreaming he'd had a falling out with that girl he liked and was starting to "big like" me. Damn! Who knew he still had a fiancée?

"You know he's in Australia at the moment, don't you?" asked Maggie. "Dave said he left after the reception to make an important meeting. He was surprised Red even went to the wedding."

"I didn't know that, nor do I care where he is." I was also a liar. *He was in Australia*? I shook my head trying to clear it of thoughts of him, not wanting to go down that road. It only led to heartbreak.

*Don't think about him. Especially since you have so many other decisions to make.*

"How are the training sessions going at the daycare?" asked Maggie, probably seeing my head shaking, and figuring it was best to stick to safer topics.

"We have a full house and they're doing well. Adding obedience and agility classes turned out to be a good thing. I'm just glad my former trainer was available to teach them."

"Good to know. And how did the date go the other night?" asked Maggie. 'You haven't said much about it."

"Okay." Determined not to let Red get to me, I'd

accepted a night out with Ron, the owner of a border collie pup I watched from time to time. We'd gone to the movies but, I had to admit, I had a lousy time. The problem was—no one could top Red.

"Oh come on, Jessie. Admit it. It was horrible," said Emma. "That's what you said the next day."

I sighed. "Yeah, it was pretty bad."

"You really do like him, don't you?" asked Emma.

"Who?"

"Don't play dumb with me. Red, of course."

"Yes," I said quietly.

Okay I said it. Owned up to it. Time to stop pretending to my closest friends.

They both looked surprised that I'd admitted it and I saw Maggie motioning to Emma to keep quiet, probably not to push me any further, but she kept right on going.

"Have you heard from him?"

"Nope."

"Not even a postcard?"

"Nothing."

"Did you see the sold sign on the house next door?"

"Yes. It's been up there for a while." That depressed me even further. I turned my head away from Emma, hoping she'd just stop talking.

"Okay," she said. "I get the point. You don't want to elaborate on your feelings. At least you finally told the truth. Later, though. We'll make you."

"Wanna play some pool?" asked Maggie.

"Sure," I said. Anything to stop the talk about Red.

After a quick game, I made up an excuse and left early, feeling I was putting a damper on the evening. Emma and

Maggie protested but I stuck to my guns. I'd be better off in my bedroom where I could mope in private, although I didn't tell them that part. I really missed Red. A lot.

Singing along to the Oldie Station all the way home, I felt a bit better when I pulled into the driveway. After greeting Sadie with a scratch behind her ears, I promptly got into my pajamas, popped some corn, and curled up in bed to watch Seinfeld re-runs, wishing I were up in my tree house watching them with Red. Man, I'd do anything to hear his laugh again. *Forget about him. He was an engaged man.*

The doorbell rang. Thank goodness. A diversion.

Running down the stairs to open it, I saw no one until a sweet smelling scent had me looking down. A gorgeous red rose sat there, pinned to a letter, beside a large green flashlight.

What the hell was this?

Curious, I picked up the flower and opened the envelope. Inside was a folded sheet of white paper. The words *I'm in the backyard* were printed on it in large black letters.

That was odd! *Who was in the backyard?*

Maggie? Emma? My parents? Trying to cheer me up by playing a joke? Had my friends left right behind me? Were they planning a surprise?

I picked up the flashlight and was about to head on back when I glanced down at my Minnie Mouse pajamas. Should I change? Nah! At least they were clean and after all, it was only my friends. I didn't have to dress up for them.

Turning on the flashlight, I walked back to the yard and

stopped in my tracks.

"What the… "

*Never had I seen anything so beautiful.*

Hundreds of twinkling tea lights lit up a path to Olive.

*Oh my goodness. Olive.*

There she was in all her glory, bathed in soft white light, both enchanting and mystifying all at the same time. Absolutely breathtaking.

Drawing nearer, I saw a spotlight centered on her and two torches holding tall candles framed the trunk of the old oak. I walked to the base of the tree and looked up, not sure what to expect.

There again I saw a gorgeous sight. Red and black bows had been tied to various branches while silver tinsel created a glittery, festive yet elegant look. Few knew my favorite colors, so whoever did this had to be a close friend or family member.

"Emma? Maggie? Are you up there?" I yelled.

Silence.

"Aunt T?"

Silence.

"Please answer. C'mon, you're freaking me out."

"Sorry," said a male voice. "Had these blasted earphones on and didn't hear you at first."

What the…?

*"Who are you?"*

Was it a burglar? I held on tight to the flashlight, ready to throw it at the intruder and make a run for it.

Hearing a branch rattle, I looked up to see… oh my goodness… Red. He was leaning out of the tree house.

I rubbed my eyes. Was I asleep? Hallucinating? I

looked again. Nope. It really was him.

"What are you doing up there?"

"You'll see. Why don't you come on up."

"Ummmm... " I glanced down at my pajamas. "Not really dressed for it. I'll go change."

He smiled. "You look fine. Cute, actually. C'mon."

He sounded excited about something.

"Well, okay."

I took a moment to smooth down my hair, then shimmied up and climbed in the door to the tree house. It was a tight fit and Red and I ended up sitting side by side, elbow to elbow, thigh to thigh. It felt damn good. Looking around I noticed two glasses of champagne off to the side beside an Ipod with speakers. To my surprise, he took hold of my hand.

I pulled away. "What's going on?" I asked. Yeah, it was exciting seeing him but I was still pissed off about the whole fiancée thing. I was too hurt to make nice right away.

"I don't blame you for being upset. I've been out of the country or I would have had this talk earlier," he said, looking dead serious. "I'm sorry about what happened at the wedding. That woman isn't my fiancée. I mean, she was once but as I told you before, it's been over for ages. She kept bothering me, showing up at my office, my condo and even at my car. I kept telling her that we had no future and eventually that I was interested in someone else. I thought she'd lay off, knowing that." He sighed. "That was a big mistake. It set her on a quest to find out who the other woman was. How she always managed to figure out my itinerary, I'll never know. She just came that night to stir up trouble."

"Really?" *He was still single?*

"Really. I've missed you, Jessie. A lot." A tender, sweet look crossed his face, as he added, "Can we please start over?" He picked up my hand again and shook it. "My name is Brian Davis. I'm your new neighbor. You may call me Red."

Going along with it, I shook his hand and said, "Jessie White. But you can't be my neighbor, the house is sold."

He grinned. "Meet the new owner."

"Are you kidding?"

"No. I arranged my business so that I can work from Hamilton. I need to be here."

"Why?"

"There's a certain woman I'd like to spend time with."

*Oh, damn. That other woman. I seemed to forget her whenever I was with him.*

Curious as hell, I asked, "Who is it, Red?"

Looking confused, he stared at me for what seemed like a long time, a hint of laughter in his eyes.

"It's you, Jessie," he said softly. "I guess I didn't make that clear. I figured it was pretty obvious that I fell for you the minute I saw you outside my office, right here in this tree."

*Really?*

I started to shake.

I'd heard that saying before about how a heart could melt and I finally understood it. Right now, I was experiencing a warmth that shot through me, head to toe.

My walls were down, my suspicions were kicked to the curb and all I was left with was a great big burning ball of heart, melting away.

*Could it be true? Had I misunderstood? He really meant me?*

"But you seemed so grouchy, at least at the beginning."

"Well, I admit I was pretty angry at first." He smiled. "You see, this brown haired minx who climbed trees and built tree houses was getting under my skin. The last thing I needed was to start to care for another woman. My ex was bad enough. I fought it at first but soon got over it. I've been waiting to tell you but knew you needed the time to get over Jim." He waited a beat before asking, "Are you?"

"Ages ago."

"Interested in going on a date with me?"

Hmmmmm… Emma always maintained that a woman should play hard to get. That guys liked the thrill of the chase. It kept them interested. *What should I do?*

"Of course I will."

It was a no brainer. To hell with playing hard to get or any other games at all.

He handed me a glass of champagne.

"To us."

"To us."

Clink.

After we'd taken a sip, he took the glass from me and placed both glasses on the floor. He turned on some music and it was then I realized that Elvis was crooning the same song as the one we'd danced to at the wedding.

All about falling in love. Man, this was romantic as hell. Candles, bows, champagne, and music. I didn't know Red had it in him.

I stared him in the eyes.

*Was he going to kiss me or would I have to do it?*

As he leaned closer, I realized that my special place here with Olive was about to become even more special.

## *Thirty-two*

Eyes closed, I leaned back in my chair, re-living the moment with Judge Stevens in her chambers. Her support stunned me and it was a meeting that changed my life. Forever.

Ever since our little talk, I'd been seriously thinking of practicing law again. It was on my mind constantly, for she'd opened doors previously closed and I'd already received several calls from law firms inviting me for interviews. I smiled, remembering sitting on the stairs at Kite's, trying to figure out what to do. That seemed so long ago. Now I had so many options I was caught up in a whirlwind, trying to figure out the best one. It was a great feeling but nerve wracking all the same.

Finally, after many long sessions with Olive, I came to a decision. The right one for me. But I kept it a secret. The only one in on it was my mother because I needed her artistic help, and of course Red, my boyfriend It felt strange to call him that, but it was the truth and man, things were going well. I couldn't be happier. But enough of daydreaming. If I started thinking about him, I'd be lost in sweet thoughts and not get anything done.

Glancing at my watch, I realized it was almost time. Time to let everyone know my decision. Time to celebrate.

Nervous butterflies tossed around my gut. Would they support what I wanted to do? Would they be angry? Laugh at me? After all their help, would they be upset? *Enough of this!* They'd all be here soon and I didn't have time to wallow in self-doubt. I needed to be confident in my choices because I thought what I'd figured out would work well. It was a different path, a new one, but one I wanted to take.

Jumping up to make sure all the refreshments were ready before my first guest arrived, I dashed into the washroom to convince myself again that I looked presentable. I smoothed down my suit, glad my Armani finally fit again, checked out my shoes, yep, Jimmy Choos always looked good, combed my hair and added a swipe of lipstick, a dash of mascara and I was ready. I walked out just as Christine arrived.

"All set for the party?" she asked, pointing to the trays of food. "Looks delicious."

"Sure am," I said. "But first, please take a seat."

Christine sat down and I could tell she was nervous by all the fidgeting she was doing. Her foot tapped a beat as she sighed loudly.

"I got my invitation but when you asked me to come early, I got nervous. Is it bad news?" she asked, as I pulled over a chair and joined her. "Give it to me straight. I can handle it."

"It's the best news possible. You've been accepted into the Diversion Program we talked about. Once you follow all the steps, your charges will be dropped." Figured I'd get right to the point and not leave her hanging, but I was unprepared for the hug she gave me, as she jumped off her chair and wrapped her arms around me.

"Thank you so much. I owe you big time. Especially sticking up for me with that crabby old judge."

"Don't be too hard on her. That crabby old judge approved the program."

"Yeah, yeah, guess she's okay after all."

She pulled away and much to my surprise, leaned over and did three cartwheels across the room, rapid fire. She then stood there grinning and let out a loud, "Yahoooo… " as she danced around, doing the "happy dance", I presumed.

I had never seen her so excited and it reaffirmed my belief in my decision. Being a lawyer was what I was born to do. I really could make a difference in people's lives. Christine was a case in point.

"And don't worry, Jessie. I promise I'll be good," she said as she stood tall, looking the most confident I'd ever seen. "I'm on the straight and narrow now and even applied to several universities. I'm going to be a lawyer, just like you. Maybe one day we'll be working together."

"Maybe," I agreed, thrilled at her choices, knowing she was really going to make it this time.

"Hey. Got your invite. What's a shingle party?" Maggie asked, walking in the door. "Is it shingle as in "hang out your shingle?" Did you get a job with a law firm?"

"You'll see," I said with a smile. "Let's wait until the others arrive."

"Hmmmmm… pretty darn mysterious," said John, as he followed behind.

"Yeah, something's up. She's been humming *Shiny Happy People* all week. I sure like the group R.E.M., after a while it drove me crazy but I'm glad to see her happy," said Emma, bringing up the rear.

So excited I couldn't wipe the grin off my face, I waited for Mom, Dad, Aunt T, Joey, Carl, Sam and Sylvia to arrive. Red walked in last as he'd been off at a meeting in Toronto, but promised to be here. I knew he'd make it because he was just that kind of a guy; however, I was unprepared when he came right over for a kiss, as this was the first time we'd been really public about our relationship. I had to admit I liked it. I'd been enjoying just the two of us getting to know each other, without anyone finding out or butting in but it was time to bring it all out into the open. No way should love be kept a secret. Ever. I looked around to see who witnessed this display of affection, and of course everyone did. Maggie and Emma just stood there shocked while Aunt T came up and whispered, "It's about time."

My face blushed as I gave my friends the thumbs up and mouthed "later". They'd want details soon.

*Time to let them know my big secret.*

Gathering everyone together in the center of the room, I said, "I asked you to come today because I have an announcement to make, and I want to share it with you, as well as thank you for all the help and support you've given me during this rough patch in my life. I've made a big decision."

"Don't leave us in suspense," groaned Maggie. "Tell us."

I went over to a space behind the desk, pulled out a large sign, and held it up.

"Jessica White: Attorney at Law," read Maggie. She stared at me in amazement. "You're practicing law again?"

"Yep," I said.

"You're giving up White's Waggles?" gasped Emma, looking shocked.

"Nope. Please, follow me."

I opened the door and invited everyone out. After they were all standing in front of the studio, I reached up and hung the Hazel Hul original sign on the nail Red had pounded in the wall yesterday. I stood back so they could see it, gleaming in the sun, in its new home, just below the White's Waggles' sign.

"What?" said Maggie and Emma at the same time.

"I'm back in business," I said. "This is my way of having it all. I love practicing law but also love my new business, so I'm placing my shingle here and I'll work with clients at the back of the room while tending to my dogs the rest of the time. It's the best of both worlds. At least, for me."

Dead silence. I held my breath. Then... a round of applause and cheers.

A smiling Maggie walked over. "Great idea, Jessie."

"A law firm at a dog daycare," said Emma. "Only you could make this work. With me as your secretary, of course."

"Thinking outside the box," said Aunt T. "I love it."

After receiving hug after hug, I approached Sylvia.

"How are you doing?" I asked, still feeling guilty for letting her down.

"I'm doing okay but I'll be even better when I'm your client again." She smiled.

"You're first in line. I have an appointment set up for

you tomorrow morning at 9:00."

"I'll be there," said Sylvia.

Looking around, I felt tears fast approaching as I gazed at all the people who'd brought me to this point. I owed them a lot. Not wanting to cry like a baby in front of them, especially when it was supposed to be a happy time, I walked over to Red and whispered, "Can you keep an eye on things for a bit?"

"No problem. Take your time." He looked at me knowingly, probably sensing what I was up to.

There was only one place I needed to be right now. The place that made me feel good, no matter what. The refuge that had been with me through good as well as bad times.

Slipping off my Jimmy Choos, I climbed up Olive and settled down on the rug in my tree house.

Patting a branch I crooned, "What do you know, Olive? I did okay. I made it. There is only one direction for me now. Straight up all the way."

Never would I have guessed that being fired, dumped and evicted would lead me on a long journey home to myself. Through times of forgiveness and second chances, as well as toughening up and learning to be gentle but firm, I found a way to have it all. A way to fulfil my law dreams, spend time with my furry buddies, be surrounded by family and friends, and be in "big like" with a man I was crazy about. I'd even accepted my mother's gift of the house.

I finally found the answer to the question that haunted me since I was fired.

Can nice girls ever finish first?

*Count on it!*

## Meet

## *Suzanne M Hurley*

Happiness to this author is curled up with her laptop creating imaginary worlds that come from her heart. Writing is her passion and dreaming up story lines is her love. Suzanne was born in Peterborough, Ontario and currently resides in Caledonia, Haldimand County, where on morning walks with Mike and Rico, she tries out her new plots on the cows, sheep and numerous wild animals she greets along the way. Please visit Suzanne M. Hurley at her website:

www.suzannemhurley.com